Copyrighted Material

Vampire Mage 2 Copyright © 2018 by Joshua King
Book design and layout copyright © 2018 by Joshua King

This novel is a work of fiction. Names, characters, places, and incidents are either products of the author's imagination or used fictitiously. Any resemblance to actual events, locales, or persons, living, dead, or undead, is entirely coincidental.

All rights reserved.

No part of this publication can be reproduced or transmitted in any form or by any means, electronic or mechanical, without permission in writing from Joshua King.

1st Edition

http://joshuakingbooks.com/

SIGN UP FOR UPDATES

For updates about new releases, sign up for the mailing list below. You'll know as soon as I release new books, including my upcoming new series, as well as sequels to *Vampire Mage*.

https://www.subscribepage.com/joshua_king

CONTENTS

Chapter 1	1
Chapter 2	9
Chapter 3	19
Chapter 4	29
Chapter 5	41
Chapter 6	55
Chapter 7	67
Chapter 8	77
Chapter 9	89
Chapter 10	101
Chapter 11	107
Chapter 12	119
Chapter 13	129
Chapter 14	141
Chapter 15	151
Chapter 16	161
Chapter 17	181
Chapter 18	191
Chapter 19	207
Chapter 20	215
Chapter 21	223
Chapter 22	231
Chapter 23	249
Chapter 24	263
Chapter 25	273
Chapter 26	285
Chapter 27	297
Chapter 28	307

Chapter 29	319
Chapter 30	331
Chapter 31	341
Chapter 32	351
Chapter 33	365
Chapter 34	375
Chapter 35	389
Chapter 36	399
Epilogue	407
Sign Up For Updates	413
About the Author	415

VAMPIRE MAGE 2

BOOK 2 IN THE VAMPIRE MAGE SERIES

JOSHUA KING

1

The sound of the explosion was so loud it was still ringing in my ears by the time the ground stopped shaking under my feet. I was so shocked that I stood and stared at Malakan's house for a few seconds before I was able to fully process what I was seeing. Massive flames overtook the entire house. It was several seconds before I came to my senses, and when I did, I took off toward the structure. My feet pounded the ground beneath me, occasionally tangling in the tall blades of grass and making me stumble as I ran. I needed to try to save Malakan. He was still inside, and even though the explosion had already destroyed much of the building and the flames were rapidly spreading across the field, I had to hold out hope he had somehow survived. Maybe he had gone into a basement or other hidden part of the house and was somehow safe.

I got as close to the building as I could, but the intensity of the heat pushed me back. The flames licked out at me like they themselves were trying to force me to stop. I took a few steps back from the flaming building to brace myself. I didn't want to give up. I couldn't just let him stay in there without at least trying to get him out. Ducking my head, I ran forward into the flames again. I tried to tap into the magic I now knew I had inside me, trying to will the heat away and stop the flames from burning me. It worked long enough for me to get a few yards further in and up the steps. As soon as my feet hit the porch, a new blast of fire burst out of the front of the house toward me. I felt the searing bite of the flames and it was too much. My tenuous grasp of my warlock abilities was no match for the ferocity of the blaze. Pain rushed along my skin and I knew I couldn't get inside the house. I ran back down the steps and toward the field.

Ahead of me I could see the fire burning across the tall grass toward the trees. It was moving faster as it ate through the grass and blackened the ground. I had to get out. I had to beat the flames across the field if I was going to survive. I didn't know what was beyond the trees; if there was anything at all. I still wasn't completely clear on all of the rules regarding areas that a warlock mirrored. The space could be limited only to what I saw, which meant if the fire got there before I did, I would be trapped. Gathering every bit of energy and strength I had inside me, I shot toward the door in the tree. My speed built with every step until even the pain from the flames seemed to fade. I watched the edge of the fire, the speed with which it was consuming the grass motivating me to move faster. Finally, I could feel cool air against my face and I knew I was getting closer. Giving myself a final push, I burst out of the wall of fire and lunged for the latch on the door. The metal had been heated by the flames even at this distance and I felt it burn into my palm. I wrenched the door open and fell into the tunnel. Rolling over onto my back, I kicked the door closed behind me and scrambled to my feet. The tunnel was even darker after being surrounded by the intense brightness of the flames. Without anything to light my way, I ran blindly through the cliff.

The silence of Malakan's chambers surrounded

me when I stepped inside. Part of me expected someone to be there waiting for me, but it was quiet and still. It was a startling juxtaposition against the roar of the fire I'd left behind. I made my way quickly through the rooms until I got back to the entryway. Rather than the many torches that had been in the walls when Ty and I first arrived here, only one was lit. Knowing the tunnels waiting for me were just as dark as the one I'd left, I reached for the torch. As soon as my hand wrapped around it, the light dimmed. I lifted it from its brace on the wall and moved it across the entryway toward another of the torches. I meant to use the flame to light the second one, but the instant the first torch touched the second, the flame extinguished. I was in darkness again. I had nothing to relight the torches, and no choice but to drop the useless thing and feel for the latch on the door blindly. I moved through the door and into the next length of tunnel.

I'd done this journey twice before and I knew the path didn't veer off at any point, but the darkness still felt disorienting. It was a relief to not to feel the heat any longer and I tried to focus on that rather than the confusion and growing panic. I drew in deep breaths to rid my lungs of the smell of smoke and burning wood. My mind was spinning with what I had just seen. It didn't make sense. I hadn't been out of the house for more than a few seconds when the explosion happened. I hadn't seen anything in the house that could explain such a sudden and horrific incident.. I knew very little about Malakan, and even less about the ways of the warlocks, but this just wasn't sitting with me well. There was something wrong. I could feel it. Malakan was far too skilled a warlock to let something like this happen on accident. Someone did this on purpose. They intended for the house to go up in flames with Malakan inside. It happened so quickly after I left, I couldn't help but wonder if they intended for me to be there as well.

The sense of danger pressed in around me as I continued through the blackness of the cliff. Even though I hadn't seen or sensed anybody inside when I first escaped the flames, I suddenly felt like I was being watched. Not being able to see around me intensified the feeling. I whirled around, retracing my steps at a run for several paces. If there was someone following me, I would have run directly into them. All I met was emptiness. I was alone in the rock, but I couldn't shake the feeling of an impending threat closing in on me. I knew I had to get out of the cliff and back to Aurora and Ashe. When I was making my way through the tunnel to visit Malakan earlier, it had felt so much shorter. Now the dark path seemed to stretch ahead of me. Every step I took ahead lengthened the way until it felt like I was never going to reach the other door. Finally, I saw a glimmer of light ahead of me. It reminded me of the first time Ty and I had traveled this way and saw the light coming from under the door leading into Malakan's chambers. Now it was the light from the first section of the tunnel. There was only one torch in this section , just like in the room I had just left. It was unnerving, feeling as ominous and purposeful as the fire itself. I hesitated to get near the torch, remembering the reaction of the other one when I touched it. Instead, I moved directly to the door and burst out into Final View.

I had run several feet into the middle of the community before anyone even realized I was there. Life was just continuing on, following the same rhythm as if nothing had happened. As far as any of the people here knew, nothing had. They didn't know about the house deep in the cliff. They didn't know about the fire engulfing the space

Malakan had created. The man wearing one shoe looked over at me sharply as if I'd said something. His head tilted, and he took several steps in my direction.

"What is it?" he asked.

"Malakan," I muttered.

It was all I could manage. I started running through the clusters of people gathered beneath the bridge. It was the first time I noticed the pain in my feet and realized I must have burned them. The sensation became sharp and almost unbearable, then faded, then worsened again. It felt like the wounds were healing and then repeatedly ripping open again. I'd need to let them fully heal, but I couldn't stop. It would have to happen as I drove across the city toward Solomon's Fang.

I hopped behind the wheel of the car I'd borrowed and raced away from the bridge. I wished I had grabbed my phone when I left. I had been almost to the bridge earlier when I realized I hadn't grabbed it, and I hadn't felt like I needed to turn around just to get it. Ashe and Aurora were both safe at the bar with Ty when I left them, and I knew if either woman needed me, they could reach out to me through their thoughts. Now I wished I could call Ty to let him know I was coming. We couldn't waste any time. When I finally got close to the portal, I parked the car and jumped out. As soon as my feet hit the ground, I could tell they had healed during the drive. I moved through the portal as quickly as I could, stumbling slightly as I passed through into the basement of Soloman's. I felt a hand grab me by the arm and I tensed, prepared to fight.

"Hayden?"

I relaxed slightly when I heard Ty's voice. He let go of my arm and his eyes traveled over me, taking in my burned clothes.

"Where are the girls?" I asked.

"What's wrong? What's going on?"

"Where are they?"

I started to move around Ty, intending to make my way through the basement and up into the bar, but Ty stepped between me and the door.

"Move out of the way, Ty," I demanded.

"No. You can't go up there."

2

"What do you mean I can't go up there?" I demanded. "You are a portal keeper, not the bouncer of my life. You don't get to tell me what to do."

Ty took a step back and looked at me firmly.

"I can't let you go."

"Where are Ashe and Aurora?" I asked.

"They're upstairs," Ty said. "But you can't go up there."

"You keep telling me that, but you haven't given me a good enough reason to keep me from doing it anyway."

I pushed past Ty and ran through the basement and up the stairs into the bar. As soon as I rushed through the door, everyone turned to look at me.

Their eyes locked on me, and a few started to whisper. I didn't care. It wasn't the first time people had talked about me when I came into a room, and I had the distinct feeling it wasn't going to be the last. I heard Ashe and Aurora before I saw them. They were laughing, the sound of their voices light and carefree. It was a sharp contrast to the adrenaline rushing through me and the danger I still felt creeping up the back of my neck. Not caring who was there, I forced my way through the people in the bar and ran up to the girls. Aurora saw me first. I noticed her eyes widen slightly, and she nodded her head in my direction. Ashe turned to look at me, and her smile melted off her face.

"Hayden," she said. "What's going on?"

"I need to talk to you," I said. "Now."

"What happened to you?" Aurora asked.

I looked down and for the first time realized the full extent of the damage to my clothes. All of my injuries had fully healed, but my pants and shirt were burned badly enough that sections hung in tatters. Blood from my burns stained the fabric. Ashe got off her bar stool and came toward me.

"Hayden, you need to go upstairs."

I hadn't realized Ty had followed me up into the bar until I heard his voice behind me. I looked back at him and saw him scanning the people spread throughout the dimly-lit space. His expression was stern.

"Come on," Ashe said.

She and Aurora got on either side of me and led me toward the stairs with Ty falling into step behind us. They hurried me up and into Ashe's apartment. Ty closed the door and locked it but didn't come any further into the room. He kept his back pressed against the door and crossed his arms over his chest as the girls brought me into living room and sat me down on the sofa.

"I'll send for some clothes for him," Aurora said.

I was starting to feel frustrated. They were more concerned about the way I looked than what I needed to tell them.

"Why do my clothes matter so much?" I asked.

"You have a bad track record recently of getting the wrong type of attention from the wrong type of people," Ty said.

I rolled my eyes.

"I swear. One more fucking cryptic speech from you and I'm going to crack."

"I'm not being cryptic," Ty said. "It's a fact. Since the first time you walked into the bar you've been catching people's eyes. You lured in Aurora, but she proved to be the least of your worries, and when a woman who was hours away from throwing you to the dogs and letting you rot is the least of your worries, you know you are royally screwed."

"Isn't being royally screwed the exact thing that got me into all this?" I asked, sliding my eyes over to Aurora.

I could see the familiar hunger flashing behind the concern in her eyes and I wished I could steal a few minutes alone with her. If there was ever a time I needed some de-stressing, now was it.

"That's not the point."

Something he said snapped back into my mind.

"Wait. There were dogs involved? No one told me about dogs."

Aurora shrugged sheepishly.

"Watching people die lost its novelty a long time ago," she said. "Sometimes I just can't stomach it. The dogs are good at making sure I don't have to witness it when pesky people decide to try to make a display of themselves at the palace."

I shook my head.

"That is messed up," I said.

She smiled and pulled out her phone. She dialed, and within seconds was telling whoever was on the other line to bring clothes. Rattling off a long list of garments, she seemed to be requesting an entire new wardrobe for me.

"That's still not the point," Ty said.

"Then what is?" I asked, my amusement disappearing and the annoyance returning. "Why did you three drag me up here to change my clothes? Aren't you even slightly concerned about what might have happened when I went to see Malakan."

"Of course we are," Ty said. "Which is why you can't be seen like this. As we've learned, we never know who is watching. When someone who has pissed off and threatened as many people as you have in the last few days shows up burned, bloody, and wild-eyed, it's obvious some serious shit went down. We don't want anyone who might be watching to see you that way. You don't know what else they might have planned."

The way Ty said it only cemented the sense of impending danger.

"I went to see Malakan," I said.

They nodded.

"You told us that was where you were going,"

Ashe said. "Remember, we wanted you to stay with us and continue the celebration of your change."

I nodded. We'd been celebrating since the night before, and while I enjoyed the revelry, I'd been drawn back to the house in the cliff. Now I felt more like I'd been lured there. Everything that had happened when visiting Malakan ran through my mind. I didn't know how much to tell them right now. My true identity as the kidnapped son of the warlock leader loomed in my thoughts, but the sight of the fire held my tongue. I couldn't talk about both at the same time. I wasn't even completely sure if I believed him, or what it meant if I did. For now, I needed time to really wrap my head around all of that. I needed to be able to absorb it before I shared it with anyone else. At this moment it was more important to tell them about the fire and Malakan. Then we could decide what to do next.

"Right after I left the house, there was an explosion."

"An explosion?" Ashe asked.

"The house was carved into the stone," Ty said. "How could it explode?"

Aurora gasped, her hand coming up to cover her mouth. She shook her head.

"Not the stone chambers," she said. "The house. His house. The one he created in the recess behind the stone."

"You knew about it," I said.

Aurora nodded.

"Of course, I did," she said. "He was my confidant. I met with him regularly. He didn't like to bring my father to that house, but I went there many times. I didn't think anyone else ever went there."

"Well, somebody did," I said.

Ty looked at me questioningly.

"What do you mean?" Ashe asked.

"The explosion," I said. "Someone caused that."

"Malakan was a warlock. He was known for being eccentric, wasn't he? Especially since his exile," Ashe said.

"What are you getting at?" Ty asked.

"It could have been an accident," she said. "He could have been experimenting and caught the house on fire."

I shook my head.

"No," I said. "This wasn't an accident."

"Malakan is one of the greatest warlocks of all time," Ty said. "He might not be as powerful and influential as he used to be, but he isn't an amateur chemist likely to burn down his own house."

"It was more than that," I said. "It wasn't just a fire. It was an explosion. I had walked away from the house and was almost back to the door when it happened. The ground shook. The house was completely consumed by the time I turned around. I tried to get inside to find him, but the fire was too intense, and I had to escape. There's no way it was an accident. It was intentional."

Aurora let out a trembling breath and hung her head. I turned and wrapped my arms around her.

"It's going to be alright," I murmured to her.

"I can't believe he's gone," she said. "I just can't believe Malakan is gone. He's always been a part of my life. I've known him for as long as I can remember, and I relied on him. Now he's gone. I don't know what I'm going to do."

I tilted her face up to look at me.

"I'm here," I told her.

"I know," she said.

A hard knock on the door made Ty turn sharply.

"Who is it?" he demanded.

There was no response, and he called out again. When there was still no answer, he opened the door slightly. A second later, he stepped back into the apartment and opened the door the rest of the way. Three large suitcases sat just outside.

"That must be the clothes for Hayden," Aurora said.

"They just dropped them and ran?" I asked.

"What else should they have done?" she asked. "The only reason they were here was to bring these to you."

I opened my mouth, then closed it again. She was being completely sincere. I didn't know it I'd ever get used to the level of dedication the Shade had to her.

Ty pulled the three suitcases into the apartment and I picked up two of them. He followed me into the bedroom with the third and dropped it onto the bed.

"Get cleaned and changed," he said. "Then we can decide what to do."

3

The water from the shower was somehow soothing even though my burns were already fully healed. I washed my hair three times trying to get rid of the smell of the fire. In the back of my mind, though, I knew there really wasn't much point to it. Standing there watching Malakan's house burn was something I wasn't ever going to forget. I could remember everything about it, from the bright orange glow of the flame to the acrid smell. I got out of the shower and dressed and went back into the living room. I expected the three of them to be talking about what was going on, but they were silent. Each was staring at a different part of the room like they were lost in their own thoughts. Aurora looked understandably devastated, but it was the expression on Ty's face that really caught my attention. He looked dark and troubled, and I remembered what Malakan had said about Ty's failings. I wondered what that could have to do with what happened.

"Let's go," I said, grabbing my phone and shoving it into my pocket.

"Where we going?" Ashe asked.

"I think we need to go talk to Darian," I said. "He needs to know what happened."

The expression on Ty's face seemed to darken even further, and he looked away. Aurora stood up, shaking her head.

"No," she said. "I want to go to Malakan's house. I need to see it."

"No," I said. "It's too dangerous. We don't know what's happening there, or if the fire is even under control. When I left, I was barely able to get through the door before the entire field was taken over. There was no one there to put the flames out."

"I have to see it, Hayden," she said. "I have to pay my respects to him."

"Besides," Ashe said. "If you're so convinced that this was done on purpose, the only way we're going to find out what happened is by going back there and trying to figure it out. Aurora said it herself, no one knew about that place except the people Malakan told about it. She was surprised even you knew. So if someone purposely blew up his house, it was someone he knew. Probably somebody he trusted."

"Either that, or someone was able to follow him and find out about the house. It's not like it was locked away or anything. Anybody who found the door at the top of that tower would be able to open it and go right in. They would just need to know where to look," I said.

"It's not that simple," Aurora said. "It might have looked like there was nothing keeping people from going through, but Malakan didn't leave anything to chance. He might have seemed like an eccentric old man, but he thought of everything. He mirrored that entire area, the house, the field, the trees, all of it, very purposefully. That was his private sanctuary. It was incredibly important to him."

"Why?" I asked.

"What do you mean?"

"Why was it so important to him? What is that place?"

"I don't know," she said, shaking her head and

swiping at a tear that was trailing down her cheek. "He never told me, and I never asked. His past is the most mysterious thing about Malakan and he is fiercely protective of it." She hesitated, the breath seeming to catch in her throat. "Was."

I nodded.

"All right," I said. "We'll go back to the house. You're right. We need to find out who did this and why."

"I want to go with you," Ty said.

"We'd have to go through the portal," I said. "I didn't think you'd want to leave it unattended again."

I didn't want to sound like I was discouraging him from coming. It felt like Ty and I had come to a mutual, if somewhat uncomfortable, agreement. We knew we benefitted each other, even if we weren't yet going to admit we needed each other. I'd admit he was useful and had helped me out of some serious shit, but I wasn't at the place where I was going to get matching best friends' tattoos with him. I didn't understand everything about the Underworld and his position in it and didn't know the implications of him not being near the portal if someone needed to use it.

"I'll seal it," he said. "Once we've gone

through, I'll seal it from the other side. No one will be able to move through it as long as it's sealed."

"So, no one will be able to go into the Underworld if they need to? Or get back to this side?" I asked.

"No one will be able to follow us through the portal if they are on this side, and no one will be able to get help in the Underworld," he said. "This happened for a reason. The attack on Malakan wasn't random. There was something behind it, and it very well could have to do with you. Going back there might be something we have to do, but it is also extremely dangerous. Sealing the portal will give us some control."

"We don't know how long we're going to be in the Underworld," Aurora said. "We should all pack at least the necessities, to make sure we have what we need."

It seemed like a strange suggestion. With everything going on, the last thing I was thinking about was picking out outfits to bring along with me. Something about the way she said it made me feel like she was just trying to fill the silence. She wanted to find normalcy after everything that had happened.

"I have everything I need here," I said. "So does Ashe."

"I have my apartment on the other side," Ty said. "Aurora, you can visit the palace if you need to."

There was a pause and then her eyes snapped to him like she just realized he was talking. She looked at him questioningly. I knew there was something going through her mind, but I didn't want to delve into her thoughts. Even though I knew I could, now that I had completed my transformation and was bonded to Aurora, it felt more like an invasion than it did before. I'd still use it if necessary, but there was something wrong about traipsing through her thoughts without her knowledge, so I decided to stay out as much as possible. Even so, I couldn't help but notice the look on her face. It was one filled with questions and confusion.

A few minutes later we made our way down through the bar and into the basement. Before we ducked through the door, Ashe glanced back at the bar, where a wiry man had taken her place. I could tell she was not impressed by his drink pouring technique. Her fingers twitched, and it seemed like she was a few seconds from diving over the bar and taking him out. I rested my hand on her hip and guided her down onto the steps. There were much more serious things for us to tend to right now. I figured that Ashe, just like Aurora, was clinging to normalcy wherever she could find it.

Ty waited while the rest of us went through the portal, then followed us. He reached into his pocket and withdrew the black object he had used when Ashe paid the blood price to pass through the portal with me the first time I journeyed to the Underworld. From his other pocket he took a small knife. I winced as he unceremoniously slashed his arm. Blood rose from a gash a few inches long. He gathered it quickly, seeming to chase it as the cut healed. Stepping back up to the wall, he brushed the blood along the bricks. It's sizzled and hissed as it sank into the wall. He tucked both implements away and turned back to us.

"There," he said. "The portal is sealed. No one will be able to move through it until I come back and unseal it."

"Then let's go," I said.

The car I'd left behind was still sitting exactly where I parked it. We got inside, and I headed directly for the bridge. I felt tense the entire drive, like I was expecting an attack at any second. Fortunately, we moved through the city unhindered and soon slid to a stop by the side of the road near where Ty had parked the first time we had come here. I was already striding toward Final View when the others got out of the car to follow me. My heart was pounding in my ears, but it wasn't enough to drown out the sound of Malakan's voice. Everything he had said to me was tumbling through my mind over and over until I almost couldn't tell one sentence from another. Part of me couldn't stop thinking about what he had told me about who I was. It explained so much. Suddenly everything Ashe had told me about my speed, my ability to read thoughts, even the bullets, was starting to make sense. But I couldn't concentrate fully on that. My thoughts kept going back to everything else about my visits to his hideout. I tried to go back through every word he had said to me, trying to find a clue or hidden message. Even another fucking riddle. Anything that might indicate Malakan knew he was in danger. There was nothing.

The noise coming from Final View was louder than it had been before. Voices rose up over each other and crashed down again until it was almost impossible to discern one word from another. As I got closer, I heard someone mention Malakan's name. The man with one shoe rushed toward me.

"What happened? Is it true?" His eyes were wild. "Was there really an explosion?"

"Yes," I said. "I don't know what happened. But I'm going to find out."

Aurora, Ashe, and Ty came up behind me.

"What are you going to do?" he asked. "There's been no sign of him. No one has seen or heard from him."

"We are going in to look for him," Ty said.

The words were barely out of his mouth when the man with one shoe stumbled to the side. I realized someone had pushed him and another man had grabbed onto the front of Ty's shirt. He looked half crazy and part of me wondered if he even realized where he was or what he was doing. Even though he was several inches shorter than Ty, the man yanked him down closer so that his face was only inches from Ty's.

"This is your fault," he said through gritted teeth. "This is all your fault. You did this." Ty shoved him away and the man fell to the ground. He crawled backward for a few feet, never taking his eyes away from Ty. "This is all because of what you did. You caused this."

Finally, a woman came up behind him and pulled him up off the ground. When he was stable on his feet, she led him to one of the trash can fires. We continued our progress toward the door in the cliff, but the man's words stuck with me. I couldn't help but notice this was the second time somebody had blamed Ty and mentioned his failings. I didn't know what it meant, but it sat heavily in my stomach.

4

SHAKEN BY THE ENCOUNTER WITH THE ANGRY MAN, but not deterred, we pushed on toward the door in the cliff. I hesitated only for a moment when we got there. I didn't know what might be waiting on the other side. Taking a breath, I reached for the handle and pulled the door open. Part of me expected a rush of heat. The fire had burned so ferociously I thought there was a chance it could have burned through the door and into the stone chambers, then traveled through and reached this end. I knew it was completely outlandish, yet I had become very familiar with the outlandish in the last week and didn't think there would ever be another time in my life when I would be able to dismiss something off hand just because it didn't sound plausible.

Damn. That was an aspect of my life I hadn't realized I was leaving behind. I'd already come to terms with knowing everything I thought my life was and would be was over. I'd already wrapped my mind around losing simple things like my apartment and the very few people I had maintained contact with over the years. Yet, it was at this moment, and the realization of not being able to trust what was around me or feel secure in my understanding of the world, that it really hit me. Somehow this felt like the most significant change I'd have to get used to.

The entryway to the tunnel was cold. The torch that had been on the wall earlier was still there. The rest of the group came in behind me and closed the door. Ty looked around and seemed to have the same thought I did.

"This was the only torch lit," I told him.

"Was it like this when you got here?" he asked.

I thought back. I realized I hadn't even considered that when I noticed the torch on my way out of the tunnel. I had been so preoccupied with getting back to Malakan and talking to him about

Aurora completing my change that I didn't really notice what was around me.

"I don't know," I said. "I know I had one with me when I was going down the tunnel toward his house, but I don't know if there were any more. But there were lights in the first room of his chambers. They weren't the same, either. I had to go through both sets of tunnels in the dark."

Ty grabbed the torch and held it high. Without another word, we walked into the tunnel. Ashe shuddered and wrapped her arms around herself. I realized it was her first time in these tunnels. This environment wasn't the most welcoming in the best of circumstances. Having to walk down them not knowing what kind of destruction and danger was waiting at the end was so much worse.

We walked along in silence for a few moments, but then I couldn't hold back my questions anymore.

"Who was that man?" I asked.

"What man?" Ty asked.

"Really?" I asked. "You're going to pretend I wasn't standing right there when that man grabbed you and shook you, and blamed everything that's happened on you?"

He let out a breath.

"His name is Philip," he said.

I waited a few seconds.

"That's it?" I asked. "That's all I'm getting? His name is Philip?"

"What else do you want to know?"

"Oh, I don't know, maybe who the hell he is? How does he know you? What did you do to piss him off so badly he decided to blame Malakan's death on you?"

Ty cleared his throat.

"You might as well tell him," Ashe said. "He needs to know everything he can. Especially about this."

"Philip was a Shade at the same time I was," Ty said. "He was on duty the night of The Incident. When everything went down, everybody involved was blamed, even if they weren't a part of the main mission or in the same area at the time. Darien wanted to make an example out of us. I lost my position that night, and so did Philip."

"But what happened to him?" I asked. "You aren't living in Final View, raving like a lunatic around a trash can fire. And by all rights, you probably should be. You have to control all the idiots who wander into Solomon's Fang, and when you aren't doing that you have to stand around watching people go back and forth through a wall. It's not exactly the most thrilling of existences."

"At least I have that. Darian demoted me to being portal keeper, but I also had Ashe waiting for me. She was willing to give me a job as a bouncer, and even though I do have to deal with a lot of idiots, at least it gives me something to do. Every day, standing by the portal is a reminder of what happened, and of the power Darian still has over me. I can't leave that position until he relieves me of it. But because Ashe made me the bouncer, I have something else. I don't have to be defined just by being a portal keeper, and I have more in my life now than I did when I was a Shade. That doesn't mean I don't hate what happened, and that I'm not bitter about the position Darien gave me, but it's something. Philip doesn't have that. Darian didn't give him a position, he just fired him. That was enough, apparently, to crack him."

"What is The Incident? And why is he blaming you?" I asked. "What did you do that would make him say all of this is your fault?"

Before he had a chance to answer me, we reached the door to the stone chambers. There was no light glimmering under the door, and the same foreboding as before feeling settled over me. We walked in and Ty swept the torch through the space, trying to see through the dark. The strange assortment of lamps scattered throughout the room were off, and when I walked closer to them, I found out why.

"The light bulbs are broken," I said.

"What?" Aurora asked.

"The bulbs," I said. "All of them are shattered."

"That doesn't make sense," she said. "None of these lamps used electricity."

"What do you mean?" I asked.

"Hayden, we're in the middle of a cliff at the edge of a vagrant community. Do you really think the power company puts a whole lot of wiring somewhere like this?"

"Honestly," I said, "I hadn't put a tremendous amount of thought into whether the Underworld has utilities at all."

"Of course it does," she said. "I told you, the Underworld is just like the other side. It just happens to have a wider variety of residents."

"All right, so there is an Underworld Power Company." I looked back at Aurora. "But you said there was no electricity here."

"Malakan didn't use electricity," she said. "As

we've established, it's not exactly practical, but beyond that, he didn't need it. He much preferred fire. He liked torches and candles. I'm not sure how old he was, but I think those just made him comfortable, like they were familiar to him."

Her talking about his appreciation for fire made my stomach turn slightly.

"But what about the lamps?" I asked. "Those weren't fire. They were just light bulbs."

"Yes," Aurora said. "He told me once that lamps amused him. I don't know why. It's not like he'd never seen them before. People have lamps in the Underworld. Something about them, though, just made him happy. So he collected them. But since he didn't use electricity, he enchanted them to glow. Not exactly the most impressive way to use his amazing powers, I suppose. But he's had a really hard time since his exile, and it was something he enjoyed."

"What could have happened to the light bulbs?" I asked.

She shook her head.

"I don't know."

"Come on," I said. "We need to keep going."

The tightness in my chest got worse as we climbed the stone steps and moved down the hallway toward the door. I held my hand against the door and was surprised to find it cool.

"Are you ready?" I asked.

"Yes," Aurora said beside me.

I opened the door and the powerful smell of smoke pushed us back. The light beyond the door reminded me of a sunset, and when I stepped through onto the charred field, I saw an orange and pink sky above me. There was enough light to see the blackened skeleton of the house silhouetted against the horizon ahead of us. We stood just outside the door, staring at it. I felt Aurora's hand grab one of mine and Ashe's grab the other. We started slowly across the grass. Nothing was burning anymore, and the lack of light made the destruction seem even more stark. The house and everything around it were a complete loss. There was nothing left but the meager remnants of a blackened, charred frame. Everything else had been reduced to ashes.

"I can't believe this," Aurora said. "How could this happen?"

"I told you," I said. "It didn't make sense. The fire was too intense and too fast, and now look at it. Like you said earlier, there was no one here to put those flames out, so what happened to them? How could this field be cool enough for us to walk on right now? I saw the things inside that house. It's not like all the rooms were full of paper and kindling. There was glass. There was metal. Those things should still be here. The fire did not burn long enough to completely obliterate them."

"Then what happened?" Ty asked.

My mind went back to the moment I heard the house explode and turned around to see it engulfed in flame. I had seen buildings on fire before. They always started small and then spread. This fire had raced across the field, but it hadn't spread in the house. The consumption of the building had been instant.

"How big is this place?" I asked.

"How big is it?" Aurora asked.

I nodded, veering away from the path to walk further into the field.

"How big is it?" I repeated. "Like you said, this place isn't real. It's mirrored."

"That doesn't mean it's not real," Aurora said. "It's just as real as the rest of Solan City."

"Yes, but it's inside a cliff. It's not really a wide open space. It's not really a field, and that's not really the sky. I don't know where it is or why Malakan chose it to be where he built his home, but where we're standing right now is barely more than a figment of somebody's imagination. It just so happens he had the ability to take that figment and put it in other people's minds too. He made it real in the sense that we can experience it, but where does it end? Solan City is a mirror of New York City. But it stops there. There's no Upstate, or Syracuse, or Catskills. Right?"

"Right," Ty said. "The warlocks only wanted to create a reflected version of the city itself."

"So, it just stops, right? The warlocks only mirrored a specific area, and once that area is finished, it ends."

"But then there's more. There are the outskirts and other areas beyond Solan."

"Yes, because there's space for that to happen. But not here. This is inside a cliff. There might be a network of caves, but there's no infinite space. So how big did he make this area? Where does it end?"

They were looking at me like they thought I should take up the position beside Phillip at the trash can. I knew they weren't following my thought process. The shock of seeing the burned-out skeleton of the house still had its grip on them. Right now, all they could focus on was the brutal contrast of the sagging ruins against the glow of the evening sky.

"I thought we came back here to see the house," Aurora said.

"We came back here to find out what happened," I clarified. I wanted to push the issue, but the look on her face was too much. I wasn't used to seeing her look fragile and emotional. She needed to work through this in a different way than I did, and I knew I needed to respect that. "All right," I said. "The house first."

I relented, but I knew it was only temporary. They weren't distracting me from the questions that had formed in the back of my mind. I had known as soon as Malakan brought me here that this wasn't a place he shared with many people, and the way Aurora talked about it only solidified that. It made the thought of someone causing the explosion in his house even more troublesome. I didn't want to think that someone he knew and trusted could have betrayed him this way. Yet at the same time, my experience with the Dragon was enough to make me doubt the entire concept of trust in the Underworld.

"We need to be extremely careful," Ty said. "Fire sites like this can be unpredictable. What looks solid could collapse with any pressure, and there could be hot spots and burning embers just below the surface."

The closer we got to what was left of the house, the more I was aware of the heat still radiating off it. It wasn't as much as I had expected so soon after the fire, but it was enough to remind me of the pain of the flames on my skin.

5

The center section of the steps was largely intact, but they led up to nothing. At the top step there was a gap where the broad front porch had been burned away. There were no signs left of the glider that had hung from the ceiling or the rocking chairs that dotted the once-welcoming stretch of wood. The image of Malakan sitting in one of those chairs, rocking slowly as he took in the area around him that he had loved so much, created a wave of emotion that made me feel like I had been punched in the center of my chest.

"You're thinking about Malakan sitting in his rocking chair, aren't you?" Aurora asked.

I looked over at her and nodded.

A hint of a smile touched her lips.

"Don't worry," she said. "I wasn't hearing your thoughts. It's just that I was thinking the same thing. Almost every time I came here to see him, that was where I would find him. Unless he had come to the palace to get me and brought me here, or the few times he was inside poring over his books, I'd come through that door and find him sitting right here on the porch, rocking in that chair. It was always the same one."

"I wonder why he liked it so much," I said.

She shook her head slightly, looking toward the spot where the chair had sat.

"I don't know," she said. "It always made me wonder why he had so many of them if he wasn't ever going to use them. Sometimes I would sit out here with him, but I know there were very few other people, if any, that he brought here. Even when I sat out here with him, it was like I wasn't even here."

"What do you mean?" I asked.

"When Malakan sat out here in his rocking chair it was like he was somewhere else. I don't know how to describe it other than that. He would sit in the chair stare out at the field and just rock. He didn't say anything or really even look around much. He just stared in front of him almost like he was seeing something I wasn't. It was the same every time I saw him in that chair."

"How long did he have this place?" I asked.

"I'm not sure," Aurora said. "I know he started spending most of his time here after his exile, but it's entirely possible he had it even before then. Malakan was never one to do what was expected of him all the time. It wouldn't surprise me at all to find out he created this place at the same time that the rest of Solan City was created, just so he would have somewhere to run off to."

"Why would he want somewhere to run off to?"

"Everyone does," Aurora said. "Don't they?"

I felt like the comment was directed at me, but I didn't say anything. I knew she was right. That was how I had ended up here. When I got to my high school reunion, I had needed somewhere to run off to, and I had ended up at Solomon's. If I hadn't run off that night, I wouldn't have met Aurora. As soon as that thought went through my mind, I wondered if it was true. I might not have met Aurora that night if I hadn't walked away from the reunion and sought solace in what I thought was just a hole-in-the-wall bar, but I couldn't believe that would have kept us from ever meeting or kept me from being here. When Malakan told me that I was the son of the Arch-Warlock, everything fell into place. It cemented for me the feeling I'd had since my first day in the Underworld. I belonged here. I was always going to find my way back, it was just a matter of how and when.

"I wish I knew where this place was," Aurora said, breaking through my thoughts.

"Maybe it isn't anywhere," Ashe said. "Maybe it's just a place Malakan imagined, or somewhere he read about in a book and liked."

Aurora shook her head.

"I don't think Malakan was the type to spend a lot of time reading story books set on sleepy farms. Even if he was, I don't think he would have chosen a place he had read about or seen in a drawing to be his personal refuge from the rest of the world. A tremendous amount of time and thought went into making this place. It has to be somewhere that mattered to him. I just wish I knew where it was and why it was important."

There was a brief moment of silence as we walked toward the pile of ashes. I walked around the remaining steps and up to where the front door had been. I was trying to orient myself and remember what the house had looked like before the fire. The frame of the front door was still standing, and I walked through it cautiously. The house had seemed so much bigger than the foundation that was left behind suggested. I knew that was just a trick of perception. I'd watched a house be built at the end of my street when I was younger, and I remembered when they first put down the foundation. It had looked so small, and I couldn't imagine why they would build a house that would be so different from the other ones in the neighborhood. I was convinced it would end up a little cottage that would seem tiny in comparison to the modest homes around it. It had fascinated me to watch the progress of that lot going from being completely empty to having a house where someone lived. I had watched them pour the foundation, then divide it up into what would eventually be rooms. I snuck onto the construction site one night to get a closer look, and walked through those spaces, trying to imagine what they would be. Even then, as I was going from room to room, it didn't seem like they were big enough.

    I was thinking the same thing as I took the first few steps into what had been the house's entryway. It was like the entire thing had closed in, as if the fire had somehow shrunk it. I carefully made my way to what had been the room where I had gone through the ritual.

"This is where he brought me," I said. "He had this room set up for the ritual. There were a ton of shelves along the walls, full of books. But look, nothing. Not even one of them is left."

"Books don't tend to survive fires," Ashe said.

"Not the books," I said. "The shelves. They weren't just flimsy pressed boards. They were solid, heavy pieces of furniture. I'd think that at least one of them would have survived, or a part of one, something." I walked further into the room. "Right here. There was a chair and a table. The chair was solid wood, but the table had metal legs." I moved the rubble aside with my foot. "Where is it? And where are the orbs?"

"Orbs?" Ty asked.

"Glass orbs," I said. "They gave me visions of my past, my present, and my future. That's how I knew Ashe was being held captive." I didn't mention what I'd seen in my vision of the past or my future. Now wasn't the time to try to understand that. "Those were solid, heavy glass. When I came back to talk to him, they were still sitting there, I saw them. No regular fire would vaporize metal and glass."

"Maybe he had already put them away," Ashe suggested.

"Why would he do that?" I asked. "He'd left them sitting out after the ritual. And where would he have put them? They would still be somewhere in the room, it wouldn't make sense for him to store them somewhere else. Besides, there wasn't time. This wasn't a fucking lawn chair he'd propped up in the middle of the room. This was a massive, heavy chair. He was standing at the door when I walked out of the house. I hadn't even gotten all the way across the field when the explosion happened. It was a matter of seconds. Less than a minute."

"Did you see anything else around the house?" Ty asked.

I shook my head.

"Just the other parlor," I said. "This was the only room he brought me to the first time I came here, when you were still in the stone chambers. He was really eager to get started on the ritual. We came into the house and he directed me right into this room and into the chair. But when I came back to tell him I'd completed my change, he brought me into the other room."

"What was in there?" he asked.

"Furniture," I said. "Some strange artifacts."

We walked back across what was left of the entryway and into the segment of the foundation that would have been the second parlor. This area was just like the first. The expanse of rubble didn't seem to contain anything but pieces of the ceiling that had crashed down onto the floor. I didn't see any remnants of anything that had been in that room when I had sat with Malakan.

"How about you?" Ty asked, looking at Aurora. "You've been here before. "

"A lot of times," Aurora agreed.

"Did you ever go into other rooms?" I asked.

"Yes," she said. "Not at first. At first, we stayed in these two rooms. I've seen the chair you were talking about, Hayden. It was always sitting in the middle of that room. It was there every time I was here, right next to the table with the glass orbs. I asked Malakan what they were one time, and he refused to tell me. He was very defensive about it and would never even let me go into the room. I guess he didn't think I needed to know whatever I would have seen in those visions."

"You said not at first," I said. "What did you mean?"

"For a while, every time I came here, we went into this room. This is where we would sit and talk. After a while, he brought me further into the house."

"What did you see?" I asked.

She walked out of the space and into the former hallway. She moved slowly further into the remnants of the house.

"Back here was the kitchen," she said. "It was one of his favorite jokes to offer me some refreshments every time I came to visit him. No matter how many meetings we had, he never got tired of that joke. Warlocks eat just like regular humans do, so sometimes we would come in here and he would make something for himself to eat or drink. He had an incredible sweet tooth." She said it fondly, with a hint of laughter in her voice. "His favorite thing was cookies. He loved lemon cookies and sweet iced tea. Sometimes in the winter he would change it up and drink coffee or hot tea. One time I even found him with a mug of hot cocoa, complete with candy cane. I don't know where he picked that habit up, but it amused him."

"Like the lamps," I said.

She nodded.

"It sounds ridiculous when you're just talking about it, but you have to remember the kind of life he had. What must have happened to him for him to refuse to talk about his past? And even if it was nothing horrible, and he just didn't like to dwell, his everyday life was something we can't imagine. He wasn't just an old man. He was one of the greatest warlocks of our time. Maybe of all time. He could make things happen that other people would never even think of, but it was the simplest things that meant the most to him. I actually had a glass of tea with him once, just to humor him."

We looked around the former kitchen. It was much like the first two rooms of the house, but in the center a large island had survived. The gray marble countertop was covered in soot, but it was still standing.

"How is this here, but there's no sign of the metal legs to that table, or the glass orbs?"

"Fires don't always burn evenly," Ty said. "Sometimes they are much more intense in some areas of the building than in others. It just depends on how much fuel is available."

"I told you, though. It wasn't like a fire started in one section of the house and then spread. There was an explosion and the entire building was completely consumed within seconds. It burned so fast and so intensely. But then what? It suddenly extinguished itself? It just doesn't make sense. Even if it did somehow burn itself out, this place should still be smoldering."

"What other parts of the house have you been in?" Ty asked.

Aurora showed us one more section of the foundation, telling us it had been where Malakan kept most of the tools and supplies he used for his rituals and magic. A single broken beaker on top of a pile of blackened dust was all that remained.

"That's it?" I asked, disappointed that we hadn't found any hint about what had happened.

"Those are the only rooms any of us have seen," Ty said. "We wouldn't know what is out of place in the others."

"Besides," Ashe said. "The rooms upstairs were completely destroyed. What's left of them is the rubble you see on the floor."

I realized Aurora had been quiet for several minutes. Her eyes swept back and forth across the area that had been the first parlor. She walked into the room and kicked a pile of broken wood. Smoke rose out of it and she stepped back.

"What is it?" I asked, walking up beside her.

"Nothing," she said.

I had resisted listening into her thoughts all day, but I couldn't anymore. I knew there was something going through her mind that she wasn't saying, and I needed to know what it was.

"Where is his body?"

The question hit me hard, but I didn't say anything. I still hadn't told Aurora about my ability to listen to her thoughts. I didn't think right now was the best moment for me to bring up that specific issue. But hearing that thought had only furthered my confusion and solidified my worry that this was done to Malakan on purpose. I tucked the question away to deal with later. Out of the corner of my eye, I noticed Ty staring at Aurora. His eyes were locked on her intently, but I couldn't discern the emotion in them.

"We should go," he said.

Aurora's hair whipped across her face as she turned her head sharply to him.

"Go?" she asked.

"He's right," I said, looking up at the sky, which was becoming darker. "We're not going to be able to find anything else tonight. We'll come back later. It'll be easier to search when there's enough light."

"Are we going back to the other side?" Ashe asked.

"No," Aurora said. "I don't think we should."

"You want to stay here in the Underworld?" I asked.

"Yes," she said. "I think we should go talk to my father. He's probably already heard about Malakan's death, but if he hasn't, he deserves to hear it from me. Besides, I think it's about time for you to see your rightful home."

"My rightful home?" I asked.

Aurora stepped closer and kissed me.

"Yes," she said. "The palace. It's where I live, and where you and I will rule over the vampires when my father is no longer Prime. "

6

I realized as we made our way back through the tunnels that I had no idea where the vampire palace was. I figured someone with the power and influence of the Prime wouldn't just hang out in a little apartment, but the word palace brought up a whole new set of images. Since I hadn't seen a castle tucked in between the skyscrapers, I had to assume the palace of the vampire royal family wasn't located in downtown Solan City.

We stepped out of the cliff into an oddly calm and quiet Final View. It seemed the chaos and turmoil had finally fizzled out, and nearly everyone in the community had settled down for the night. A few people were still standing at the trash cans, but their voices had been lowered to murmurs.

Around the edges of the open space I saw piles of blankets, sleeping bags, plastic bags, and cardboard. Occasionally one of the piles would shift and I knew these were makeshift beds for everyone who lived under the bridge. No one paid any attention to us as we made our way back through to the other side of the bridge and got into the car. We drove in silence in the opposite direction of downtown and soon we'd reached the outskirts of the city. It was similar to the area where Ashe had been kept captive in the church, but even that had been within the bounds of the city. Now, we ventured away from the city and into a darkness unbroken by street lights or glowing windows. Finally, ahead of us, I saw a huge stone arch. We passed through it into a village that could have existed centuries ago. Standing in complete opposition to the glittering glass and steel buildings of downtown, this village was a collection of houses and stores made of wood and stone. Many had thatched roofs that looked like they had been there for generations.

"Where are we?" I asked.

"The area you were talking about earlier," Aurora said. "The place beyond Solan City. This is the underworld that wasn't made to mirror a city on the other side. It exists on its own, just as always has. The palace isn't much further."

"You can drop me off here," Ty said.

Those were the first words I had heard him say since we'd walked through the door in the tree. I'd noticed as we were traveling that he seemed more distracted and distant than usual. Not that Ty had ever been the most effervescent person I'd ever met, but he seemed even more disconnected now. The way he had been staring at Aurora loomed in the back of my mind, and I wondered what he'd been thinking. On the other hand, I could understand him not being in the best mood. I would probably be mopey too if everyone was blaming me for all kinds of awful shit..

"Why here?" Aurora asked.

"I'm not going to go up to the palace with you," he said. "I'll just stay in the tavern."

"Why?" Ashe asked. "We're not far from the palace. Just come with us."

"No," Ty said. "I'd really rather stay at the tavern. There are some people I know who were planning on being there tonight, and I could use some time to unwind."

It was a lie. I could hear it in his voice. I didn't know why he was lying, but after everything he'd already been through, I didn't think Ty needed to be pushed any further. I pulled off on the side of the road and stopped.

"That's fine," I said. "We can just meet up tomorrow. Call if you hear anything. We'll do the same."

He gave an almost imperceptible nod and got out of the car without another word. When he was gone, I looked over at Aurora. She pointed ahead of us.

"Keep going," she said. "I'll tell you where to turn."

It was the same as it had been since we got into the car. She would only give me directions one or two turns at a time. At first, I was a little bit offended by it. It made me feel like she didn't think I would be able to handle anything more complex. The further we went from the city, however, the more I realized and why she was actually doing it. We were quickly leaving everything that looked familiar, and as soon as Solan City was behind us, I had no frame of reference. Every mile we traveled was completely new to me. As soon as that sank in, I started trying to absorb everything I was seeing. I wanted to remember how to get to all the places I needed to be, just like I did when I was in

New York. This was my new world, my new reality, and I needed to be comfortable and confident in it.

We hadn't gone far beyond the village when I saw my first glimpse of the palace. It was exactly what I had imagined. Sprawling and opulent, it rose out of the ground like a gothic castle. Which, by all rights, was exactly what it was. A huge iron gate blocked the wide, winding driveway that led up the hill to the palace. As soon as we approached it, a Shade guard stepped out from behind one of the columns and glared into the car.

"Let us through," Aurora commanded.

He stepped back and an instant later the gate slowly slid open. I drove in and followed the driveway around the side of the palace. Another guard stood waiting there, and I stopped the car. He approached, and I realized he wanted me to get out so he could park the car. Aurora took my hand as we walked onto a cobblestone pathway leading to a side entrance of the palace. I felt a little flicker of disappointment. I'd really wanted the drawbridge to go down and an announcement of our arrival to be made. Maybe a couple of trumpets. Nothing fancy. Instead, she led Ashe and me to a small wooden door at the side of the building and through a narrow passage that spiraled upward toward a breezeway.

"My father hates it when I use that entrance," Aurora said. "He says I should let the guards escort me through the main portion of the palace."

"Then why don't you?" I asked.

"Because she doesn't have to," Ashe said.

I laughed. No truer words have ever been spoken.

"This is one of my favorite spots in the palace," Aurora said, holding out her arms as if to encompass the entire breezeway. "I love coming out here and just looking out over the grounds."

I walked to the edge and leaned on the stone railing. it was too dark to see much beyond where I was standing, but I got the impression of grounds that stretched far out around us. A short distance away I could see the dark shapes of hedges, and I imagined a maze. I glanced over at Aurora.

"Did your parents have the groundskeepers make that maze for you?" I asked. "For you to play in when you were little?"

Aurora laughed.

"I was a child so long ago I barely remember it," she said. "But, no, that maze was not designed for me to frolic in."

"Why is it there, then?" I asked.

She followed my gaze and I knew she could see more of the meticulously kept grounds than I could, because she was seeing it through the filter of memory.

"I'm not sure," she said. "It's just always been there. My mother and the other women who raised me never let me go over there when I was playing outside, and when I got a little bit older, my father warned me that I was never to go in."

"And you actually listened to him?" I asked. "That surprises me."

Aurora shot me a glare.

"Are you saying I am disobedient?" she asked.

I laughed.

"That's exactly what I'm saying," I said. "Are you going to argue?"

She tilted her face and scrunched up her cute little mouth like she was thinking about it.

"No," she said. "And no, I didn't actually listen to him. Not at first, anyway. When I was younger, I didn't have the opportunity to try to go into the maze. I was never alone. Either I was with my mother or I was with one of the other women who took care of me. Everywhere I went, they were right there with me. When I got a little bit older and was given more freedom, I tried to sneak over and see what was in there. That's when I discovered that even when I thought I was alone, I wasn't. No matter how hard I tried, or how sneaky I attempted to be, I was always caught. Jaxxim pulled me down off the side of the hedge and blocked my way into the maze on more than one occasion. That's when my father assigned him to me as my personal bodyguard. Then I got a little older and it didn't matter to me so much anymore. I discovered far more interesting things in the world, and new and creative ways to get in trouble."

She gave me a mischievous grin.

"What about now?" I asked. "Do you want to know what's in there?"

She looked out over the grounds again and shrugged.

"Honestly, I don't really care anymore. I learned a long time ago that my father loves control and power. For a lot of people, it can be intimidating, but I got over that not long after he started to be more a part of my life. Now I think of things like him not wanting me to go into the maze the same was I think of Malakan and his lamps. It amuses him, so whatever. It seems like a waste of energy to try to get around it."

I turned to Aurora and wrapped my arms around her waist, pulling her in close and kissing her.

"Well, when the palace is ours and we are ruling the vampires, you won't have to humor anyone, and you can go in the maze whenever you want to. You can even frolic."

Aurora smiled, but out of the corner of my eye I saw Ashe's head cock to the side.

"You do realize you just fantasized about her father dying, right? The only way you're ever going to take over the palace and become Prime is if Darian meets his end."

My arms fell away from Aurora.

"You sure do know how to take the fun out of a situation," I said.

Ashe grinned and kissed me.

"You know my skill set," she said.

"Come on," Aurora said. "I want to show you more of the palace."

She led us down to the end of the breezeway and through another door into the palace itself. We were in a dark corridor lit only by torches.

"What's with all the torches?" I asked. "You

already told me the Underworld has electricity, so why do so many of the buildings seem to ignore it completely?"

"Tradition," Aurora said. "The palace has been here since well before my father was Prime. There are sections of it that have all of the modern amenities you'd expect, but a lot of it was kept the way it's always been. I guess you could say tradition is important to royalty."

"Like the guards in London wearing the big furry hats?" I asked.

Aurora laughed.

"Something like that," she said. "You'll get used to it after a while. It can actually be really nice."

At the end of the corridor I saw a door leading to a stone staircase that curved up into a tower.

"What's that?" I asked.

"That leads to the guards' quarters," Aurora said. "There's another one on the other side of the palace."

We took another set of steps down into a wider hall. This one looked much more like it was designed to be seen. Rather than bare stone, the floor was covered with a thick carpet, and tapestries hung every few feet down the walls.

"Do you know what was wrong with Ty?" I

finally asked. "Do you know why he didn't want to come here?"

"He said there were people waiting for him. People go and stay at the tavern all the time," Aurora said.

"Do you actually believe that?" I asked.

"No," Ashe said. "She knows that's not the truth."

"That's not exactly accurate," Aurora said. "The tavern is where people go and get together, and a lot of times the ones who still drink will drink too much and end up stumbling into one of the rooms for the night."

"But you know that's not why Ty is there tonight," Ashe said. "I wouldn't exactly say he frequents the tavern anymore."

"Then why is he there tonight?" I asked. "Why didn't he just come back here with us?"

The women exchanged glances, and I could see Ashe looking at Aurora significantly. Without saying a word, she was pressuring Aurora to tell me something. Finally, Ashe sighed and turned to me.

"Do you remember when I told you Ty was really high up in the Shades? He wasn't just one of the guards. He was near the top of the hierarchy."

"Yes," I said.

"The hierarchy is really important among the Shades," Aurora said. "Working their way up through the ranks takes time and a lot of work. There have been guards who have served for centuries and never made it as high as Ty had. He was extremely good at what he did, and he had earned the trust of the rest of the guards, and of my father. That's why he had been chosen to be the personal errand runner for the Prime. It was his responsibility to make sure that messages were safely delivered from my father to others, and vice versa. That in, addition to his other responsibilities, made him extremely important among the guards, which was why it was such an incredible fall when The Incident happened. Not only did Ty lose my father's trust and his position, but also his reputation. It was humiliating, and he hasn't wanted to come back to the palace. He hasn't stepped foot back here since that night.

7

"Let's keep exploring," Aurora said, obviously trying to move the conversation on. "There's a lot more in the palace I want to show you."

She was trying to gloss over the conversation we were having, and I was willing to let it go for the moment. I knew I would find out more when the time came. For now, I would indulge Aurora.

"I'm exhausted," Ashe said. "Is there somewhere I can sleep?"

Aurora nodded.

"Sure," she said. "I'll show you to one of the guest rooms."

We moved along several more hallways, going up and down stairways until I lost track of where we were in the building. It felt like the first time I had gone through the tunnels to Malakan's stone chambers. Finally, we walked out into another lavishly decorated hallway and Aurora stopped in front of arched white double doors.

"Here," she said. "There's a private bathroom and everything in there. If you look in the dresser, you'll find some pajamas. I'll have one of the servants come for your clothes and they'll be clean for you in the morning."

"Thank you," Ashe said.

I could see the change that had happened between the two women since the night I met them. It was obvious then that they had some sort of history and experience with each other, but it was tense. There might have been a friendship of some kind, but the separation in their status within the vampire community was clear when I looked back on it. Now they seemed to be drawing closer together. They were getting accustomed to a sense of equality and reliance. They needed each other as much as I needed each of them, and they both needed me. Ashe disappeared into the room and closed the door behind her. Aurora turned to me.

"Are you tired, too?" she asked.

"I'd like to see more of the palace," I said.

She smiled and took my hand again. I liked the

way it folded so easily into my palm. We walked slowly through the palace and I listened as she described the different rooms and pointed out all of the incredible features of the seemingly endless home. Just like she had said when I asked about the torches, most of the palace was equipped with every modern amenity I could possibly think of. All of it had been layered on top of the existing structure, creating a fascinating juxtaposition between the ancient and the progressive. Some hallways were like the first and lined with torches, but then opened out into rooms filled with technology; like the media room that was bigger than my apartment. I stood in the middle of that room looking around, trying to take it all in. I'd never seen anything like it. Even in my glory days when recruiters from colleges and NFL scouts were doing everything they could to woo me, I'd never experienced this level of luxury and indulgence.

"Do you like it?" Aurora asked.

"It's amazing," I said. "I just..."

"You just what?"

"What do vampires watch on TV?" I asked.

I knew I sounded stupid, and Aurora's laughter confirmed it, but I couldn't help the curiosity. The screen in front of me rivaled movie theaters, but I was having trouble figuring out what would be on it when Darian or Aurora kicked back at the end of a long day.

"What do we watch on TV?" she asked. "That's your big question?"

" I have other questions, but right now, I'm curious about this whole situation. Are you football fans? This could host one hell of a Superbowl party."

"Football?" she asked, narrowing her eyes as she pronounced the word like she'd never heard it before. "No," she shook her head. "Mostly we watch the televised executions and the news bulletins about where to go to collect blood."

I felt like I was going to throw up. I had made major progress in the last week, but that statement was enough to make a good chunk of the new badass me drain away.

"What?" I asked, my voice weak.

Aurora stared at me for a few seconds before her face finally softened and a laugh bubbled out of her.

"Hayden, seriously. You honestly think that we sit around a room like this and watch people get murdered?"

"It was more the going and collecting blood

part that was getting to me," I said. "I could probably pretend a televised execution was fake. I've watched enough television to be desensitized to most violence. A good old-fashioned drawing and quartering would be nothing to me."

"Oh, we don't do that anymore," Aurora said. "That fell out of fashion years ago. All those animal rights activists worried about the horses having to work too hard. Now we just all go out to the middle of the village and watch the hangings."

I couldn't breathe again.

"Are those on a regular schedule?" I asked.

Aurora laughed again.

"Hayden! Have you not learned anything about the vampire culture in the last week?" she asked. "I know Ashe gave you her 'Vampires Fact versus Fiction' speech. Sunlight is fine. Garlic is delicious."

"A stake through the heart just pisses you off."

"Yep," she said. "That's the one."

"How do you know that?"

"Ashe never changes," she said. "She won't admit it, but she'll always swoop in and help someone going through their transition if she thinks they're going to survive."

"She does this a lot?" I asked.

"I said if she thinks they're going to survive,"

she said. "That's not as often as you'd like to think. Does she do what she's done for you often?" She shook her head. "Never."

"Why does she help them?" I asked.

The smile played at Aurora's lips again.

"She likes her strays."

I lunged for her and scooped her up by her waist, tossing her over my shoulder. Aurora squealed in response.

"Strays?" I asked. "Is that right? I'm a stray?"

I gave Aurora a hard smack on her ass and she giggled again before I set her back on her feet.

"Come on," she said, pulling me by my hand. "There's something else I want to show you. One more room."

She led me down a few more hallways and through a heavy black door. She opened it and we walked through into a room that looked straight out of a picture of ancient Rome. A massive sunken bath took up the majority of the center of the room and huge round columns accented the marble floor.

"This," she said, walking backward a few steps as she reached behind herself to release the zipper on her dress, "is all yours now. This is the life you can enjoy now that you are my Lord."

The dress dropped away, revealing only the tiny scrap of panties beneath. She kicked off her shoes as I walked toward her. My hands ran across her skin and I pulled her up against me.

"Yes, I am," I said, ducking my mouth down to kiss her.

Our mouths played against each other for a few seconds, then I felt her fingers working at the button on my pants.

"You missed our celebration of your change," she said.

"I know," I said.

"Why don't we do some celebrating of our own?"

The rest of our clothes fell into a pile on the marble floor, and I followed Aurora down the steps into the warm water of the bath. The water felt smooth and soft, like it was laced with oil. She walked me into the middle so the water was over her waist, then guided me to sit on a ledge along the side. She ran her hands down my chest and over my belly, then one found my hard cock. My head fell back as she stroked. I could only take it for a few seconds before I grabbed her hips and pulled her forward into my lap. I sank into her in one hard thrust. Filling my hands with her breasts,

I used them for leverage as I thrust into her. The effect of being inside her now was even more powerful than it had been before. All my depleted strength rushed back, and I felt my abilities becoming sharper. The connection between us made me feel like I was more in touch with the new aspects of myself I was just discovering. It was like parts of my brain were lighting up. I knew some of it was from being transformed into a vampire, but that wasn't all. Some of it had always been there, I just hadn't known it before. Somehow, now that I had found it, it felt natural.

Aurora's hips rolled, grinding down into my lap so I plunged even deeper into her welcoming body. I didn't slow down. I didn't want to lessen the intensity or make it last. I wanted to indulge my every craving and need and take every bit of her she would offer me. I let out an animal roar as I came deep inside her, and at the same moment Aurora cried out too. Her walls clamped down around my cock and our bodies throbbed and pulsed together in frantic rhythm.

Spent and satisfied, I climbed out of the water a few minutes later and took one of the towels from the shelves carved into the back of a column. I reached for my clothes, but Aurora eased my hand back down to my side.

"Don't bother," she said. "One of the servants will get them. You have fresh clothes. Come on, let's go to bed."

"How will the servants know?" I asked.

Aurora walked over to one of several staircases leading up and out of the room.

"Their job is to anticipate every need we have and fulfill it."

"I might be able to get used to that," I said.

She started up the steps.

"I'm sure you will," she said.

8

The steps lead up to what Aurora called her bedroom. In reality, it was a network of several rooms that made a luxurious apartment. We walked into the second room and my suitcase was already sitting on an oversized bed positioned on a platform.

"See?" Aurora said. "Needs anticipated and fulfilled."

She let the towel she had wrapped around herself drop to the floor and walked over to a large bureau against the wall. Reaching inside, she took out a sheer nightgown. I reciprocated by dropping my own towel and walking over to the bag I'd packed before we left Ashe's apartment. I pulled out a pair of black sweatpants and a gray t-shirt. We crawled under the thick blankets and I felt my body relax into the soft mattress. Aurora turned off the light and curled up beside me. Even with her cuddled up close to me and the soothing darkness settling over me, I couldn't completely relax. My brain wouldn't stop turning, and I couldn't will myself to go to sleep. I stared up at the ceiling, thinking through everything that had happened. I didn't know how long I'd laid there, but Aurora's breath was slow and deep when I slipped out from under the blankets and grabbed a sweatshirt from my bag. Dropping it down over my head, I made my way back through the palace.

I'd been leaning against the stone railing on the breezeway overlooking the maze for long enough that my eyes had become accustomed to the dark and I could see more of the meandering pattern of the path through the hedges. Around me, the night air was thin and cold, but I didn't mind it. It made me feel more awake and my thoughts were sharper as I breathed in each fresh breath. Why wouldn't Darian let Aurora go into that maze? What was it about it that made him want to keep his daughter away, not just when she was a child, but even now as an adult? I understood what she had said about his sense of power and control amusing him; that explanation wasn't enough, though. Even if Aurora wasn't serious about it anymore, it was still strange. Maybe it was even stranger if she wasn't curious about it anymore and Darian was still not upfront with her about what was there. I could understand a father being worried about a little girl venturing into a huge maze, especially a little girl as hard-headed and determined as Aurora. But she said he'd actively prevented her from entering it even when she was grown and had gone through her transformation. It just didn't make sense.

"Are you trying to find the end?"

I turned to look over my shoulder and saw Aurora coming down the breezeway toward me. She was wearing a white robe over her nightgown, and she wrapped her arms around herself to stay warmer.

"What?" I asked.

"You're staring at the maze like I used to. Are you trying to see if you can find the end of it from where you're standing?"

It was like I'd drawn her toward me. I shook my head.

"Not exactly," I said.

"Good," she said. "Spoilers. You can't see the end from here. At least I was never able to. What are you thinking about?"

"Did your father ever tell you why he didn't want you to go in the maze?"

"No," Aurora said matter-of-factly. "He just said he didn't want me to go in there. Then when I kept trying, he told me I wasn't allowed to go in there. Then when I continued to keep trying, he told me I was forbidden. He said I didn't need an explanation, that I was to do as I was told and that was it. Like I said, it lost its novelty after a while and I decided to just..."

"Humor him," I said.

"Exactly," she said. "It's just a maze. It's not worth the argument. What are you doing out here, anyway? You can't sleep?"

"No," I said. "I've got too much on my mind."

I thought back to my reaction when she came out onto the breezeway. It had been like I had drawn her to me with my thoughts, only I knew that wasn't the case. She had just woken up and I wasn't there, so she came looking for me. I knew then, however, that I needed to tell her what I'd told Ashe. Telling her felt different. When I mentioned it to Ashe, I didn't have any reason to think it was strange. It was one more thing in a string of changes I was going through, and new abilities I was discovering about myself. I had no idea until she told me that being able to read her thoughts wasn't something that was normal for vampires. Now that I knew it was unusual, it was harder to face Aurora. I hadn't been honest with her. I hadn't been honest with any of them. With everything going on, I didn't know if I should tell her the whole truth, but I could at least tell her this part of it. I took a breath.

"What is it, Hayden?" she asked.

"There's something I need to tell you," I said.

"Go ahead," she said.

"I can hear your thoughts," I blurted out, knowing there was no eloquent way to say it.

I wasn't sure what I expected her reaction to be, but the blank stare surprised me. I waited for a few seconds before she actually responded.

"You can what?" she asked.

"I can hear your thoughts," I repeated. "I realized I could do it before you finished my transition. I can hear Ashe's thoughts, too."

"You can hear what I'm thinking?" she asked. "And you can hear what Ashe is thinking?"

"Yes," I said. "I haven't tested it out yet, but I'm fairly certain I would be able to hear Stephana's thoughts, too."

"Oh," she said. "So, you're telling me once you have sex with a woman, you can hear her thoughts? That's a unique side effect."

"Yes," I said. "And sometimes I can make them hear my thoughts, too."

Aurora looked like she was getting ready to ask me more questions, and I didn't want to risk her asking something I wasn't willing to answer. I knew I was hitting her with something major that she didn't expect, and she was having to a process it like I had, but there was too much going on. I really didn't want to contend with the 'How does that make you feel?' conversation. Now was not the time for me to practice for appearing on afternoon talk shows.

"Hayden, that's --"

"I know," I said. "The only reason I'm telling you right now is because I heard what you were thinking when we were at Malakan's house."

"The only reason?" she asked. "So, what? You just weren't going to tell me at all?"

"I didn't say that," I said. "I just think there's enough other shit happening right now that we need to be focusing on that. I don't need to be sharing all my growing pains with everybody. I would have told you eventually, when things calmed down some."

"You can't keep things like this from me, Hayden."

"I'm sorry, Aurora. I promise it won't happen again. Why were you wondering about Malakan's body?"

"What about his body?"

Ashe was coming at us from the other side of the breezeway.

"You two really need to stop just popping out of nowhere," I said.

"I'm sorry," Ashe said. "Would you prefer it if I announced myself first?"

"That would be nice," I said.

She walked back out of sight.

"Hayden? Aurora? Just so you know, I'm on my way out."

"Hilarious," I said as she came back into view.

"What are you talking about?" she asked. "What about Malakan's body?"

"I heard Aurora wondering why there was no sign of his body in the house," I said.

Aurora looked back and forth between us.

"You told her?" she asked.

"Yes," I said. "She's the first one I heard, and I told her about it. But again, now is not the time to be focusing on that. Right now, I want to know why that was going through your mind."

Before she could say anything, I heard another voice reverberating through the palace. It sounded frantic as it grew louder.

"Aurora! Aurora, are you here?"

It was Darian.

"I'm out here," she called.

The Prime appeared in the doorway and then rushed toward Aurora. He threw his arms around her in an embrace I could only describe as awkward. She looked uncomfortable, like it wasn't a gesture she was accustomed to. When he released her, she took a step back toward me.

"Is it true?" Darian asked. "I heard there was a tragedy and that Hayden was involved. What's going on?"

"Yes," Aurora said. "It's true. There was a tragedy, and Hayden was there, but he didn't have anything to do with it."

Her voice was careful, each word measured as she built herself up to telling her father what had happened.

"Then what's going on?" Darian demanded.

"Father," she said, taking a step toward him. "Listen to me. There was an explosion at Malakan's house. Hayden was there."

"An explosion?" Darian asked.

"Yes," Aurora said.

"Where is he?" Darian asked. "Where is Malakan? Is he here?" He looked around Aurora toward me. "Did you bring him back here?"

"No," I said.

"His house was destroyed," Aurora said. "It burned down. He didn't get out."

The Prime's mouth open, but no sound came out. He stumbled back a few steps, reaching for the wall to support himself. He looked shocked.

"His house burned down?" he asked. "Are you sure he was inside?"

"I had just walked out," I said. "I was there talking to him, and I left. I hadn't even gotten all the way across the field to the door when it happened."

Darian looked at me questioningly.

"The field?" he asked. "He brought you to his

house? This happened at the house in the cliff? He never even wanted *me* there."

"I sent Hayden to him," Aurora said. "You know that, Father."

Darian's eyes opened wider.

"I can't believe this," he said. "Malakan, my dear friend. I can't believe he's gone. How can he be dead?"

"I'm sorry," I said. "I know Malakan was an important confidant for you."

Even as I said it, something was pricking at the back of my mind. Darian sounded shocked and devastated, which I would have understood, but there was something about it that wasn't right. The dramatic extent of his reaction rubbed me the wrong way. I didn't know exactly what it was, but I was immediately on edge. Was he simply acting?

"Yes," Darian said. "He was. More than I can say. And I will find out who is responsible for this."

This perked up my attention. I hadn't said anything about the suspicion I had that someone had planned the explosion. Why would he jump to the conclusion that someone was responsible for it? I took a step closer, so I stood next to Aurora.

"What do you mean you will find out who is responsible for this? How do you know it wasn't an accident? Only a few chosen people knew about the house, right?"

Darian met my eyes and held them for a few seconds.

"It's late," he said. "Everybody needs to get some sleep. We've all been through a lot."

9

Darian pulled his eyes away from me to look at his daughter.

"Bed, Aurora," he said. "All of us will feel better after some sleep, and we can figure this out in the morning."

He turned and stalked away from us.

"He's probably right," Aurora said. "Maybe we should try to get some rest." Ashe started to turn away, and Aurora reached out for her. "Ashe come with us. I'd feel better if we were all together."

We walked back through to Aurora's bed chamber. I crawled into the warm bed, and one woman curled up on either side of me. They both rested their heads on my chest and let out long breaths as they tried to go to sleep. I didn't feel any different than I had the first time I laid here trying to sleep. There was even more on my mind now. it was just too much. Something about Darian's reaction made the hair on the back of my neck stand up even now.

I'd been lying there for what felt like hours when I felt Ashe's hand come up to the side of my face. She traced the curve of my jaw with one finger and then propped herself up to look down at me.

"Can't sleep?" she asked.

"No," I said.

"Feeling tense?" she asked.

"A little," I admitted.

Ashe tucked her head and kissed the side of my neck. Her mouth ran up my neck and she sucked my earlobe into her mouth briefly.

"I can help you with that," she said. "Do you remember the last time you were feeling tense?"

I nodded, and my body immediately reacted to her. My cock got so hard it lifted the blanket away from me, and Ashe made a happy sound.

"Let's go over there," I said, gesturing to an armchair and ottoman.

Ashe nodded, and we climbed out of the bed. I stripped out of my pants as I approached the chair, then sat. She sat on the ottoman and reached forward to wrap her hand around my cock. Her soft palm ran along my shaft and swirled over the engorged head. The lust I felt the morning I came down the stairs at Soloman's and saw her behind the bar was nothing compared to what I felt now. Just like she had told me it would, my need for sex was only stronger now that I had gone through my change and was fully a vampire. The craving was irresistible, and I had no patience to go slow. Fortunately, neither did Ashe. She held the base of my cock firmly and opened her mouth. She took me in fully and without hesitation. Her little moan as I filled her mouth and dipped close to her throat told me she was as hungry for me as I was for her. Sliding the ottoman closer to the chair, Ashe opened her legs so they were draped on either side of the cushion where she sat. The position pushed the skirt of the pale blue nightgown she was wearing up to her hips and revealed she wasn't wearing anything under it. Her hand ran up her thigh and over her belly before pushing one shoulder strap down. The thin fabric fell away from her breasts, and she immediately cupped her hand over one. She kneaded into it for a few seconds before letting her hand drop down over her belly. I watched her fingertips trace up along her inner thigh, then finally find her wet pussy. I felt the vibration of her mouth as she groaned in response to the sensation of her fingertips sliding over her clit.

I tilted my head to give myself a better view of Ashe dipping her fingers into her opening. She thrust two fingers inside herself as she mimicked the speed with her mouth on my cock. Out of the corner of my eye I saw something moving on the other side of the room, and I lifted my gaze to see Aurora coming toward us.

"You two are playing without me?" she asked.

"You are more than welcome to join us, " I said.

Aurora grinned and stripped out of her nightgown as she walked toward us. I reached for Ashe and slid further down in the chair. Turning Ashe around, I guided her so she came down in my lap, letting me sink deep into her. I pressed my hand to the center of her back so she fell forward onto the ottoman. The position spread her wide open and drove me deep, while giving me an incredible view of her ass bouncing as I started thrusting into her.

I didn't have the view for long before Aurora swung her leg over the chair so she straddled my chest, presenting her pussy to me. I took one hand from Ashe's hip and slipped it between Aurora's thighs so I could grab her ass and pull her down to my waiting mouth. I ran my tongue through her folds, hungrily lapping up the sweet, hot juices already flowing from her. I wondered how long she had been listening to Ashe and me, getting herself hot and wet before joining us. Sliding my hand down, I pushed two fingers deep into Aurora and focused the tip of my tongue on her clit. Her head fell back as she rolled her nipples between her fingers and rocked her hips against my mouth.

Ashe's hips shifted just slightly, and I knew she'd tucked her hand beneath her so each thrust massaged her tight pearl. She was gasping, her skin slick and sweaty, and Aurora was moaning. I knew both were close and I could feel my own orgasm rushing up through me. I pounded into Ashe harder, holding Aurora close as I flicked my tongue against her at the same intense rhythm. Seconds later both women screamed out and I felt Aurora's pussy tighten around my fingers as Ashe's closed around my cock. My tongue gathered a fresh wash of Aurora's fluids as she came, and I continued to lick her until she cried out for me to stop. It was enough to send me over the edge and I shot deep and hard into Ashe. She pushed her hips back and whimpered with pleasure as I filled her.

Finally, after giving ourselves a few moments to recover, we disentangled ourselves from each other and went into the bathroom attached to Aurora's bedroom. There we took a long, leisurely shower, washing each other slowly. We explored each other, and my fingers brought each woman to another shuddering orgasm before we emerged.

I looked at the bed, but though I was completely satisfied, there wasn't a single part of me that wanted to get in.

"I don't feel like sleeping," I said.

"Neither do I," Aurora said. "I feel better and stronger than I have in a long time. I don't want to waste any time."

"Exactly," I said. "I don't want to waste any time, either. We need to figure out what happened. You wouldn't happen to have any human food or drinks here, would you?" I asked.

"Sticking to it, huh?" Ashe asked.

"For now," I said. "I think Stephana might be onto something. Besides, it's not like it hurts me. I consumed plenty of things before my change that were terrible for my body and I knew it. I did it anyway. Why don't we just think of my occasional cup of coffee and chocolate chip cookie as my Underworld vice."

The women laughed.

"Well, it just so happens we do keep the kitchen stocked with a few things," Aurora said. "We occasionally have visitors from species that eat, and I might be known to occasionally have a snack."

"Really?" I asked, surprised.

"Don't be so shocked," Aurora said. "I told you I had tea with Malakan."

"You told me he gave you some sweet iced tea and you didn't like it."

"I don't do it often," she said. "But I'm not as militant as Ashe over here. There are a few things that I still enjoy every now and then."

"Good," I said. "Because if I get through this, you better believe I'll be using that media room to watch football, and I can't watch football without munchies."

When we were dressed, we spiraled down into a deeper part of the palace and Aurora showed us into the kitchen. Three men were already there, filling platters with a huge array of food. I was starting to think the palace might be bugged. I definitely didn't love the idea of the servants being able to listen into everything that was happening, but like I had told Aurora, I could get used to not having to wait for the things I wanted.

"How do they know what we want?" I asked, leaning toward Aurora.

"Concerned you aren't the only one around here who can read thoughts?" she teased.

"I was thinking more along the lines of subtle spying," I said. "Maybe there are a couple of microphones in each room, or tapestries with the eyes cut out and secret passages behind the walls."

She shook her head and kissed me again.

"I don't know if I should let you into that media room again," she said. "I think you have watched enough movies and TV for a lifetime."

"How about an eternal existence?" I asked.

She tilted her head and made a sound like she was contemplating.

"Why don't you check back with me in a couple hundred years?"

"You've got it," I said.

Rather than having the servants follow us, we each took a platter of food and made our way into a lounge decorated in dark wood and brown leather. Depositing everything onto a wide coffee table in the middle of the room, we sat and I reached for a cookie.

"Is that really what you're going to eat from now on?" Ashe asked.

"Not the only thing," I said. "But they're so good. You said some people say certain foods taste better to them after they become vampires. Apparently, chocolate chip cookies are my thing now."

She laughed and grabbed another of the cookies off the platter. She nibbled the corner, then tossed the cookie back onto the plate.

"I still don't get it," she said.

"I'm going to find something you like," I said. "Mark my words."

She reached over and ran her hand along the inside of my thigh.

"You already have found something I like," she said.

"And you will have a steady diet," I said, leaning over to kiss her.

Her tongue dipped playfully into my mouth and I smiled as I sat up. I had to focus if I was ever going to get through this conversation.

"All right, before I get distracted again. Aurora, you and I were talking before your father interrupted. Ashe, you asked why we were talking about Malakan's body."

"Yes," Ashe said. "I heard you talking about Malakan's body. Why?"

"It wasn't there," Aurora said. "It wasn't in the house."

"There was almost nothing left," Ashe said. "I don't want to hurt you, but did you think that maybe his body was destroyed? The fire was strong enough to obliterate metal and glass. He could have been turned to ash like everything else."

She said it as carefully as she could, but the words obviously disturbed Aurora.

"There should have been some indication," she said. "Even when there are other disasters and entire areas are wiped out, you can still see signs of where people were. You might not be able to find a whole body, but you can see an outline or bits of bone or teeth. Something. But it's not just that. Don't you think the timing is a little strange?"

"What do you mean?" I asked.

"Nothing like that has ever happened. Malakan has been alive for centuries, he's seen war and destruction, but he's never had a disaster like this happen to him. He has survived everything people have thrown at him, even after his exile. But then this happens right when you've come to ask for his help? You show up and he helps you, and then his house bursts into flame, and there's no sign of his body left behind?"

"What do you think it means?" I asked.

She shook her head as she sat back.

"I don't know," she said. "I have no idea what it could mean. But it's bothering me. I haven't been able to stop thinking about it. It just doesn't seem right. Something about this whole thing doesn't seem right."

"Why did you send me to Malakan?" I asked.

"Don't you know?" she said.

10

"What?" I asked.

"Don't you already know?" Aurora asked. "I would think by now you would have figured it out."

"Ashe told me some," I said.

"But that was mostly a guess," Ashe admitted. "I told him what I knew, and what I thought might be your reasoning."

"I want to hear it from you," I said. "I want you to tell me why you sent me to Malakan before you would complete my change."

"I knew as soon as I bit you what I had done," Aurora said. "I couldn't resist. The second I saw you walk into that bar, I was completely entranced by you. There was something so incredibly different about you, something I've never experienced in any other man. I looked at you, and I knew in that instant I had to have you. When I went to bite you, I couldn't control myself. I gave the bonding bite, but when it was all over the reality hit me. I've never been bonded to anyone in my entire existence. In all of the years I have been on this Earth, there hasn't been a single man I have wanted to align myself with for eternity. I always saw it as tying myself down and limiting what I could do and experience. When I left you in that room and my mind cleared, it occurred to me what had just happened, and the gravity of the decision that I had to make."

"Did the decision really matter to you?" I asked.

"How could you ask that?" Aurora asked. "Of course it mattered to me."

"I'm sorry if I needed some confirmation," I said. "Ashe was all too quick to let me know how easy it is for you to just abandon the people you've bitten. And you didn't seem too concerned when your father threatened to kill me himself. It seemed like a game to you. Especially when you told me the only way you would do it was if I went to Malakan and got the answer to your question."

"I didn't mean for it to seem like a game,"

Aurora said. "I wouldn't do that to you. This is the most serious decision I've ever made, and I put a huge amount of thought into it. It might not have seemed like it to you, but that's just how I am. I'm not going to lie to you and say I immediately knew I was going to go through with the ritual to complete your change. I was attracted to you like I've never been to anyone else. I was drawn to you in a way I didn't expect, and I wasn't ready for. I didn't know if I wanted to make that sort of commitment. There had to be more than just that attraction to help me make the decision."

"So, you sent me to Malakan to get his opinion," I said.

"It was much more than that," she said. "I sent you to him because I knew he was the only person who would be able to give me the information I needed about you. From the second I saw you, I knew there was something that set you apart from everyone else, but I didn't know if it was the type of difference I needed."

"I don't think I'm following you," I said.

"Malakan wasn't just someone I talked to," Aurora said. "He wasn't just a friend I went and spent time with when I felt like it. He was a confidant, but more than that, he was someone I trusted completely. He had been around my family since before I was born, and even though we didn't get close until I was much older, he had been a part of my life since I was very young. He made prophecies about my life and even though most vampires, and even a lot of warlocks these days, don't believe in prophecies, I took them to heart and carried them with me my entire life. When I met you, I needed to make sure I was making the right decision, and only he would be able to tell me if I had made the wrong choice."

"What were the prophecies?" I asked.

"He said my name wasn't an accident. Just like it implied, I would see many dawns, but they wouldn't always be beautiful. I would see the dawn of war and the dawn of torment for my people. When I found my Lord, I would see the dawn of healing. But then there would be more pain, more turmoil, before the final resolution. But that final resolution could only come if I chose the right man. When he came, he would be back from the dead and ready to follow the destiny of his blood."

"What does that mean?" I asked.

"I never knew," Aurora said. "That's the point. He wasn't able to give me any more information than that. But I was always confident that if there was ever a time when I found a man I considered completing the bond with and accepting as my Lord, he'd be the one I could trust to tell me if I had found the right one. That's why I sent you to him. I first wanted to know if you were brave enough to go find him. Then, if you survived that journey, Malakan would meet you. I told him about you, but very little. It was only enough to let him know to expect you and that I wanted to know something about you. If you could then return to me with that, I would know you were the one I was supposed to choose."

"But I didn't get the answer," I said. "I went to him and he made me go through that ritual. When I was done, he gave me a choice. I could either get the answer to the question you wanted, or I could find out where Ashe was, so I could go save her. I wanted you Aurora, but I had to save Ashe. I couldn't let her die because of me."

"Once I was safe, he decided he wasn't going to sit around and wait for you. I believe he told me he wasn't going to jump through your hoops anymore," Ashe said.

Aurora glanced at her and then back at me.

"Oh, really?" she asked. "You weren't going to jump through my hoops anymore?"

"I don't think I used those words exactly," I said.

Ashe nodded, a smile curving her lips.

"Yes, you did," she said.

"OK, fine. Yes, I decided I wasn't going to let you decide whether I lived or died. That wasn't your job. You'd decided to bite me and put me on the countdown to death. I decided I wasn't going to let that happen."

"But don't you get it?" Aurora asked. "That's enough. Malakan gave you the answer when you decided not to ask the question. What sets you apart is the same thing that made you willing to give up eternal life in order to save Ashe. You weren't going to let someone, not even me, tell you what you were going to do. You knew what you needed and wanted, and you have the courage and strength to take it. That is the type of man I knew was meant to be my Lord."

She had just finished talking when I felt something prickle at the back of my neck. I could feel eyes on us and sensed someone close by. Aurora started to speak again, but I held up my hand to stop her and touched my finger to my lips to keep her quiet. We weren't alone. Someone was listening to every word we said.

11

STILL HOLDING MY FINGER TO MY LIPS TO KEEP THE women quiet, I got up and slowly made my way over to where I'd sensed the person watching us. When I was nearly to the door, I moved quickly to try to catch whoever might be there. I didn't see anyone, but I heard a rustling sound down the hallway that told me someone had been there and was running away. For a brief moment I considered chasing whoever it was, but I restrained myself. It was probably better for them to just go. I crossed the room back to the women. Both looked at me questioningly.

"What's going on?" Aurora asked.

"Someone was listening to us," I said. "We need to go."

"Why?" Ashe asked.

"No questions right now," I said. "I need you to just trust me and let's go."

The women nodded, and we hurried to gather everything we needed from the palace before rushing out toward the carriage house where the valet had parked my car.

"What did Malakan mean by all those warnings?" I asked Aurora when we were pulling out of the driveway.

"I told you," she said. "I don't know. He wasn't able to give me any more information than exactly what he said to me. That was it."

I shook my head, frustrated. "It was the same when he did the ritual with me. He said he wouldn't be able to explain any of my visions to me because they were meant only for me and I would be the only to understand the significance. So if his words were significant to you, what do you think they mean? Can you think of anything that might make sense?"

"Actually," she said thoughtfully. "Yes."

"What is it?" I asked.

"I believe when he said I'd see the dawn of a time of war he was talking about what happened forty-five years ago."

I looked at Ashe.

"Is that something that should be in the manual?" I asked. "Maybe in a history addendum? You know, at this point, I'm thinking a full online course for the newly minted vampire would be a good idea. Just a self-paced thing. An overview of vampire history and culture. Special project on wooden stakes."

Ashe laughed.

"It's seeming more and more like a good idea," she said.

By this point we had gotten away from the palace grounds and the risk of eavesdroppers didn't seem pressing. I wanted to keep talking to Ashe and Aurora, but didn't know where to go, so I pulled off on the side of the road and turned to them.

"What are you doing?" Aurora asked.

"I want to be able to talk to you, and I can't do that while I'm driving. Besides, if we are in the car, it's going to be a lot harder for someone to be able to listen in to what we're saying. What happened forty-five years ago? Does this have some sort of name too, like The Incident?"

"No, there's no name," Ashe said. "But there probably should be."

"I told you the palace is the same as it was even before my father was Prime," Aurora said.

"Yes."

"I probably should have said, well before my father was Prime. You see, he actually hasn't been Prime for very long in the greater scheme of things. Only since this event happened."

"But you said you were here when you were a child and that you weren't allowed to play in the maze," I argued.

"And that's true," Aurora said. "My parents were members of the Prime's court of trustees. They lived here with the Prime and his family. I grew up alongside some of the Prime's children, but for the most part, we lived very separate lives. I didn't spend much time with him, even though my parents did. I always had the feeling my mother was trying to keep me from getting too close to the inner-workings of the Prime's rule. She didn't want me to get wrapped up in it or obsessive about it the way so many people do."

"So, you just lived here?" I asked.

"Yes," she said. "For a very long time. Then, forty-five years ago, everything changed. The Prime and his entire family underwent a ritual very similar to the one you did when you went to see Malakan. But something went wrong during the process, and the entire family was killed. In an instant, they were gone. A lot of the vampires blamed the warlocks who were conducting the ritual. They blamed them for the deaths of their leaders and accused them of doing it on purpose. There was a tremendous amount of upheaval, and the vampires swore revenge. This led to seventeen years of war. It was horrible. But then my father came up with a plan. He had been installed as Prime after the tragedy, and he said he had come up with a way to create unity between the two species again, while also exacting his revenge. This would soothe the angry masses of vampires but would still let him work toward bringing the species together again in peace. He said it existed before and it could exist again. Nobody knew what his plan was, but there was hope."

"What happened?" I asked.

"The Incident," Ashe said. "Darian's plan went wrong. It was devastating for everyone. Those he had told about the plan had been so optimistic, sure this would be the way for the war to finally end and everyone to go back to their lives. When

The Incident happened, it took all of that hope away."

"I keep hearing that term," I said. "The Incident. You keep saying it like it's something I should just know about, but I don't. I want to know what it means."

Aurora drew in a breath. She and Ashe exchanged a look before Aurora continued.

"We already told you Ty was progressing through the hierarchy of the Shades, and had reached the rank of official errand runner," she said.

"Yes," I said. "And after The Incident, he was wrapped up with everyone else who was on duty and given the boot."

"Not exactly," she said. "He lost his position because of The Incident, yes, but it wasn't because he had gotten wrapped up in it along with all the other guards. He was there that night. He was blamed for it."

"For what?" I asked. "I'm really tired of all this roundabout stuff. I want to know what happened. If this might have anything to do with Malakan, then I need to know."

"My father knew the ArchWarlock had just had

a new baby. His little son was his entire world, and he was absolutely thrilled to have him. He and his wife hadn't been able to have children for many many years, no matter what they did, and this little one was the fulfillment of all their dreams."

I felt my chest starting to tighten, but I didn't say anything.

"Darian knew the best way to get to the Arch-Warlock, and therefore, the rest of the warlocks, was through that baby. His plan was to have the Shades kidnap the baby. Obviously, this would be horrible for the ArchWarlock and his family, but that was just the revenge part. The plan was much bigger than that. Darian knew the entire warlock species would be in mourning for the loss of the child, which would cause the pain he wanted them to feel. It would be some minor retribution for the pain the warlocks caused when they destroyed the Prime family."

"How did he think that would bring unity to the vampires and the warlocks?" I asked.

"Remember, the plan had two parts," Ashe said. "The kidnapping was just the revenge. The bigger part was what he believed would eventually bring the species' back together. He intended on raising the baby as his foster son. As he raised him, he would teach him all the ways of the vampires. Of course, he wouldn't have the same powers, but he would know the culture and the history. He would feel like a member of the species just as much as any other child raised in the community. He wouldn't tell him he was actually a warlock. Then, when the boy came of age, my father planned on reconnecting the baby with the Arch-Warlock. He would be able to learn about his warlock heritage but also share what he knew about the vampires. That baby would be a bridge between the two species."

"He seriously thought that would work? He stole a child and was just going to raise it to think one thing about itself, then spring on him years later that he's something totally different? And instead of the true parents of that child coming down on his ass with the wrath of the gods for stealing their baby and keeping him from them for his entire childhood and into his adult years, he expected they would just think it was wonderful to see him again? Then what? He'd go to them and tell them the wondrous stories of the vampires, and they would see how futile their feud had been, come together, and bond over the joy of that completely fucked up kid with no real identity?"

Aurora shrugged. "Darian truly believed if he could prove a vampire was able to raise a warlock child as his own and teach him the life of a vampire, when the warlocks did get him back, they wouldn't be able to hate the vampires anymore because they had raised him among them. And the vampires wouldn't be able to hate the warlocks anymore because they would find out the child of the Prime, that they had loved, was actually the child of the ArchWarlock. He believed this would force the two sides to set aside their disagreements and feuding and come together. Then there could be a lasting peace."

I felt like I'd been hit by a truck. What Malakan told me wasn't just the rambling of an old, eccentric man, or some sort of allegory he wanted me to understand. It wasn't another infernal riddle. When he gave me that answer, he was telling me the truth. Now I needed to know the rest of it.

"So, what happened?" I asked. "Obviously the plan wasn't carried out the way it was supposed to be."

Aurora shook her head.

"No," she said. "It wasn't. For several weeks

before the planned night of the kidnapping, my father had Ty infiltrate the warlocks. He wanted to know as much about them and their movements as he possibly could. In his mind, this would make it easier to slip the baby away. He thought Ty could handle it. Ty assured him he could, and even laid out plans for my father so he would know exactly what was happening. Then the night of the kidnapping came, and it didn't go according to that plan. No one knows what exactly, but something happened along the way and the baby was lost."

"Lost?" I asked. "What do you mean lost? How could they lose a baby?"

"Nobody knows," Ashe said. "All they know is when Ty and the others came back to the palace, they didn't have him with them. There was never any trace of him. He was lost and presumed dead."

"That is what we call The Incident," Aurora said.

"It's a hell of an incident," I said.

She nodded in agreement.

"Of course, my father tried to cover up what happened, but by then too many people knew. When the ArchWarlock found out, it drove him completely mad. Enraged by the kidnapping and murder of his son, he called for the blood of all the vampires. He wanted the species wiped from existence. This started the next war. It's been absolutely horrific, even worse than the first. There has been a tremendous loss of life on both sides. Recently, though, there's been a stalemate."

12

I shook my head, my body trembling with the emotions coursing through it.

"It's not a stalemate," I said. "It's a cold war."

"What do you mean?" Ashe asked.

"Neither side is ever going to give up. Things aren't just going to simmer away and fade into nothing. There hasn't been a resolution, so neither the vampires nor the warlocks are going to be willing to let this go." I looked at Aurora intently. "Do you believe what Malakan told you? Do you really believe what he prophesied for you?"

"Yes," she said. "I trusted him and knew he wouldn't tell me something that wasn't true."

"And you fully believe that's true for everyone?

He wouldn't tell someone something he didn't believe to be absolutely true?"

"No," she said. "Not unless there was a very specific reason for it. He would never do it to hurt someone. He didn't give those answers casually."

"How do you know?" I asked. "Why did you trust him?"

"He had always stayed loyal to the Prime family. As a whole, the vampires and the warlocks got along. But just like with everyone else, there were always some underlying tensions and prejudices. There were always members of both sides who looked down on the other, and there have always been members of both sides who have thought they should be in power in the Underworld. That's why the wars got so bad, so fast. The people who already hated each other just saw what happened as an opportunity to finally act out those aggression without prejudice. Malakan never wavered, though. Not even through the wars. Not even after his exile. He always remained completely loyal and willing to do what he believed was best, not just for his kind, but for the family, and for all of the Underworld. That's why I sent you to talk to him, Hayden. I knew I could trust what he told me about you. Whatever he said, I would be able to trust it was true and make my decision from there." She drew in a shaky breath. "Now, I'm never going to know what he was going to tell me."

"I know what he was going to tell you," I said.

Her eyes lifted to me and I could see tears in them. She shook her head slightly, searching my face.

"What do you mean?" she asked.

"I know what he was going to tell you," I repeated. "After I went through with my ritual and I made the decision to ask him where Ashe was being held captive rather than getting the answer to the question you asked, he only gave me that information. He did exactly what he said he was going to do and only answered one question. But he did have one thing to tell me. He said I was long since thought dead. I left there knowing I wasn't going to get the help from him that I needed. After you completed my transformation, I wanted to go back to talk to him so he would know what happened. I couldn't really explain it, but I just felt like I needed to tell him it had worked out. I guess there was a part of me that still wanted him to tell me something, anything that might explain what I didn't know and what everyone had been saying about me."

"He told you that people thought you were dead?" Ashe asked.

I nodded. Her eyes slid over to Aurora and I knew she was thinking the same thing. Those words aligned with the prophecy Malakan had given her, telling her she would find a Lord who had come back from the dead.

"What did he tell you when you went back?" Aurora asked.

"Nothing at first," I said. "He congratulated me on my transformation, and on our blood bond. It wasn't until right before I left that he told me…"

I hesitated. How was I supposed to word this? I felt more like I understood why the old warlock didn't come right out and tell me from the very beginning. It was really hard just to find the words. I decided I had no choice but to just push ahead.

"The son of the ArchWarlock didn't die the night of The Incident," I said.

"I don't understand," Aurora said. "Why would that be what he wanted to tell you? How could that have anything to do with me wanting to know what was different about you?"

Time to rip off the Band-Aid.

"Because I am the child they kidnapped that night," I said.

Both women gasped.

"What?" Aurora finally asked.

I nodded.

"It explains what he meant when he said I was long since thought dead. He wasn't talking about the human world and the people I'd left behind. That's what I thought at first. I thought maybe he meant that I didn't have to worry anymore about learning how to be a vampire. He could tell I felt like I had come into my own here and wanted to completely commit rather than drifting back and forth between my two existences. I remembered Ashe had told me the transition was much harder for some people, and that they sometimes tried to cling to their former life. I never had that compulsion. I'm not going to say it was completely easy for me to believe what I was being told, or to accept what was happening to me. But once I did, I was all in. When Malakan told me people thought I was dead, I thought he was reassuring me. He didn't want me to worry that they were still looking for me or that I had any obligation to go back and make explanations to people."

"But that's not what he meant," Ashe said softly.

"No," I said. "He meant I was long thought dead here in the Underworld."

"I don't understand," Aurora said. "How could this be possible?"

"I don't know," I said. "But he was completely sincere about it. He told me I am the son of the ArchWarlock and I was kidnapped when I was a newborn. He didn't explain anything else to me. He didn't tell me that was what everybody calls The Incident, or that it had anything to do with Ty. But it made me realize what he was talking about the first time I saw him. Ty and I had just gotten to the stone chambers when we saw Malakan. Even though Ty didn't introduce himself, the warlock looked at him like he knew who he was and said he was glad to see him taking responsibility for his failings. I had no idea what he could be talking about and Ty wasn't feeling in the mood to share. I thought he might be as confused as I was, but that's not the case. He must have known exactly what Malakan was talking about. Malakan knew who I was immediately, he just didn't tell me. Seeing Ty with me was a reminder of what happened that night."

"How could you not tell us?" Ashe asked.

"I'm sorry," I said. "I felt like it was more important to try to find out what happened to Malakan and that telling you could come later. I didn't understand that it could be a part of everything. Now I realize he wasn't the only one who knew."

"What do you mean?" Aurora asked.

"The Dragon," I said. "When I went to The Foundry with Ashe that night to meet with Ty and try to find out where you were, the Dragon decided to meet with me. Stephana had told me a little bit about Lunaris and warned me to be careful while I was at the bar, but I didn't realize just how careful I actually needed to be. When the Dragon brought me in to meet with them, they told me I was a powerful hybrid just like them. At the time, I thought the two bloods they were talking about were human and vampire."

"They meant vampire and warlock," Ashe said.

I nodded.

"They had to have. That means they know who I am and that I'm still alive. But how long have they known that?"

"Why does that matter?" Aurora asked.

"Because if they found out when I showed up,

then they are as shocked as everyone else and don't know what to do with the information other than use it to connect with me. But if they've known this entire time, if they knew I didn't die as a baby during the kidnapping, then there is something so much bigger going on."

"That is just one of the issues this brings up," Ashe said. "Not the least of which is what actually happened that night. We know you were kidnapped. That's documented. Ty and the rest of the team planned out how they were going to get into the ArchWarlock's palace and get out with you without alerting anyone. We know they got inside and that they did get you. But what happened after that? They said you were lost. You didn't just vaporize and end up with your foster parents. That's not how that works. Something happened between them taking you from the palace and you ending up on the other side with a human family."

"I need to talk to Ty," I said. "He's at the center of this. He was there that night. He's supposedly the one who took me. I need to know what happened after he got me."

"I'll call him," Ashe said. "Maybe we can meet him at the tavern."

She pulled out her phone and dialed, but a few seconds later ended the call.

"What's wrong?" I asked.

"He's not picking up," she said.

"Maybe he's asleep," I said.

"No," Ashe said. "Ty can't sleep through his phone ringing. It's a habit from being one of the Shades that never really left him. The Shades don't work. They don't have shifts or set time off. Being a Shade is a responsibility that completely takes over their existence. They are expected to be available at all times, just in case the Prime might need them for something. He still keeps his phone right beside his head when he sleeps, and the ringer is at full blast."

"Maybe there really were people at the tavern who he knew, and he is catching up with them. He could have put his phone down to go do something for a second. He's not a Shade anymore. Maybe he's starting to get used to that. Let's drive over there and we can try again on the way."

Ashe nodded. She looked like she was trying to stay calm, but I could see the worry etched on her face. I tried not to admit to myself I was feeling the same thing. The day Ty showed up at Ashe's apartment and asked me all those questions came back into my mind. He had wanted to know everything about me, including where I grew up and about my parents. At first, I thought he was just marking his territory, trying to intimidate me because he didn't like that I was spending so much time with Ashe and going after Aurora. Now I wonder if it was because as soon as he saw me, he knew who I was. If that was true, it meant he had been keeping it from me, and from Aurora and Ashe, this entire time. I couldn't help but wonder why, and how long he was planning on waiting to say anything. If he was ever planning on saying anything at all.

13

As I moved to start the car, I realized Aurora was staring at me strangely.

"What is it?" I asked.

"It just explains so much," she said.

"What do you mean?" I asked.

"The fact that you have the blood of the mages in you. This whole time, we've been trying to figure out why you're so different from the other vampires. Your abilities came on so fast and so strong, and you've been able to do things vampires can't. Being a warlock explains why you were so much stronger and faster when you were still going through your change than many other vampires are when they are fully transitioned and have been training for years. It also explains why you are able to read our thoughts and can sometimes put your thoughts into our minds. That's a warlock power. Mages, especially strong ones, can make a connection with their lovers that can be incredibly powerful. They can share their thoughts and communicate without speaking, but it also makes their abilities sharper and more pronounced. Combining the lust of the vampires with the reaction to sex from the warlocks created something unbelievable."

"It must also be why I was able to fight off the warlocks when they were holding Ashe captive. I did things during that fight I didn't know I was able to do, and still don't even know how I did them."

Ashe nodded.

"Your vampire abilities seemed so much more pronounced to you because they were a change. You made the transition as an adult, so you knew what it was like to not have those abilities and to have to learn to use them. Your warlock blood has been there since the day you were born. You might not have known about it, but it was always there. It is a part of you."

"This is also why being with you makes me feel so much stronger," Aurora said.

"Why would you say that?" I asked.

"I told you after we had sex that I felt better than I had in a long time. I thought maybe it was just because you are incredible. But from the minute I met you it felt like you were fulfilling my need for lust and sex more than any other man has ever been able to. Now it makes sense."

"I appreciate the compliment and all, but I don't understand," I said.

"When a vampire bites a human and changes them into a vampire, they create a link. For most, it's like a parent-child relationship."

"Think of Stephana and me," Ashe said. "She is my Sire. She created me a long time ago, and since then has been in the role of my parent. I rely on her for guidance and she is very protective of me. She has a certain amount of control and influence over me. It's not as strong now as it used to be because I don't spend as much time with her as I did at the beginning of my existence as a vampire, but it's still there. In most relationships, the new vampire doesn't have their full control over their abilities for a while after the change, so the Sire is responsible for them. This responsibility also means being able to influence their thoughts and actions. It's both to protect the new vampire and make sure they are able to get through those first challenging months, or even years, until they develop their full strength. But it's also a way to force training on them. Most people don't take too well to being completely controlled. They don't like the idea of someone else being able to actually affect what they think and how they act. Especially if the person who changed them is a stranger or someone they don't particularly like. The instinct is for the new vampire to try to resist that control. They try to push back against it and stop it from actually having an effect."

"And so they learn to fight," I said. "It's like shoving a baby bird out of a nest and just hoping it figures out how to use its wings before it smashes into the ground."

"Exactly," Ashe said. "As the new vampire gets more confident and starts to fight against the influence over them, they learn to use their abilities more. But this doesn't always happen. Sometimes the vampires don't mind the control and never fight it. Sometimes they aren't strong enough. And sometimes they don't know they can do it. Most relationships keep at least some influence no matter what, but the degree varies widely from person to person."

"But for others, the parent dynamic isn't there,

but the reliance and influence still are," Aurora continued. "That's why a very long time ago, some of the vampires who wanted to establish total and unquestioned vampire control over the Underworld and have the warlocks as their subjects, got an idea. They decided they would change as many warlocks as they possibly could and keep them close, so their influence stayed strong."

"They wanted to create an army," I said.

The women nodded.

"They believed that if they were able to change the warlocks and influence them completely, they could then use them to infiltrate the warlock areas and take down the ArchWarlock and the rest of those in power. Then the vampires would be able to establish control."

"That's a pretty diabolical plan," I said.

"It is," Ashe said. "And it would have worked. As a matter of fact, it started to."

"What do you mean it started to?" I asked.

"The vampires knew this couldn't be a sudden onslaught. They couldn't just storm into the warlock neighborhoods and start changing people right and left. It never would have worked that way. The second they bit someone, they'd be attacked by the other warlocks. They had to go about this in a much more subtle and gradual way. So, they carefully infiltrated the group. Like I said, there were tensions between the two species, but not unanimously. For the most part, we got along. There was harmony and even talks of balancing the power so that there would be both vampire and warlock control over all areas of the Underworld rather than division. I think that's what drove that group to get started on their plan. The idea of having to cooperate with warlocks and accept any type of warlock control over their lives was unimaginable to them. So, they pretended they didn't feel the way they did. They eased themselves in with groups of warlocks and created what looked like friendships. I wouldn't be surprised to find out there are actually quite a few vampire warlock hybrids that don't even realize they are both."

"Why would they do that, though? If they hated the warlocks so much and we're trying to figure out a way to get rid of them, why would they make relationships with them?"

"To get close to them," Aurora said. "Like she said, it's not like they could just go out on the streets and start taking down person after person. The other warlocks wouldn't just stand there and watch and wonder what was happening. They might have been able to get one person, maybe two, but they most likely wouldn't have gotten back here alive. And that would have eliminated the whole point. They knew they had to go about it in a way where they would be able to make the change and start exerting their influence without other warlocks really noticing what was happening. That's what would make it so effective. After they had the warlock children in their control, they would be able to send them back in among the other warlocks without it seeming like there was any change. Those warlocks could then start doing the bidding of their Sires."

"You said it started to work," I said.

"It did," Ashe said. "Those vampires were extremely effective in creating those relationships. Then they decided it was time to take their plan to the next step. They started changing the warlocks. It was really rather effective at first. They managed to influence their group of minions to do a lot of things. Including some pretty horrific things. For a while, the warlocks couldn't figure out what was happening. There were attacks and disasters with seemingly no explanation. Buildings were being destroyed, people were dying. They knew there was something going on and they had to figure out what it was. Unfortunately for those few vampires, there was still such thing as loyalty. The Prime family got intelligence about what was happening and told the warlocks. They put together a posse and took those vampires out."

"What about the warlocks who were already under their control?" I asked.

"The link between a vampire Sire and child only exists as long as both of them do. As soon as those vampires were executed, the warlocks were released from their control. Of course, they were still vampires. There's no way to take that away. There's no vampire cure or anything. But they no longer had to do the bidding of the vampires who created them. They could go back to living their lives essentially just like other warlocks. The only real difference was they now had vampire abilities and needs. Fortunately for them, fulfilling those needs isn't so bad."

She smiled at me and I returned it.

"I don't understand, though," I said. "What does that have to do with us? You're the one who changed me, so you have that influence?"

"Not exactly," Aurora said. "I made a blood bond with you, so we are linked to each other for the rest of our existence, but because you are a warlock, it goes beyond that. After what happened with those vampires and the warlocks they changed, the Prime and the ArchWarlock met to talk about what needed to be done. Obviously, they couldn't just let something like this slide."

"You said the vampires were executed," I said. "I don't think that sounds like anybody let it slide."

"Not for them," Ashe said. "But that wasn't the worry. If one group of vampires came up with that plan and actually executed it, what was going to stop any other group from doing it again in the future? There needed to be something to stop them, and something to give retribution. They came up with the swapped link. It was all done completely in secret and nobody really knows how it happened. The only thing we were told was that the most powerful warlock of the time created a spell that changed how the link developed between a vampire and a warlock. After that, if a vampire bit a warlock, they didn't get power over that warlock. Instead, the influence and control went to the warlock. Now that vampire was completely reliant on the warlock. Only that warlock could sustain the vampire. All of the vampire's needs, blood, lust, everything, had to be fulfilled by that warlock, no one else. It provided protection to the warlocks because they could no longer be turned against the rest of the warlocks by vampires. It also meant that any vampire who tried would be immediately tied to that warlock. They would have no ability to resist them or leave them because they relied completely on them, and they could never kill them because of the control. In essence, they are addicted to the warlock."

"So when I turned you into a vampire, I created an especially strong bond with you," Aurora said. "It's not just the blood bond that unites us for all existence and makes you my Lord. It also makes me totally reliant on you. Only your blood and your body will be enough for me ever again. You are my addiction."

I leaned over and kissed her, feeling the rush of need passing between us. When I pulled back, I had another question.

"Why don't the vampires just not turn the warlocks?"

"What do you mean?" Ashe asked.

"If the problem is that they become addicted to the warlock when they change them, why don't they just let them die if they want to get rid of them?"

"The addiction would still exist," Ashe said. "The vampire would just have nothing to sustain them. They would starve and weaken until eventually they would die."

"Good thing I forced you to change me," I teased Aurora, flashing her a grin. "That would not have been fun for you."

She swatted me playfully and pointed at the road ahead of us.

"Go on," she said. "Let's get to the tavern and find Ty."

14

"He's still not answering," Ashe said a few minutes later.

She had tried to call Ty several times since we started toward the village again, but he hadn't answered. It was obvious she and Aurora were getting more worried every time there was another failed call.

"It's just not like him," Aurora said. "He's always available. Even if he doesn't answer the phone the first time because he's in the shower or doing something else, he calls back immediately."

"What could have happened to him?" Ashe asked.

"I don't know," I said. "But the only way we're

going to find out is by going to the tavern and looking for him."

I could hear the bitterness in my voice as I said the words, and out of the corner of my eye I saw Aurora staring at me.

"Hayden?" she said. "What's wrong?"

I didn't want to admit to the anger I was feeling toward Ty. It had been building up inside me since I found out about his involvement. No matter how hard I tried to push it away, I couldn't get it out of my mind.

"He let me down," I said.

"He let you down?" Aurora asked. "Who, Ty?"

"Yes," I said. "I know it doesn't make any sense, because I obviously didn't know him at the time, but now that I know about his involvement in my kidnapping when I was a baby, I feel like he betrayed me."

"But he was following orders," Ashe said.

"That's the thing," I said. "It's more than that. It's a really strange dichotomy. On one hand, he was ordered and trained to be my kidnapper. I'm angry with him for coming into what was supposed to be my home and taking me from my family. He took my entire life away from me, and me away from my parents and everything I was supposed to know. So in that way, he betrayed me. But at the same time, Darian chose him because he trusted that Ty would be able to go into the palace, get me, and bring me back to him safely. That made him my protector. He was supposed to take care of me, and instead I somehow got lost and shuffled off to a foster family nowhere near what was supposed to be my world and my existence. So in that way, he also let me down. He failed me on both accounts."

"Do you think he knows what happened?" Ashe asked. "His official report to Darian was that he didn't know what happened to you; that you were lost. Do you think that's true?"

"I don't know," I admitted. "I was thinking about the day he came to your apartment right after Aurora bit me. He showed up and start asking me all those questions, do you remember?"

"You told me he asked you about yourself," Ashe said. "But he just met you. Like I told you, Ty has never been a trusting person. Having you just show up and Aurora immediately make such a connection with you, not to mention me, probably seemed really strange to him. Remember, his entire purpose in life has been to protect Aurora and her family, and then me and the portal. He was probably just trying to find out as much about you as he could."

I shook my head.

"No," I said. "I think it's more than that. He wasn't just asking me normal 'get to know you' questions, and he seemed angry when I wasn't able to give him the answers he wanted. He was really interested in knowing everything he possibly could about my childhood and my parents. I told him I didn't really have parents. I have my foster parents, of course, but they never adopted me. They never even mentioned the possibility. I know absolutely nothing about my birth parents." I paused. "I guess it's not really true anymore, is it?"

"So, you think Ty knows?" Aurora asked.

"I think he at least has his suspicions," I said. "But that just brings up a whole new set of questions. If he thought I was dead, why wasn't he more surprised to see me? Actually, he might have been surprised, but not in the way I would have expected."

"What would you expect?" Ashe asked.

"You've told me over and over how important being a Shade is. It's a higher calling and really important to the men who do it. To the point that it's been almost thirty years since Ty lost his position and he still thinks and acts like one of them. That means he took his responsibility extremely seriously. Don't you think if he's thought for all this time that I was actually lost, even dead, and I showed up again, he would be more than just curious? I would think he would be thrilled. Even if he wasn't completely convinced just from the very beginning, even if he had an inkling that I might be that baby who was lost so many years ago, he'd be happy first and question it second. There would be at least some indication that he was glad I was alive, if nothing else."

"So, you don't believe he thought you were dead," Aurora said.

"I don't even know if he thinks I was lost," I said. "That's why I need to talk to him. I need to know what happened and why he hasn't said anything about this to any of us."

"Are you sure about this, Hayden?" Ashe asked.

"The ritual I did with Malakan," I said. "I told you it showed me an image of my past, my present, and my future. The image I got of the present was of you being held captive in that church. I saw every detail, exactly like I was standing in the room with you. I saw you tied up and hanging from the ceiling. I saw the blood under you. I even saw the engraving of the dragon and the moon in the altar. That carving is how I knew when I found the first sanctuary that we weren't in the right place. That image was exact, so I have to believe the other ones I saw were accurate, too."

"What did you see in your other visions?" Aurora asked.

"The vision of my past was of Ty. He looked exactly like he looks now, which I guess is something I'm just going to have to get used to. I couldn't see where he was. Everything around him was dark, but I could see him clearly, and he was carrying something. I followed him and saw that he was carrying a tiny baby. No more than a few weeks old, if that. He was running, and he looked completely frantic. That baby had to be me. I had to be seeing the night I was kidnapped."

"What did he do with you?" Ashe asked.

"He brought me to a portal," I said. "It looked like the wall that leads through to Solomon's, but I can't be completely sure. It could have been any wall. What matters is I saw him take me and hand me through that portal to a woman who was waiting on the other side."

"Who was the woman?" Aurora asked.

"I don't know," I said. "I didn't recognize her.

But she was wearing a necklace with the dragon and the moon. She took me and ran. When I saw the vision, I didn't know the baby was me. I don't have any pictures of myself as a baby or even as a toddler. I didn't realize what I was seeing. All I really focused on was how strange it was to see Ty looking exactly the same, when I knew I was looking into the past. I told Malakan that, and he pointed out that I have no idea when that vision was. It was just sometime in the past. That could have been years, or it could have been days, there was really no way of knowing. But I had the distinct impression it wasn't just a few days before." I fell silent for a few seconds. "Am I?"

"Are you what?" Aurora asked.

"Am I going to get used to things not changing? Am I going to get used to looking like I did when I was twenty-eight years old and never aging? Am I going to get used to nobody around me ever looking any different, but knowing that time is passing?"

"You will," Aurora assured me. "It's something every vampire who is created and not born has to go through. You had a normal life before I changed you, so you have an idea of what it's like for time to pass and everything to go along with it.

Eventually, that will fall away. You'll get used to what it's like here in the Underworld. Everything will start to melt and flow, and it will just one day seem completely normal to you."

"And if you're anything like me," Ashe added, "you'll have a strange moment one day where you see someone you know who isn't a mage or a lycan, or a fae, and they will have aged. It won't even occur to you that they are human, and it will seem completely odd to you that they look different. That's when you'll know you're fully immersed."

"That makes me wonder, though," I said. "Am I not going to change?"

"What do you mean?" Aurora asked.

"Being a hybrid alters everything. I'm not reacting to becoming a vampire like everybody else does. You didn't change a human into a vampire. You changed a warlock into a hybrid. It means I'm stronger than most vampires, and I obviously have abilities that come from being a warlock. So how else is my warlock blood going to impact my existence as a vampire? Am I going to age? I know you said warlocks have extremely long lives, but will I have a long life like them, or immortality like you? Or will it be something in between? Maybe I will live two or three times as long as the average warlock and then start aging. Or maybe I won't start aging at all, but I'll just suddenly die."

The questions were pouring out of me at an almost frantic speed, but I couldn't control them.

"Hayden," Ashe said, but I just kept going.

"And what if it's not a matter of one of them outweighing the other. Maybe it's not that the vampire part will take over the warlock part, or the warlock part will take over the vampire part. Maybe they will both stay in control of part of me, which means that eventually the warlock part is going to reach the end of its life. So does that mean that the warlock part of me is going to die? I'm just going to wake up one day and the abilities I have because of my warlock blood are just going to be gone?"

"Hayden," Ashe said again. "Calm down. You are not the first hybrid, remember? And I promise you, you won't be the last. Now, there are special circumstances with you it because of who you are and how you came to be, but this isn't uncharted territory. When Aurora changed you, she gave you everything that being a vampire entails. You have fangs now and eventually, as much as I know you don't want to hear this, you will crave blood. You have an insatiable desire for sex. You don't need to eat or drink any type of normal food or beverage in order to stay alive. Becoming a vampire means taking the existing form and transforming it into something elevated. You didn't lose anything when you became a hybrid. You gained everything. You will maintain all of the abilities that your warlock blood gives you, and you will be able to use them forever."

It was a powerful thought, and it got my heart racing. A rush of adrenaline rolled through me and I was even more driven. Pushing down on the gas, I sped faster toward the tavern.

"Speaking of what's going to happen," Aurora said. "What happened in the other vision?"

I glanced at her briefly before looking back at the road.

"What?" I asked.

"You told us what you saw in your vision of the past and in your vision of the present. What about the future? What did you envision for what's to come?"

A heavy weight settled in my chest.

"Something I intend to stop from happening at all."

15

It felt like it took hours to get back to the village, but finally I saw the tavern ahead of us and pulled up in front of it. Despite it being the middle of the night, the lights were still burning brightly inside the building, and when I got out of the car, I could hear the voices of people inside. It was the same type of noise from Solomon's Fang. Some were laughing and singing. Others sounded serious, like they were locked in deep conversation. Occasionally there was a burst of yelling or the crash of something falling over. Part of me expected that crash to be followed by a fight, but everything seemed to carry on like normal. We walked inside, and I saw that this place was nothing like Solomon's Fang. The noise coming out of that might have sounded the same, but that's where the similarities ended.

Much like the outside of the building, the inside of the tavern looked like we had stepped backward into another time. The light I had seen glowing through the windows came from lanterns and torches strategically positioned around the room. Rough-hewn wooden beams were still visible on the ceiling and mimicked in the columns that supported it. All of the tables tightly packed on the unfinished, straw scattered floor looked like they were crafted out of the same type of wood. Even the chairs showed the unmistakable unevenness and dips that proved they were not manufactured in some factory somewhere; they had been handmade an unknown number of years ago.

We walked up to the scarred wooden bar and the man behind it looked at us without reaction.

"Hi Benson," Aurora said.

"Good evening Aurora," he said. "What brings you here tonight? I thought your father didn't like you hanging around here with the likes of us."

There was a hint of a smile on his lips, but I got the impression the touch of bitterness in his voice was real. The uneasy feeling I had about

Darian was growing stronger with every story I heard and person I met.

"Since when did that stop me from doing anything?" Aurora asked.

"You've got a point there," Benson said. "So, to what do I owe the pleasure of your visit? You haven't been in for a while."

"I know," she said. "I've been very busy lately. There's someone very important I want everybody to meet."

She tilted her head back toward me, and Benson narrowed his eyes slightly, like he was having trouble seeing me in the flickering light.

"Hayden," I said.

"It's nice to meet you," he replied. "And Ashe. It's always good to see you, even though you'd rather spend time in that newfangled bar of yours."

Ashe laughed.

"I wouldn't exactly call Solomon's Fang newfangled, Benson," she said.

He opened up his arms as if to encompass the entirety of the tavern.

"Newer than this," he said.

She nodded.

"I'll give you that," she said.

"I'm sorry, Benson," Aurora said. "I'd like to

hang out and catch up with you, but that's actually not why we're here tonight. We were looking for Ty. Do you know where he is?"

"He's not here," the bartender said. "I saw him earlier. He came in, but he didn't even stay long enough to say hello. He walked around like he was looking for someone or wanted to be seen, but then he left. He was only here for a couple of minutes."

"And you have no idea where he went?" Aurora asked.

"No," he said. "Like I told you, he was only here for a couple of minutes. He didn't even speak to me. He did look really preoccupied though; like the weight of the world was on his shoulders."

Aurora nodded and pushed back from the bar.

"Thanks," she said. "I appreciate it."

"No problem," he said. "I'm sorry I couldn't have been more help. I'll let him know you're looking for him if he comes back in here."

"Please do," she said. "Tell him it's really important that we talk to him. Have him call me or Ashe."

"I'll do that," he said.

Not really knowing what else to do, we walked back out of the tavern and got into the car. I let out a breath as I leaned my head back against the headrest.

"What now?" Ashe asked.

I rolled my head to the side to look at Aurora.

"Do you know if Malakan was involved in planning the kidnapping?" I asked.

"I don't know," she said. "I was never a part of things like that. My father kept me very strictly separated from his rule."

I sat up straighter.

"But do you think it's possible that he was?" I asked.

"Why?" she asked.

"He knew who Ty was as soon as he saw him. He mentioned his failings. It was very specific."

"I really don't think he was," Aurora said. "I suppose it's possible, but that's just not how my father operates. He is extremely secretive and likes to keep things to himself, especially when he's planning something. It wasn't even until he started working with Ty and the other chosen guards that people found out what he was planning."

"I thought Malakan was his confidant and someone he trusted to help him with major things like that?" I said.

"He was," Aurora insisted. "But my father

wouldn't want to be discouraged. After everything happened, I confronted him about it. I asked him why he wouldn't tell me what was going on. He said he didn't tell anyone but the Shades he had chosen to be involved. He didn't want too many people to know about it, because that only increased the risk that something could go wrong. He told me he intended to tell Malakan about it only after he already had the baby so Malakan could be your mentor. He wanted you to have the very best in guidance and teaching, and for Malakan to be there to help you with any warlock-specific issues you might face growing up. That way he would also be there for you to help you after you came of age, and he would be the one to train you."

"Do you believe that?" I asked.

"He could have been lying," she admitted. "But Malakan never mentioned anything to me, and when he found out what happened after The Incident, he seemed just as shocked and devastated as everybody else. It didn't strike me as being shocked that something went wrong, but genuine surprise that it happened at all. I got the impression he felt really guilty."

"Guilty?" I asked. "Why?"

"Because he couldn't stop it. If my father had entrusted Malakan with his idea from the beginning, the warlock would have been able to show him the flaws in that plan and discourage him from carrying it out. Of course, that's exactly why my father didn't tell him. He didn't want to hear that his brilliant idea for reuniting the species and creating partnership and understanding wasn't going to work, or even that it could cause more damage. But I think Malakan had carried that with him ever since. He always wondered what he could have done if he had only known about the plan sooner. Even if he hadn't been able to dissuade my father from going through with it, he might have been able to change the outcome."

"So you don't think Malakan knew what happened to me," I said.

"Do you?" she asked.

I thought about the question for a beat.

"No," I said. "He seemed genuinely surprised to see me. He was expecting a man to show up and talk to him about you because you told him I was coming, but the way he looked at me when I walked into the stone chambers -- it was genuine. He didn't know it was going to be me. He wouldn't have reacted like that if he knew what happened, and he wouldn't have mentioned Ty's failings. I didn't know who I was at the time. There was no reason to try to impress me or fool me into thinking they weren't working together. That was a true reaction.

"Ty knows who I am," I said. "Malakan knew who I am. And they knew the other did. But Ty never said anything to me." I looked from Aurora to Ashe and back again. "Maybe he thinks that has something to do with what happened to Malakan."

"He'd want to find out more," Ashe said. "If he thinks there's any chance that whoever set off that explosion in Malakan's house did it because of The Incident, then he would want to know. He's been carrying this with him for the last twenty-eight years. I always knew what happened that night bothered him and that he was still devastated over losing his position in the Shade, but I never knew just how much it was hurting him."

"I don't think anyone does," Aurora said. "If what Hayden saw in his vision of the past is even close to accurate about what happened that night, then there is something much bigger happening."

"If that vision is right," I continued, "it means Ty didn't lose me the night of the kidnapping. There was no accident or mishandling that resulted in me being gone and everyone thinking I was dead. He knew all along where I was and that I hadn't died."

"But why did he do it?" Ashe asked. "What made him want to hand you over to someone else and then take the blame for losing you?"

"I don't know," I said. "But maybe Ty feels like twenty-eight years of holding onto a secret has finally caught up with him and now he's paying the penalty. He's going to want to try to make things right."

"Where would he start?" Ashe asked.

"He could have gone back to Malakan's house or the Final View," Aurora said. "Maybe he went back to talk to Phillip and find out what he knows."

"There's only one way to find out."

I turned on the car and started back toward the city.

16

Things seemed to have gotten back to normal in the community under the bridge. By the time we got there, I was even more worked up and everyone gathered under the bridge turned and looked at me strangely as I ran toward them. It was almost as though they had forgotten what had happened or had chosen to just move on. I guessed that was the way things were in a community built on the idea of watching people end their lives. When something happened, they reacted intensely, but just as quickly were able to put it behind them and move forward. They didn't really have much of a choice. There was nothing any of them could do.

As I went from person to person, asking them if they had seen Ty, I hoped I wasn't just as helpless. There had to be something I could do. I had to have some sort of control over what was happening now and what *would* happen. Malakan couldn't have just died and left me with this impossible piece of information he'd given me and no way of knowing what I was supposed to do next.

"Have you seen him?" I asked the next person I approached.

She looked at me with the same type of fear and confusion I was sure most people had when they looked at the people under the bridge. Especially those who crawled out of the river thinking they were dead, only to discover they had entered a world they never could have imagined.

"Who?"

Not wanting to bother to take the time to explain myself, I ran past her and up to the next trash can fire.

"Ty," I said. "Have any of you seen him?"

"Wasn't he here with you?"

I shook my head at the man who had spoken to me.

"After that," I said. "Have you seen him since then?"

"No," he said. "What happened to him?"

"I don't know," I said.

I knew I sounded harsh, but I didn't care. I didn't have the patience or compassion to deal with any of this. I was making my way to the next cluster of people when I saw Philip ahead of me. I ran up to him and he took a few steps back. His eyes searched my face and then a flicker of recognition lit his gaze.

"You," he said. "He's been waiting for you."

"Who?" I asked. "Ty? Is he here?"

Philip shook his head.

"Not Ty. He's not the one waiting for you."

"Is he here? Have you seen Ty?"

"It's his fault," Philip said. "All of this. All of this is his fault. He shouldn't have done it."

"Shouldn't have done what?" I asked.

Phillip stared at me again and his head tilted to the side like he was looking at me for the first time.

"You," he said. "He's waiting for you."

I let out a sigh of exasperation and pushed Philip away so I could move further into Final View. The man with one shoe came up to me.

"You're back," he said.

"Yeah," I said. "I need to find Ty. Have you seen him since the last time we were here?"

He shook his head.

"No," he said. "I'm sorry. I wish I could help you."

"If you see him, tell him we're looking for him. It's extremely important that we talk to him."

"Is it about Malakan?" he asked.

"I just need to talk to him," I said.

Even though this man had been as helpful as he could be, I didn't trust him. I couldn't trust anybody. Trusting anybody right now would be putting myself in even more danger than I already was, but I knew it wasn't just me. Aurora and Ashe were inextricably a part of this now. There was no way they were going to be able to get out of it, and that meant I was obligated to protect them. They got involved in this because of me, even before I knew anything about it, and I couldn't let them get hurt because of it.

Aurora walked up behind me.

"Nobody seems to have any idea where Ty is," she said. "We asked everybody who would respond to us."

"Me, too," I said. "I didn't have any luck. I don't think he's been back here."

"So, what do we do next?" Ashe asked.

"I want to go back to Malakan's house," I said. "There's something about it that's still bothering me, and I need to figure it out."

"What is it?" Aurora asked.

"I'm not sure," I said. "But I need to look. I feel like there's something there that we missed."

The women nodded, and we walked away from the man with one shoe. I paused when we were a few steps away and rushed back to him.

"What's your name?" I asked.

He looked at me questioningly.

"Name?" he asked.

I looked over my shoulder at Ashe.

"Don't tell me that there aren't names in the Underworld, or that there's some sort of mystical naming protocol and people can lose their names if they live within a certain proximity of water or some other ridiculous, nonsensical shit like that."

She shook her head.

"No," she said.

I looked back at him.

"Sorry," I said. "I'm still kind of new around here. I'm still learning the ropes. There's a manual in the works, but I don't really think it's going to be very helpful to me right now. Publication date is still a little bit off. Maybe for next Christmas season."

He looked at me like I was several neon hues short of a Crayola box. It is a challenging moment of self-realization when you're standing in front of a man wearing one shoe and living beneath the bridge, and he is looking at you like you're the one who's lost his mind.

"I'll keep my eye out for it," he said.

I nodded and turned away.

"Thanks," I muttered.

"Bugs," he said.

I turned back around to look at him.

"What?" I asked.

"You asked my name. Bugs."

"Bugs?"

"It's what everyone calls me. Have for as long as I can remember."

I stared at him.

"Bugs?" I said again.

He took a few steps toward me and leaned close. His eyes flitted around for a second before he spoke.

"You never know what you're going to find in computers," he said. "Or where you'll end up because of it."

He spoke in a conspiratorial whisper, but there was something in those words that was more genuine and stable than anything I had heard him say before. I felt like I was seeing past the circumstances he was in now to a life he had lived unknown years before. I nodded.

"It's nice to meet you, Bugs," I said. "I'm…"

"Hayden," he said. "I know. We all do."

Well, that's good. Nothing unnerving about that.

"Hayden, come on," Aurora said.

I felt locked in place by the other man's eyes. There was something in them I couldn't explain. Finally breaking myself away from his stare, I jogged up to meet the women. We walked to the entrance to the tunnel and I opened it without hesitation. I didn't even feel like I needed the torches anymore. I was so familiar with every inch of the tunnels and every room of Malakan's chambers that I could have done it even in the pitch blackness. I already had.

I didn't think about what we might find on the other side of the door in the tree until we were almost there. All I had been thinking about was the house and whatever it was that was bothering me so much about it. When we approached the door, however, I started to wonder what might have changed. Would the door even be there anymore? The house? The land? What happened to a place like that when it had fulfilled its purpose and was no longer usable?

"Is this place real?" I asked, looking at Aurora.

Her eyes glowed in the light of the torch she held over her head.

"What do you mean?" she asked.

"Is it real?"

"Of course, it's real. You've been there."

"I know," I said. "But I don't know how this works. Malakan created this place out of nothing. He literally came into the middle of a cliff and crafted an entire environment out of his imagination. So, does that mean we are just existing in his thoughts when we are here, or is it actually here? Does a place that was designed and created on a whim by magic stay even if that magic isn't there anymore?"

"It's just as real as anything else," Aurora said. "When the warlocks mirror a place, it comes into being just like anything else. It is as real as any other place."

The way she answered me told me she knew I was thinking about more than just the house and the torched fields. I was struggling with what Malakan had told me about myself. It made sense. It explained so much about my life and how I had always felt, and yet at the same time I couldn't understand it. How could it possibly be that I had lived throughout my entire childhood, as a teenager, a young adult, and now, and never knew that there was something so extraordinary about me? If I was born the child of the ArchWarlock, what did it say about me that I had never known and had never experienced the abilities it should have given me?

Philip's words flashed through my mind again. I wanted to tell myself he was just rambling, but I knew deep within me that wasn't true. There was more to what he was saying, but I didn't know what it could mean.

"Are you ready?" Ashe asked.

I nodded and reached for the handle to the door. Pushing it open, I stepped out into darkness. Just like the world beyond the cliff, it was night here in the world Malakan had created. A huge full moon prevented the area from being completely pitch dark, and I used that light to guide me into the fields. The heat that had radiated off the ruins of the house had cooled completely, but little else had changed. I started in the same direction I had gone earlier and had only been walking a few moments when the burn marks stopped. I looked down at my feet and saw the precise line where the singed grass gave way to untouched ground.

"Look at this," I called back to the women.

They rushed up to me and stopped on either side.

"What is it?" Aurora asked.

"Look at the grass," I said.

"It's burned," Ashe said.

"Right but look how it ends. The burned part just stops."

"The fire burned out," she said.

"So perfectly?" I asked. "Right in this exact spot?" I shook my head. "No," I said. "That's not how fires work. A fire doesn't just stop because it gets tired of burning. Something has to stop it. It stops because it runs out of fuel or oxygen. There's plenty of both here. There's more grass right there, there's air. So what made it just stop?"

"What do you think it means?" Aurora asked.

I shook my head.

"I don't know. But it's strange."

I stepped out of the burned grass and continued in the direction I had been walking.

"What are you looking for?" Aurora asked.

"The end," I said.

"The end?" Ashe asked. "What do you mean?"

"The last time we were here, I asked you how big this space is. Malakan created it out of the inside of a cliff, which means it's not infinite. It doesn't just stretch on and on. There is some point where the area he mirrored has to end. That's what I'm trying to find."

"Why?" Aurora asked.

I didn't answer, but just kept walking. The truth was, I didn't know what I was really looking for. I didn't know what about the edge of the area he mirrored might mean. But the questions in the back of my mind just kept coming and every time I tried to figure out what they were or what they could be trying to tell me, it brought me right back to wondering how big this space was and what I would find at its edges.

We'd been walking for almost half an hour when the field started to change. Instead of just being an open space of waving tall grass, I noticed scruffy shrubbery. After a few more yards, there were more trees like the ones in front of the house. I examined each one of them as we approached, wondering if I might find another door. None of the trees I could see seem to have a handle or a gap of any kind, so I kept going. The further I walked, the deeper the woods around me grew. And soon even the moonlight was almost completely obscured. There was barely enough illumination to guide me along my way, and I had to wait for Aurora to catch up with the torch. I took it from her and held it high above my head to light up as much of the space around us as I could.

"I didn't know this was out here," she said. "I've never come this far."

"You said you don't know where the real place is that Malakan mirrored this after," I said.

"No," she said. "He never told me. Why?"

"I'm just wondering if he kept it exactly the same way. If we did know where that was, and we walked away from the house, would we find woods like this? Or did he create them for another reason?"

We hadn't gone much further when the light from the torch touched something in front of us. It took a few seconds for me to realize it was rock. The stretch of woods had ended abruptly at a jagged rock face that stretched high above us. I took a few steps back and held the torch up to try it to light it up more.

"This is it," I said. "This is the end. This is the wall of the chamber."

"So, what does it mean?" Ashe asked. "You found what you were looking for. What does it tell you?"

I shook my head.

"Nothing." I gazed at the rock.

Suddenly, it was all clear. I pressed my hand to the rock and started walking along its edge.

"What are you doing?" Aurora asked.

"I'm following it," I said.

"Why?" Ashe asked.

"We got in here by going through a tunnel, right? Yes, Malakan's chambers are in the middle of it, but he built those out of the caverns. He crafted that entire area out of what was already there. He just manipulated the rocks. All of this is a cavern, which means that there are probably other tunnels. How often have you heard of a cavern that has just one tunnel that leads all the way in, and no other way out?"

"I don't know," Ashe said. "I've never really thought about it."

"Probably never," I pointed out. "Usually there are a few different access points to caverns. Sometimes there will be a chamber or two that are only accessible through one particular tunnel, but not something this big. Everybody seems to know about the door in the cliff in Final View, but no one but us will go into it. I don't know what they know about it or why they are hesitant, but for some reason they stay away."

"Would you have been eager to go inside if you didn't know who Malakan was?" Aurora asked.

"I didn't know who Malakan was when I first came," I pointed out. "I still don't really know anything about him. I came in because I had to. But I don't doubt for a single second that the only reason I was able to get all the way in with Ty was because Malakan let it happen. If he didn't want us going through that tunnel, we wouldn't have made it."

"I don't understand what that has to do with this cavern having another tunnel access," Ashe said.

"If there is another tunnel, it means the door in Final View isn't the only way to get inside, it's just the only way people know of. Malakan made that one obvious. It's just sitting out there for all the world to see. There's nothing concealing it or trying to make it look like it's not there. You don't have to do any sort of special incantation or ritual or anything to go through it like you do the portal. You just have to open a door. Being that open and upfront about it means Malakan wanted people to know where he was."

"Doesn't much sound like someone in exile," Aurora said.

"No, it sounds *exactly* like someone in exile. He wanted everyone who he thought mattered to know where he had gone when he was ousted from the warlocks. Creating this place was his way of hiding away, but also being readily found by people who knew where to look. He was hiding in plain sight."

"Sneaky," Ashe said.

"Essentially," I agreed. "When he set this place up, he was making it obvious he didn't stop being a warlock or following his beliefs just because he'd been pushed aside. He made the entrance to his private lair obvious to anyone who saw it. They just had to be able to pass through it. Something that visible is made for attention, and it's been my experience that when things are made for attention, they are covering up something that someone wants to keep hidden."

"But you didn't know where to find him," Ashe pointed out. "We had to go to Stephana for help. If he wanted to make it so obvious, why would you need help finding it?"

"Remember, I said 'everyone who he thought mattered'. There's a difference between being out in the open and being able to be found. He was still hiding, still in exile, just in a place where if you knew where to look, you could get to him. I was only able to find him because I asked the right questions and Ty and I followed the clues. Those weren't accidental. Malakan knew we'd find him. We were supposed to find him. But if he made it seem difficult and we had to go through several channels, it would seem much more significant when we did."

I was still following the rock, running my hand along it as we walked along the edge of the cavern. In my mind, I tried to imagine what this place would have looked like before Malakan mirrored the house and its surroundings into it. How big was it? Was it completely empty, or were there rock formations dividing it up? If I could envision just how big the cavern was when he first discovered it, I could better determine how much further we had to walk until we had traced the entire outer edge of the space.

"Why would it matter to him if the door to his

chambers seemed significant?" Aurora asked. "I told you, I went to visit him all the time, and he never made a big deal out of where he was, or me knowing it."

"No, but he did try to keep your father away from here," I said. "You said yourself he didn't bring Darian to the house. He wanted to keep this place safe and private. You were allowed in here because he wanted you to be able to come here. But you always went through that tunnel, right?"

"Of course," Aurora said. "That's how to get in here."

"Is it?" I asked.

I kept walking and suddenly my fingertips ran over something that felt different than the rest of the rock. I went back a few steps and traced over the area again.

"What are you doing?"

"If I've learned anything in the past few days, it's that things aren't always as they appear."

I ran my fingers along the same uneven area and then started pressing my fingertips into it. I could feel the stone starting to move slightly, so I kept going.

"What does that have to do with Malakan?" Aurora asked.

I handed the torch to her and added my other fingers into the gap in the stone. As I forced it apart, the stone started to move more.

"There's this entire world that nobody knows about, and the entrance to it is in a bar that anybody can just walk into. Vampires are real, but they're almost nothing like most people believe. They mingle almost perfectly with humans."

"Hayden, what the hell are you talking about?" Aurora asked.

I smiled.

"The people of the Underworld seem to like hiding things in plain sight," I said. "That's the door in Final View. It draws your attention, so you don't notice what's really important."

I gave another tug and the stone shifted just enough to reveal it wasn't a solid wall, but a piece that had been slid into place over the mouth of another tunnel. Ashe gasped and nearly dropped the torch. Aurora rushed up beside me and stared into the tunnel.

"It's another entrance," she said.

"Yes," I said. "Malakan made a big deal out of that entrance to the cavern so that everyone would think he was protecting it so carefully. Of course, he was. He didn't want just anyone to be able to get inside. But the main reason he was doing it was so no one would even consider there might be another way. A passage just for him so he could get in whenever he wanted, without anyone noticing."

"Or out," Aurora said.

17

"That's why there's no body," Aurora said.

Her voice was powdery and soft, like she couldn't even believe the words she was saying. She looked at me with hope in her eyes and I wanted so much to confirm it to her, but I knew I couldn't. There were still too many questions left to tell her anything in absolutes.

"I think it's possible," I said. "I told you from the beginning that something about this fire doesn't sit well with me. It didn't happen like a normal fire and it didn't burn like a normal fire. There were too many things about it that just didn't make sense, and not being able to find any trace of his body just confirms it more for me. I can't be positive he's still alive, but I think finding this entrance is enough that we can say we don't know everything yet."

"You think he did it himself, don't you?" Ashe asked. "You think Malakan set the fire on purpose."

"Again, I think it's possible. There's a very strong chance he faked his own death."

"But why?" Aurora asked. "He adored this place. Why would he destroy it?"

"Exactly because of what you just said," I said. "He absolutely loved this place. It was his private refuge from everything that was going on in the world around him. Anyone who was close to him would know that. Which means if anything ever happened to it, anyone who knew him would immediately think someone had done it to him rather than him doing it himself."

"Another distraction," Ashe said.

"Maybe," I said. "If he really did do this himself, there was a reason. We need to find out why, and I think it has to do with me."

I started toward the entrance of the new tunnel and Aurora grabbed me by the back of my shirt and pulled me out of it.

"What do you think you're doing?" she asked almost frantically.

"I'm going in," I said. "This was obviously Malakan's private entrance to this place. If he set that fire himself, this is how he got out of here without anybody knowing. I want to know where it goes."

"No," Ashe said.

"Why not?" I asked.

"Because you don't know where it goes," she said. "Malakan had some of the most powerful magic abilities of anyone who has ever existed. I'm positive he had some sort of spell or magical object that would allow him to transport himself without having to use tunnels. There would be no need for him to use some tunnel like this."

"No," Aurora said. "He didn't."

"What?" I asked.

"Malakan didn't have any sort of spell or magical object that he could use to transport him rather than having to go through the tunnels."

"How do you know that?"

"That's part of being sent into exile for a warlock. That type of magic does exist. It's very rare and extremely difficult to master. As you can imagine, that means it's also very dangerous and desirable. Any warlock who is able to transport themselves without use of conventional channels is a serious threat to anyone who is against them. It means they could just appear wherever they wanted to and then disappear without anyone being able to follow them, or even know for sure they were there. When a warlock is put into exile, their abilities are closely evaluated. While there's no one who can completely take away all of the magical powers of someone as powerful as Malakan, there are locks that can be put into place to prevent certain skills from being used. No warlock is born with the ability to transport themselves. It's something they have to learn and develop over a long time. That means it can be controlled. When a warlock is exiled, their ability to do that is taken away from them. It's a way to keep them under the control of the other warlocks and to prevent them from being able to use that ability against the others. Malakan would have been able to transport himself that way before his exile, but he hasn't been since then. He has to move from place to place in the same ways everybody else does."

"Which means this tunnel is our closest link to him. This is what he used to move from place to place without everybody knowing, and the fact that he put that piece of rock in front of the entrance means he was trying to protect it. He didn't want other people to find it. If we can find out where it leads, we might be able to find him," I said.

"That is, if you're right and he's still alive," Ashe said. "Right now, it's just a guess. We can't guarantee he did light that fire or that he went through this tunnel to escape. And if he did, what does that even mean? If he wanted you to find him, he would have told you he was leaving. Somebody doesn't blow their house up and fake their own death if they want other people to know where they are."

"Maybe there are only specific people he doesn't want to know," I said. "It doesn't matter, though. I need to find him. He knows about my past in a way that nobody else does, and I want to know what he knows. I need him to tell me who I am and what I'm supposed to do now."

"You don't need him to tell you that," Aurora said. "You know who you are. It's just going to take some time for you to get used to it."

"And how do you suggest I do that?" I asked. "It's not like I can roll up to the other warlocks and say 'Hey everybody it, guess what? I'm your long-lost prince who you thought was dead for the last twenty-eight years. But I'm back now, and I would really appreciate if you would teach me how to be a warlock so I can go about my life with my vampire princess mate.'"

Aurora stared back at me for a few seconds and then blinked.

"Yeah," she said. "That probably wouldn't go over very well."

I shook my head.

"I didn't think so," I said.

I started into the tunnel again and was yet again yanked back.

"You're not going in there," Ashe said.

"You've got to stop doing that," I said.

"Look, Hayden, I understand that you're upset. I get that you want to figure all of this out and that you think chasing down Malakan is going to give you what you need."

"And you don't think it will?" I asked.

"I'm not saying that. I didn't think so before, but now I think it's completely possible Malakan is still alive. And if he is, he might be the one to tell you what you need to know about yourself and your past. But I also know you aren't ready to just throw yourself into something you know nothing about."

"That's what I've been doing the entire time

I've been in the Underworld," I snapped back. "Ever since I walked into that bar and she bit me, I've been neck-deep in shit I don't understand. And I've had to get through it."

"You've had Aurora and me to help you," she said. "We knew what you were going through and were able to help you figure it out. Neither of us know anything about this. You're about to throw yourself into something completely unknown to all of us, and you need to think about that. You have no idea where this tunnel leads or what might be waiting on the other end. Whether Malakan is out there or not, if you go through that tunnel, you will have to face whatever is there. Right now, you would have no idea what to do and might end up getting yourself killed. I can't imagine that's what Malakan wanted. If he's alive, finding him is going to be on his terms. If he's not, there's nothing you can do about it. Either way, you need to focus on what you have ahead of you."

I didn't want to hear it, but I knew she was right. Like I had already told the women, this was not a stalemate, it was a cold war, and I felt it heating up around us. I knew it was going to build up until it blew. We had to stop it in any way possible. I already knew I was going to be a vital component of what was to come, but it was up to me to find out why and to know what role I was going to play.

"We need to focus on Ty," Aurora said. "He knows more about this than anyone, possibly even Malakan. There's a reason he walked away, and I think if we find out that reason, it will tell you what you need to know."

"Where do we look now?" I asked. "He's not at the tavern, he's not in Final View, and he's not here. Wherever he went, he had his reasons. There's something he needed to do, and I don't think we're just going to be able to find him."

"What are you saying?" Ashe asked.

"I'm not always going to be able to rely on all of you to tell me what to do and how to do it. This is who I was born to be and what I was meant to do. I have to be able to rely on myself. I've been learning about being a vampire and understanding your ways. But that's not all of me. I need to know more about my warlock side. It's already come out of me in a lot of ways since I started this change, but I need to learn to control it. I can't just walk up to the warlock clans and tell them who I am. I don't think I can tell anybody right now. There was someone listening to us in the palace and I think they've been following us. There's danger all around us and if I'm going to be effective at fighting this war, I need to be in control of both sides of me. If I don't have Malakan to train me, we need to find someone else who can."

"I agree," Aurora said. "But who can we trust? If we can't reveal your identity to anyone, how are we going to find someone who has the ability to train you the way you need?"

"We should go back to Stephana," Ashe said.

"Why Stephana?" Aurora asked.

"She's considered an outcast herself," Ashe said. "She's never really fit in with the vampires and has always reached out to people who are struggling while going through their transformations. Even after, she's there for the ones who don't feel like they are really a part of the community. She's known to help all kinds of people who are in a bad way. Hayden, you noticed all the food and clothes in her house. She eats human food, yes, but the main reason she has all of that is so she can help anyone who might need it. The Underworld isn't always the most welcoming place, especially for those who are new to it."

"Really?" I asked sarcastically. "Because I was just thinking it would make the most charming setting for the next women's network Christmas movie."

"There are rumors she maintains friendships with species that other people won't even get near. She also has affiliations with the Dragon, though she doesn't consider herself friends with them or a supporter of what they do. The point is, she might be able to help. I know she says she didn't know Malakan personally, but she might be able to get in touch with other magi. If she knows anyone who could train you, she will get in touch with them and set it up."

"We need to be extremely careful," I said. "We can't be sure who we can be loyal to or who we can trust. We don't know their loyalties or who they might want to help. I don't want the truth about my identity to come out before I want it to. That's something I need to be able to control on my own."

"We can trust her. She is my Sire and has always been there for me. She has already helped you. She would never put you in danger, and we can figure out how to keep your identity under wraps until the right time."

I nodded.

"It might be our only choice."

18

I knew I wouldn't see him, but I couldn't stop my eyes from scanning the sidewalks for Ty as we made our way back through the city. Every time I saw someone who I looked to be his height or had some of his mannerisms, I would get a spike of hope only to be disappointed when the person turned around and I saw it wasn't him. I knew it was ridiculous to be looking for him this way. He left for a reason. It wasn't like he just got bored and decided to go for a ridiculously long walk. He intended on leaving before he even asked us to drop him off, and until he wanted to be found, he was going to stay gone.

We had been driving through the streets of the city for several minutes before I noticed the car behind us. At first, it seemed like just another car on the road. After a few turns I realized it was following us. I didn't want to alarm the women by bring it to their attention, so I sped up slightly, then made a turn that let me backtrack and come up two cars behind the one following us. Aurora looked at me strangely, but I didn't acknowledge it. She had enough on her mind right now and didn't need me worrying her further.

When we got to Stephana's building, Ashe took out her phone and sent her a text. A few moments later, the door opened and the older woman looked out at us. She had a curious expression on her face and met Ashe's eyes when we got out of the car.

"Hi, again," she said, following Ashe with her questioning gaze as she made her way up the front steps and into the house.

"Hi," Ashe said.

"Aurora," Stephana said. "It's nice to see you. It's been a long time."

Aurora smiled, but the expression didn't warm her entire face. Stephana close the door behind us and we made our way into the living room. Ashe was already sitting in the overstuffed chair when I walked into the room.

"Well, this is a nice surprise," Stephana said,

looking at us. "I don't think I have seen you this many times in the last six months, much less a week, Ashe."

She glanced over at me.

"She's much more of the birth-death-Christmas-Easter-High Holidays type child that all those human parents complain about. She never comes to visit me this much."

Ashe rolled her eyes and I held back a laugh. It was hilarious to see this strong, feisty woman being treated like a sullen teenager.

"Come on, Ashe," I said. "You don't visit your sire any more often than that? Don't you think you could at least just make an effort to come see her on Sundays?"

Ashe narrowed her eyes at me.

"I don't think I'm exactly the type to come over for a family meal," she said.

"I think it's a wonderful idea," Stephana said. "I could put together a whole spread. I'm sure if I got in touch with Final View, I could scoop up somebody to have over for dinner."

"Do we think we can move on from the guilt trip portion of the night?" Ashe asked. "There actually is a reason we are here."

"I wouldn't expect anything less," Stephana

said. "Like I said, Ashe only comes to see me for the major things."

"This is pretty major," Aurora said. "It actually ticks pretty much all the boxes for one of Ashe's visits."

"Seriously?" Ashe said, shooting a glare at Aurora.

Aurora shrugged, and I swooped in to keep the momentum of the conversation going.

"It's kind of a birth-death-High Holidays type situation," I said.

"What's going on?" Stephana asked. She seemed to notice for the first time that Aurora and I were still standing at the edge of the room. She gestured at the couch. "Why don't the two of you sit down? Hayden, can I get you something to eat?"

I hesitated.

"Well," I said.

"What's wrong?" she asked.

"I'm just thinking," I said.

"Is it that hard of a question?" she asked.

"Kind of," I said. "I mean, I don't really need it. On the other hand, a big ass chocolate chip cookie does sound really awesome right now."

Stephana laughed.

"Well it just so happens I have a cookie jar full

of freshly baked big ass chocolate chip cookies right in the kitchen. I'll get you one."

She walked out of the living room and into the kitchen. She came out a few seconds later carrying a plate with two cookies on it.

"Thank you," I said.

"Remember, Hayden, you can make your own rules. Always keep that in mind. You don't have to do what anyone else does or what anyone else thinks you should do. This is your existence, and you're going to have to experience it for a long time. You need to do what's right for you."

Out of the corner of my eye, I noticed Aurora and Ashe exchange glances, then they both looked at me. I knew exactly what that look meant even without having to read their thoughts. That was as good a segue is anything. I took as big a bite of my cookie as I could fit in my mouth, chewed, and swallowed.

"That's part of why we came here," I said. "It turns out I might have to figure out my own way even more than we thought."

She looked at me questioningly.

"What are you talking about?" she asked.

"Hayden isn't just a vampire now," Ashe said.

"I know," Stephana said. "He just told me he

completed his blood bond with Aurora. That makes him her Lord."

"It's more than that," Ashe said.

Stephana listened intently as we filled her in on everything that had happened since the last time we were there. I expected her to have a huge reaction when we told her that I was the stolen son of the ArchWarlock, but she hardly seemed to notice. She gave a barely perceptible nod and continued to listen. When Ashe stopped talking, I picked up and continued. I told her everything we had seen at Malakan's house and what we discovered about the second tunnel. By the time I was finished, I felt breathless, but she still hadn't reacted. She waited for several seconds like she was processing through everything we had just told her. Finally, she sat up a little straighter and a hint of a smile curled her lips.

"I always knew there was something special about you," she said. "From the moment I first saw you, Hayden, I knew there was something different. This really does change everything."

"It does," Ashe said. "That's why I said we should come back and talk to you. I figured if there was anybody who would be able to help us, it was probably you. We don't know if Malakan is dead or alive, or where Ty went or why. There are so many questions right now, but the most important thing is that none of us is going to be able to stop the war that's coming. It's been inevitable since the day that they took Hayden. The fact that he's come back here doesn't change that, but it does mean he needs to get ready for what's ahead of him. We need your help finding somebody who can train him in his warlock ways."

Stephana nodded.

"You were right to come to me," she said. "Hayden is the hope for the future. Him coming back here now is no accident. But if he's going to be able to do what he needs to do to save his kind -- both of his kinds -- he has to know everything he can."

"Can you help?" I asked.

"I have connections with many warlocks, but I don't know if any of them would be the right choice. I'm not sure if I could trust any of them to be as discreet as we would need them to be. They could definitely give Hayden the training he needs, but knowing them, they would immediately go to the tavern and spill everything to anybody who would listen."

"Yeah, we need to avoid that," Ashe said.

"What about the other exiled warlocks?" Aurora asked.

"Others?" I asked. "There are more than just Malakan?"

"Yes," Aurora said. "There have been dozens of warlocks who have been exiled since the beginning of the war. It hasn't been as popular in recent years, but there was a while where any warlock who seemed to have any vampire sympathies or was linked to vampires or their ally species in any way would be exiled. Some were just sent into temporary exile for a few months if what they were accused of was minor, or if there wasn't enough evidence to completely justify total exile. But there were others, like Malakan, who were sent into lifelong exile, completely cut off from the rest of their kind. Wouldn't that make them the perfect choice? If they were treated that way by the Warlocks, don't you think they would want to help anyone who was trying to bring this conflict to an end?"

"No," Stephana said. "I can understand why you would think that, but it's just not true. I've spent enough time with those who have been exiled and others who voluntarily left the faction to know the loyalty to their kind is incredibly strong. Even if their ultimate goal is to live in a society where there's peace and cooperation between the vampires and the warlocks, they are desperate for the acknowledgement and praise of their kind. Many of them believe if they can return to the ArchWarlock and his advisors, they will have influence. They would jump at the opportunity to offer such a valuable piece of information to the other warlocks."

"They can't all be like that," I argued.

"You're right," Stephana said. "They aren't. There are some, like Malakan, who were hurt by their exile because it cut them off from the world and the people they loved but accepted it because they are strong in their beliefs against the war. They want to end the conflict and corruption and see an Underworld that is united rather than fractured. But it's almost impossible to really know which of them thinks that way. Especially when it comes to something as groundbreaking as what we're talking about here. I don't know if you understand the power of this revelation, Hayden. This isn't just about you finding out your life wasn't what you thought it was. Your birth was the greatest moment of joy your parents had ever experienced. You were foretold to be one of the greatest warlocks to ever live, greater even, perhaps, than Malakan. You were to lead the warlocks into power. The moment you disappeared, the entire future of the warlocks, the vampires, and the entire Underworld was changed. You still being alive and finding your way back here changes the course of everyone's life, and the impact it will have has truly yet to be seen. Anyone who found out about you might be tempted to share it with the warlocks. Imagine being cut off from everything you've ever known, from the world you believe you are a part of and being so desperate to be accepted again and seen as valuable. Then you are offered a piece of information that is like the most precious jewel in existence. Telling the warlocks who you really are would be giving their people back the prince they have mourned for twenty-eight years. The reward that would come from that…" her voice trailed off for a moment. "Even the strongest of the supporters who left the faction may be swayed by that."

"Do we have to tell them who he is?" Aurora asked. "Can we just say he needs training?"

Stephana shook her head.

"Even that is too risky," she said. "There's far too much suspicion. Hayden is still new, and people don't know him yet. A mysterious friend of the vampires who wants to know more about the warlocks would be intriguing to the warlock leaders as well. And if they were to somehow find out that Hayden is bonded to Aurora, it would look far too suspicious that the princess's Lord suddenly wants to know more about the magi. It would seem like an omen of war."

"Then who?" Ashe asked.

She sounded exasperated, almost desperate.

"The Dragon."

I didn't realize I had linked myself in to Stephana's thoughts until I heard those words in her voice moving through my mind.

"What about them?" I asked.

She looked at me with confusion and I realized I hadn't yet told her about my ability to read her thoughts. There was no turning back now.

"What?" she asked. "What about who?"

"The Dragon," I said.

Stephana looked over at Ashe and then back at me.

"You heard me?" she asked. Then she nodded. "That's right. You would have the abilities of the warlocks even if you don't know about all of them. I'm going to have to remember that. It definitely takes away a lot of the mystique, doesn't it?"

"I try not to listen all the time," I told her. "It's not like I can hear everything that's going through your mind."

"Good," she said. "Let me make a suggestion -- don't play around with that. There's a reason thoughts are silent. You might not always like what you hear, and the people around you probably don't like the idea of not having any privacy even inside themselves."

I nodded. "Why were you thinking about the Dragon?" I asked.

"They aren't really the type that most people would want to associate with," Stephana said.

"I'm aware," I said. "I'm not exactly eager to have another run-in with them anytime soon."

"Why not?"

I realized we had skipped over everything that happened between Ashe and the Dragon.

"They captured me as payment," Ashe said matter-of-factly.

"Payment?" Stephana asked. "What do you mean?"

"Ty didn't lead me to Malakan," I admitted. "Not exactly. When we went to The Foundry that night to meet with Ty, the Dragon was there. Or, at least, they somehow figured out that *I* was there.

They brought me to them and told me they knew I was a powerful hybrid. Of course, at the time I thought they were just talking about me being a human and a vampire."

"They knew," Stephana said. "Somehow, they knew who you are."

"I think so," I said. "I asked them what they knew about Malakan and if they could help me find him. They gave me a riddle to direct me to him and then sent me away, but to them that was enough. I was already out of the club by the time they told me they'd taken Ashe as payment for the council they gave me."

Stephana gasped and covered her mouth. That gesture told me she knew the type of brutality the Dragon was capable of, and what it meant for Ashe to be taken by them.

"I'm all right," Ashe reassured her. "Hayden rescued me."

"How can you associate with people who would do something like that?" I demanded.

"You have to understand," she said. "The Dragon is an ancient organization. They've been around far longer than most people realize. In many ways, they still operate by the standards of the time when they were first established."

"They captured her," I emphasized. "They tortured her. Just because they gave me some vague piece of information that may or may not lead me to a man I was looking for. How can you possibly justify that?"

Stephana looked at me strangely.

"How long did they have her?" she asked.

"Why does that matter?" I asked.

"Because it does," she said harshly. "How long?"

"Several hours," I said. "I'm not sure exactly how long."

"It took you that long to rescue her?" she asked.

"Do you know what I had to do to find her?" I asked. "The shit I had to go through? It's not like they gave me a receipt for her and a handwritten thank-you note. Ty and I had to break their fun little code, go traipsing through the fucking roadside motel of the damned, and find Malakan. Then I had to go through a ritual that showed me my past, present, and future, and then decide whether I was going to find out where they were keeping Ashe, or what I needed to do to convince Aurora to complete my change."

I felt like I couldn't stop the words that were

pouring out of my mouth. I told her everything I experienced in the church fighting against the magi guards and rescuing Ashe. Finally, I was back to the moment where I had started the story, telling her about finishing my transformation and going to Malakan to tell him, only to watch his house explode.

Stephana was staring at me when I finished.

"They didn't kill her," she finally said.

I blinked at her.

"Because I saved her," I said. I grabbed my now-empty plate and started for the kitchen, feeling like I needed to move around to expel some of the energy that was ramping up inside me.

"No, Hayden, you don't understand. Taking a person for payment isn't unusual for the Dragon. It has fallen out of favor over time, for obvious reasons, but it's still done. But they don't keep them. They have no reason to hold them captive. The payment is a blood sacrifice, similar to the one given to go through the portal. If they had intended her only as payment, they would have killed Ashe within a short time of her getting to the church. But they kept her there long enough for you to get to her."

"So, you're telling me it was a really warped

Easter egg hunt?"

"No," she said, smiling as she shook her head. "They wanted to know if you would come for her, and if, when you did, you would fight for her. It was how they tested their theory about you. They wanted to see how you would perform."

"And if I hadn't found her? Or if I hadn't been able to fight the mages? What then?"

"They would have accepted they were wrong about you and Ashe would have been sacrificed."

"That is a risky little game," I said. "And a really shitty thing to do to the warlock guards. I didn't exactly leave them in the best condition."

Stephana looked distracted for a few seconds, like she was trying to figure something out, then shook her head and turned back to me.

"They already know you, Hayden. I doubt they've shared that piece of information with anybody beyond the Supreme Eight, but it's still significant. Lunaris, the larger group that the Dragon controls, is made up of all the misfits, outcasts, and extras of society. They are the ones who aren't wanted and who are left behind when species are culled. If there is anyone who would be willing to accept someone who has as muddled an identity as you, it will be them."

19

"Call them," I said. "Find out where they want to meet."

"You look exhausted, Hayden," Stephana said. "You need some rest."

"No," I said. "I can't waste any time."

"How long has it been since you've slept?" Aurora asked. "Really slept?"

I tried to remember, but I couldn't. I shook my head.

"It doesn't matter," I said. "I need to keep going."

"No, Hayden," Stephana said. "You need to get some rest. You're running on adrenaline and rage right now, and that's not enough to keep you going. Eventually, you're going to crash, and that could be dangerous. You need to get some sleep, and we'll try to find you a trainer in the morning."

I didn't want to give in. Every moment was important. Wasting even a second felt like it could derail me and push me further away from accomplishing what I needed to. But I could feel the exhaustion weighing on me. I knew I would be much more effective if I let my body and my mind rest for a while. I also knew if these three women had gotten it into their minds that I needed sleep, they weren't going to let me get out of it. It would be easier to just go along with it than it would be to argue.

"Fine," I said. "I'll sleep."

"Good," Stephana said. "The three of you will stay here. You're already here, and it's safer than trying to go anywhere else. Hayden, you can go to the same room as before. Ashe, Aurora can stay in the guest room beside yours."

"Thank you," Aurora said. "I appreciate your hospitality."

"It's the least I can do," Stephana said. "We need each other more than ever now."

Ashe and Aurora each came up and kissed me goodnight before heading further into the house to go to bed. I said goodnight to Stephana and went into the bedroom where I had napped the first time I had come there. A fresh pair of sweatpants was draped across the end of the bed.

"I thought I'd be ready for you. Just in case."

I turned around and saw Stephana standing at the doorway. I looked down at the pants in my hands and smiled at her.

"Thanks. I really appreciate it. All of it. Everything you've done for me."

"It's nothing," she said, shaking her head.

"Of course, it is," I said. "I wouldn't be here right now if it wasn't for you."

She narrowed her eyes and tilted her head.

"I would hope you wouldn't be hanging around in my house if it wasn't for me," she said. "I think that would indicate a problem."

I laughed.

"You know what I mean."

She smiled.

"I know," she said. Her eyes dropped to the sweatpants in my hands. "Aren't you going to change?" she asked.

"Um," I said, glancing down again. "Yeah, I was just…"

"Too tired?" she asked. Her voice had dropped slightly. "Here, let me help you."

She pushed away from the frame and came into the room, closing the door behind her. Her gaze traced my body as she approached, and her hands reached for the button on my pants. By the time she had released the button, all pretense was gone. Her mouth rose up to mine and I plunged my tongue in past her lips as her fingers moved down to my zipper. It felt like it had been a lifetime since I had been touched. The lust coursed through me intensely and I remembered what Ashe told me about the power of the cravings for lust. They weren't just desire or want, they were necessity. I needed sex the way I used to need food, and right now I was starving.

I kissed her passionately, my hands pulling her clothing away as she stripped me bare. When there was nothing between our bodies, I grabbed her close to me. Her skin felt soft against mine and each breath made her breasts rise and fall against my chest, so I could feel her nipples tightening. I wrapped one arm around her waist and toppled her backward onto the bed. Sliding back, I parted her thighs with my hands. Without hesitation, I sank my tongue into her. The taste of her filled my mouth and I dug my fingertips into her skin. Stephana lifted her hips up to press harder against my face and I obliged by nuzzling into her. After a few seconds of coaxing her to open for me, I rose up over her and caught her mouth in another kiss. She didn't close her thighs, making it easy for me to settle my hips between them. I was already hard, and the engorged head of my cock sought out her dripping entrance eagerly. Her slickness allowed the cushiony tip to slide over her easily and I circled my hips for a few seconds to trace her opening and explore her folds. The touch made a rush of sensation flow through me and my need for her spiraled even higher.

"Why do you always make me wait?" she purred.

"You don't want to wait?" I teased her.

"No," she murmured. "I want you now. I've needed you inside me since the moment you pulled out of me.

"Then I guess it would be unfair of me not to oblige you," I said.

In one movement I plunged into her, and Stephana's head fell back, her eyes closing as she savored the feeling of me filling her. Rather than sliding back immediately, I held my hips in place, pressing further until I felt like I couldn't get any deeper. Then with a sharp push, somehow managed it anyway. Stephana cried out and I repeated the thrust. Finally, I couldn't control myself anymore. Rolling my hips, I moved inside her with tight strokes, so I continuously felt her hot, slick walls against every inch of me. Stephana brought her legs up and wrapped them around my waist. I took hold of her hips and lifted them a few inches to give myself a better angle. Holding her in this position, I began thrusting harder and faster. The slam of my body against hers made her breasts bounce. I watched them for a few seconds, then cupped one with my palm.

Ducking my head, I took the other nipple between my lips and nipped at it with my teeth. Her fingers dug into my hair and suddenly she pulled my head up to crush her mouth against mine in another kiss. The harder I pounded into her, the more aggressively she kissed me, and soon our bodies were locked in battle. In the same movement she clung to me and pulled me away from her, and in return I chased her and demanded she chase me. Sweat ran along my skin and I licked salty drops from hers. Stephana pushed against me to flip me onto my back and landed straddling my hips. She sat up, arching her back and letting her hair brush against my legs. She looked magnificent, in her element as she rode me. Her body handled mine masterfully and without hesitation. It was obvious she wanted me every bit as much as I wanted her, and that only made her sexier.

I ran my hand down the center of her chest and stopped it on her lower belly. Turning it, I pressed the pad of my thumb to her clit and massaged in slow circles. She moaned and rocked her hips against the touch, encouraging me to go faster. I pressed into her and let the speed of her movements control the swirl of my thumb on her taut pearl. Soon, she was gasping, and the tremble of her body told me she was getting close. I held her hip with my free hand and lifted my hips to slam into her a few more times. Stephana suddenly let out a cry and I felt her body clench down on mine. It was enough to push me over the edge and I came hard. She ground her hips down into me as she rode the waves of pleasure rolling through her. Her walls met each pulse of my cock with a squeeze, and she whimpered when I pushed deeper into her.

Finally, we dropped down onto the pillows and she smiled at me.

"You've gotten even better since your transformation," she said.

20

"He still not answering?" I asked.

Ashe looked up at me from where she sat at the table positioned near a window at the back of Stephana's house. She shook her head.

"No," she said. "I've called him at least ten times this morning. His voicemail inbox is full now. I'm pretty sure it's all messages from me."

"Have you talked to anybody from Solomon's Fang?" I asked.

"Why would I have talked to anybody from Solomon's Fang?" she asked.

"Don't you have a phone tree or something? Just for this type of situation when people suddenly go missing and other people need to find them?"

"No, we don't have a phone tree, Hayden," she

said. She picked up her phone and pressed the button to dial Ty again. After a few seconds, she let out a sound of exasperation and dropped the phone to the table. She looked up as Aurora came into the room. "We need a phone tree," she said.

"A phone tree?" Aurora asked.

"Yeah," I said. "For Solomon's Fang. Haven't you ever heard of a phone tree? You call a couple of people and they call a couple of people and they call a couple of other people? Spreads the word really quickly? 'Hey, guys, Ty seems to have disappeared at a super inconvenient time and we really fucking need to talk to him, so if you hear from him, send him our way?' No?" I looked between the two women, who were both staring at me. I shook my head. "Underworld PTA must seriously suck," I said.

Ashe laughed.

"I take it your parents were really active in the PTA?" she asked.

I shrugged.

"Do we know anybody we could call?" Aurora asked, "There has to be somebody that you know from the bar who might have some idea where Ty is. We're not the only people he associated with."

"Just about," Ashe said. "He interacted with

fewer and fewer people as the years went by. But I can probably call Jake, the other bartender. Maybe one or two of the waitresses. They might know of some other people he keeps in touch with or might be able to tell us if they've seen him."

"I can call Jaxxim," Aurora said. "He probably doesn't know what to do with himself, not following me around all the time. He could use a project. I'll ask him if he's heard from Ty, or if any of the other Shades know anything. As far as I know, he hasn't associated with any of them in a long time, but things seem to be changing pretty quickly around here. We probably shouldn't discount any possibility."

I grinned.

"See? Phone tree."

Both women shot me glares, but I just kept smiling at them until they smiled back. Stephana came into the room a few minutes later carrying a mug of coffee. She sat it down in front of me and I took a long sip. Both Aurora and Ash walked out of the room with their phones and I could hear them pacing as they talked. There were a few starts and stops to their muffled conversations and then Aurora came back into the room.

"Nothing," she said. "Even just mentioning his name made Jaxxim uncomfortable."

"Does everybody know what he did?" I asked.

"Not the details," Aurora said. "But they know he did something that made my father really angry and lost his position. That's enough to make none of the Shades to want anything to do with him. And that's pretty much what he just told me. I asked if he had heard from or heard anything about Ty, and he bristled. He said that he hadn't heard from him, didn't know where he was, and still didn't think I should associate with him."

"All right, so that wasn't very successful."

Ashe came into the room shaking her head.

"I wasn't, either," she said. "Nobody from the bar has heard from him since we left. And it turns out, we're not the only ones looking for him. Apparently, there are a lot of people who are pretty pissed off about not being able to move through the portal because he's not there. They seem pretty eager to find him and get him back to his post. Getting knocked down to portal keeper didn't make Ty happy, but the Underworld doesn't really function without him."

"So, what do we do now?" Aurora asked.

"I've reached out to my contact with the Dragon," she said. "I asked her to meet with us later this morning. I didn't want to talk to her about the specifics over the phone."

"That was probably a good idea," I said. "I'm going to go take a shower and get ready."

I could feel their eyes on me as I walked out of the room, but I didn't turn back to look at them. I was lost in my own thoughts.

I was back in the bedroom, staring down at my bag of clothes, not even remembering why I was looking at it, when Aurora came into the room. She stepped up beside me and stared into my face like she was waiting for me to say something.

"What's on your mind?" she asked. "You seem really quiet."

"Your father," I said.

She looked at me strangely.

"My father?" she asked. "Why are you thinking about him?"

I turned to her.

"How can I not be thinking about him?" I asked. "I just found out that he's the reason my life went completely off course. I can't stop thinking about how he schemed to have me kidnapped as a baby twenty-eight years ago. For all that time, people thought I was dead. Darian even thought I was dead, and because of something he did. How does he keep going?"

"What do you mean how does he keep going?"

"How can he possibly just keep going about his life like there's nothing wrong when he thinks it's his fault a newborn baby was killed?"

"He has to," Aurora said. "He doesn't have any other choice. He has people to lead who trust him and are relying on him. Besides, if I was carrying something like that around with me, I would want to do anything I could to try to get it out of my mind and not have to think about it all the time."

"I just don't understand," I said. "I don't understand how he could have even come up with a plan like that. What kind of a person wants to kidnap a baby to use as a weapon?"

Aurora cupped my face with both hands and touched a kiss to my lips.

"I can't tell you I understand what you're feeling," she said quietly. "I've never been through anything like it. But I do understand why you're feeling it. If I found out about myself what you found out, I would feel the exact same way. But I want you to know that my father is, for the most part, a good man. He has always wanted what was best for his kind and is fiercely protective of the vampire people. He thought he was doing the right thing. He knew losing you was going to hurt your family, but he also believed in his heart that in the long run, it was going to heal all the conflicts and damage that was being done throughout the Underworld. The tension between the warlocks and the vampires didn't just affect our species, you know. It wasn't just about Solan City or it's outskirts. The war had effects that reverberated throughout our entire world. What my father planned to do might not have been good, or even right, but war rarely is."

"How can you defend him? You just said you know what he did wasn't good. He meant to cause pain by kidnapping me."

"I know," she said. "I know he intended on hurting the ArchWarlock and his family with the kidnapping."

"Those are my parents you're talking about," I said.

"I know," she said again. "And I know my father meant to hurt them by taking you. But he only did it in retaliation for the deaths of the Prime and his family years before that. He never intended on killing you. That wasn't the point of it. He really thought good was going to come out of it.

Sometimes you have to act brutally in order to make things change."

I wanted to agree with her. I wanted to be able to think about it that way, but I couldn't. I admired how she looked at her father. She saw such strength in him, and that, in turn, gave her strength. Even though it was obvious to anyone who looked at them that their relationship was far from close, she was steadfast in her belief in him as a powerful leader and that he always did what was best for her people. As much as I wanted to believe in him that way, and as much as I wanted to be able to let go of what had happened at the start of my life, I couldn't. Even if I could put aside the tragedy he caused, I couldn't bring myself to trust him.

The way he reacted to the news of Malakan's death still stuck with me. It didn't sit right, though I couldn't place why. I only knew that every time I thought of the look on his face when he rushed in to confront us about the news. His eyes stood out to me. There was something in them, or more accurately, something that wasn't in them. For all his hysteria and dramatic words, there was no compassion or fear in his eyes.

21

THE TRIP TO MEET WITH STEPHANA'S CONTACT brought us out of the city, beyond even the outer edges where I had been. We drove in tense silence until we reached a thick forest. Stephana stopped just inside the first rows of trees and we got out.

"Where are we?" I asked.

"It's better known now," she said, "but Lunaris has always been an extremely secretive group. They have had to operate in the shadows and outside the awareness of others in order to protect themselves and their work. When I told my contact I needed help, she said we needed to meet here so no one else would hear what we were talking about. She knows if I am getting in touch with her and asking for help, it's serious, and to her, that means it might be dangerous."

"Is it?" I asked.

"Yes," she said. "This could be extremely dangerous. You need to understand that before we go any further."

"I do," I confirmed. "And I'm ready for it."

It took several minutes of us walking through the trees before I began to notice the signs of a path beneath our feet. It appeared as sparse spots in the fallen leaves and pine needles at first, but after a while it became more defined, and I could see it meandering through the woods ahead of us. There was no indication of where it was leading, but we just kept following it. Finally, ahead of us, I noticed the dark line of the trees seemed to lessen and the path opened into a clearing. The only thing in the clearing was a small cabin, and Stephana walked up to it without hesitation. She knocked on the door and then hung back with the two other women and me. Only seconds after the knock, the door opened a few inches.

"Yes?" a voice asked from the darkness inside the cabin.

"Diane?" Stephana said. "It's me."

The door opened further, and a woman peered out at us. Her eyes scanned each one of us, then she nodded.

"Come inside," she said.

We all walked into the cabin and I noticed it was only one room. There were signs the building hadn't always been that way. Deep gouges in the walls and ceiling marked where there had once been rooms, but these walls had been removed to create the large open space where are we now stood. In the far back corner of the room a black cast-iron stove heated a kettle. The smell of burning wood and herbs filled the air around us.

"Thank you for meeting with us today," Stephana said.

I looked at the woman's face as she turned to us. She didn't look familiar. I didn't think she was one of the women I had seen in The Foundry, but she could have been one of the people who hadn't removed their masks.

"You told me you needed help," Diane said. "What can I do for you?"

Stephana stepped back and reached for my hand. I stepped up beside her.

"This is Hayden," Stephana said.

Diane gave another slight nod.

"I know," she said. "I had the pleasure of making his acquaintance recently."

This confirmed to me she was one of the people in the shadowy room, but the fact that I didn't recognize her face was unnerving. I didn't like the idea of not knowing who was around me. It reminded me of the person who was watching us, and it put me on edge.

Her eyes shifted behind me and I saw her lips curl up slightly when she looked at Ashe. Stephana stepped protectively between them to block Diane's view.

"No," Stephana said.

Diane gave a short, dismissive laugh.

"Don't worry, Stephana, Ashe is safe. Hayden already paid the price with her once. She won't be the price again."

"There will be no price," Stephana said in warning. "You made a very serious mistake messing with my child. You will not make another."

I was surprised at just how quickly the woman caved to Stephana. She had been built up to me as being mysterious and powerful, and yet she relented instantly to Stephana. I knew there was a story there. Something happened that put Stephana in a role of power over this woman, and likely the entirety of the Dragon. I didn't know what it was, but it made my curiosity even stronger.

"What do you need?" Diane asked.

"I need someone I can trust," Stephana said. "Someone who knows the ways of the warlocks."

Diane drew in a breath. She walked out of the cabin through the back door and a few moments later came back in with the others I'd seen the night I met the Dragon. None looked surprised to see me, and I wondered how much they knew about me and my past. Or possibly, my future.

"Hayden," one of the men said to me. "It's good to see you again."

He said it less like he was actually happy to encounter me again, and more like part of him was surprised I was still alive. I nodded in acknowledgement.

"Do you know your secret yet?" another of the men asked.

"Yes," I said. "I am a hybrid."

I didn't go any further than that. Even though these were people Stephana believed could help me, I still didn't know if I could trust them. I didn't want to reveal everything until I was more confident in them.

"Yes," the man said. "You are. A very strong one, if I guess correctly."

"Hayden has learned his vampire side well," Stephana said.

"Yes, but I've never known much about my warlock side," I continued. "I'd like to know as much as I can."

"He needs to learn about his abilities," Stephana said. "He needs a trainer who can teach him about the very basics of his magical capabilities, but who will also push him to his potential. We need someone we can trust."

None of the Dragon responded. They exchanged glances, all of them looking hesitant. If we were right and they did know who I actually was, it was obvious none of them was sure if they wanted to get involved. I knew I would have to be the one to convince them. I took a step closer.

"I know all of you are like me," he said. "You are all hybrids and so you understand the special circumstances I face. But I have something that you don't. I am both vampire and warlock, but I am also blood bound to Aurora, princess of the vampires. As the Lord to the daughter of the Prime, I am both a hybrid and a person in a position of power. This means I could make things much better for you if given the opportunity."

This seemed to reach them. Diane met my eyes.

"You say you want to be trained in the ways of the warlocks," she said. "But we already know you have used your magic before."

"I've used it when I didn't know what it was," I admitted. "In situations when I was under extreme stress, it seemed I was able to use an ability I didn't know I had. I need to be trained to understand what's inside me and how to use it when and how I need to."

"What do you plan to do with these abilities once you have them?" she asked.

"Whatever needs to be done," I said.

My response seemed to satisfy them, and the man who had spoken to me the night I was at The Foundry came closer.

"We will arrange for a trainer," he said. "They will make sure you are given all of the skills you need, and you have our word no one will know about this."

"Thank you," I said.

Now that I knew my training would be under way soon, excitement pumped through me. There was still so much I needed to know, but for now I would concentrate on myself and what I could do to claim back what had been taken from me.

22

"How long will it be until the trainer gets here?" I asked.

"We will get in contact with him as soon as we can," Diane said. "It shouldn't be too long. You can wait here."

I expected them to stay with us, but instead the entire group walked solemnly out of the cabin and closed the door behind themselves, leaving Aurora, Ashe, Stephana, and me alone in the quiet of the room.

"So, we just wait?" I asked. "We're expected to just sit around here and not do anything, even though we have absolutely no idea how long it's going to take before this person shows up? When do we just give up if he doesn't show?"

"He'll come," Stephana said. "For now, all we can do is wait."

I paced around the cabin trying to work off some of the energy and adrenaline. I wanted something, anything, that could distract me and keep me from letting my thoughts venture further into the places they were trying to go.

"Tell me more about the war," I finally said.

"What do you mean?" Aurora asked.

"I want to know more about the history of the war between the warlocks in the vampires," I said. "If I'm such a big part of it, and I'm going to keep being such a big part of it, I need to know what happened and why."

"What do you want to know?" Ashe asked.

"All of it," I said. "You told me the Prime and his family were going through a ritual with the warlocks. Malakan told me it was like the one I went through with him. Why were they doing it? Why would the Prime vampire and his family need to go through a ritual with the warlocks to show them their past, present, and future? I don't understand the significance of that."

"The tensions between the warlocks and vampires have existed since the beginning of both species," Stephana said. "Throughout the ages, there have been intermittent efforts to create peace and even cooperation between the two. The family went through the ritual during one of the longest and most successful stretches of peace between the two species the Underworld has ever seen. Of course, there were some forces and secret organizations still determined to destroy one or both sides, but for the most part, things were going very well. But then the Prime said he felt that he was going to be betrayed. He didn't understand it and couldn't explain it, but he said he felt deep within him that someone was against him and his family, and something horrible was going to happen. Immediately, there were advisors and factions like Lunaris that stepped forward and warned him that the feeling he was having was about the warlocks. They said the warlocks had been planning to overthrow him and war was coming. He didn't want to believe it. He was one of a strong group that had been very vocal about creating strong relationships between the vampires and the warlocks, and how those relationships would promote the greatness of the entire Underworld. Lunaris simply played on his deepest fears."

"So, he didn't believe them," I said.

"He didn't know what to believe," Stephana

said. "For months, he tried to ignore the feelings and fears. But soon things started happening that made him worried he was right."

"What kinds of things? What do you mean?"

"Just little things that seemed threatening to the Prime and to the rest of his family. Honestly, most of them were so minor he probably wouldn't have even noticed them if it wasn't for people whispering of conspiracies in his ear. The battery was disconnected on his car several times. Windows were broken in the palace. His daughter said she felt like somebody was following her or watching her. They found animal bones scattered around outside of the palace. They were things that happens sometimes, and of course they were unpleasant, and even a little weird, but they were deeply disturbing to the Prime. Finally, he decided to approach the warlocks. He believed strongly that if it was warlocks doing this, they weren't the majority, and they weren't working under the command or the support of the ArchWarlock. He truly believed in the alliance he and the ArchWarlock had. When he went to them, they assured him they had absolutely nothing to do with any of it and were still just as committed as they had been to the alliance between the species and to continuing to build relations and create a stronger and more united front."

"Then why did they tell him to go through the ritual?" I asked.

"The Prime told them about his fears. They had been getting worse and more prevalent, and the rest of his family were starting to feel it as well. They were getting more anxious and fearful, and he was worried about their health. He told the warlocks it felt like there were people around him all the time and someone was against him and was trying to hurt him or his family."

"It sounds to me like somebody was gaslighting him," I said.

"A lot of people thought the same thing," Aurora said. "The problem was, there was no evidence of what had been happening. You can't see fear, at least not usually. People saw the bones, but not as many as the Prime said he saw, and not in the places he said he saw them, or even in the shapes they were supposedly in when he first found them. They knew his car wasn't working properly, but by the time the Prime said anything to people, he had already reconnected the battery, or put gas in it when he said it had been drained. People didn't know what to think. Finally, the warlocks suggested he undergo the ritual. They told him they couldn't tell him what was happening, but they could help him and his family clear their minds and connect to pinnacle moments that would help them understand what was going on and prepare for what might happen in the future."

"Just like Malakan told me," I said. "He couldn't tell me what I was going to see or even what the visions meant, but he could help me see them."

"Yes. The Prime agreed and they made plans to go through with the ritual. Usually such a ritual is only performed on one person at a time, with one trusted warlock with them. I'm sure you understand as well as anybody how intense the experience can be," Stephana said.

"Yes," I said. "It was not like anything I'd ever gone through. I don't even know how to explain it. I do know that by the time I was halfway through, I didn't want to do it anymore."

"That's probably why the warlocks agreed to let the entire family do it at the same time. They knew that it could be intense and difficult for all of them, especially the Prime's children. They thought it might be easier for all of them if they were together. Even if they weren't fully aware of each other's presence throughout the ritual, maybe just being in the same space would be comforting. Of course, that also meant including more warlocks. Each person would need their own warlock to oversee their specific personal experience, and they also wanted the ArchWarlock present to oversee the entire thing."

"That seems like a lot of magic to try to stuff into one place at a time," I said.

"It is," Aurora said. " Which very well might be why things went as badly as they did."

"What happened?" I asked.

"They brought the family to one of the warlock temples and set up the ritual," Stephana said. "At first, everything seemed to be going well. As well as it could, anyway. Very few people were there that night, so the details of exactly what happened are a little shaky. What we know is that during the first part of the ritual when the family members were shown the vision of their past, they all got through it. They seemed a little bit shaken up, especially the Prime, but they all agreed to continue. During the vision of the present, though, something went extremely wrong. The Prime apparently lost control."

"What do you mean he lost control?" I asked.

"Nobody but the people who were there that night really know," Ashe said. "That's just how it was described. There is a lot of question as to what really happened. Some people say it all ended then. Other people say the warlocks kept pushing and went through with the next stage of the ritual. Whatever happened, by the end of that night, the Prime and his entire family were dead. It was like a bomb had fallen on the Underworld. The aftermath was instant and horrific. There wasn't even a question of blame. Essentially everyone was completely convinced it was the warlocks. They figured the Prime knew something, that he really was having these visions and experiences that were warning him about something horrible that was going to happen. It was only a matter of hours after everyone found out about their deaths that vigilante groups formed and attacked the warlocks."

"How do the Primes come into power?" I asked. "Is this an inherited monarchy situation? Elections? Gladiator fights every few years? I know you said, Aurora, that we will reign over the vampires if and when Darian is no longer Prime. But how does that work, exactly? It can't always be passed down to a child, can it?"

"Usually it is inherited," Aurora said. "But, obviously, that doesn't happen very often. When you are the leader of an immortal species, your reign tends to be fairly long. And the concept of inheritance also relies heavily on the child itself, if there is one. Vampires can have children just like humans. That's how I was born. My father is a vampire and so was my mother. For children like me, we are born with certain abilities and powers, and they grow through childhood. When we reach maturity at the age of twenty-one, we are fully transformed into vampires."

"Twenty-one?" I asked.

"Yes," Aurora said. "That's why when a human is transformed into a vampire, they look young again. Being transformed ages you backwards, for lack of a better way to explain it. Not everybody will get all the way back to twenty-one, but everyone gets younger. If a vampire has a child with a human, things are a little different. The baby is born is essentially human. They might show some hints of vampire powers, but they don't need blood and aren't going to have fangs. They might be a little faster or a little stronger than their human counterparts, but for the most part they blend in. This allows them to make a choice when they get to the age of maturity. As they get older, they are encouraged to visit both worlds and experience what life would be like as a human and as a vampire. It is an unwritten rule that human and vampire parents are to give their children as much exposure to both worlds as they possibly can, and help them learn everything they can about both sides of themselves. In these situations, it often means there is a pairing between a vampire and a human who has decided not to be changed, or a human who was changed after the baby was born. The most widely-accepted belief about pairings like this is that the parents chose to have that child when both weren't vampires, so the child should be given the choice about the type of life they are going to lead. They want the children to be given as much opportunity to see life from both perspectives as they can, so they can then make a good decision about their future. You can think of it kind of like Rumspringa among the Amish. As they are getting closer to turning twenty-one, they are expected to make that decision. They need to decide to either go through the transformation and fully embrace their vampire side, or to live as a human. If they decide to be human, they are accepting all of it, including the limited lifespan."

"If vampires reach maturity and transform at twenty-one, and humans who are changed age backwards, why are there some vampires who look much older?" I asked. "Like Darian. I'm assuming he was born to vampire parents. But he looks a lot older than twenty-one."

"Individual vampires can look older for a variety of reasons. Some used to be human and were much older when they were changed, so they weren't able to age backwards as much. Others were aged when they were touched by black magic. Some look older because of an interesting detail of hybrid aging. A child born to a human and a vampire is primarily human until they are changed. They are not yet immortal. This means they are going to age as long as they aren't transformed. Though they reach maturity when they are twenty-one, this doesn't mean they are obligated to go through with the ritual then. It's what's expected of them, of course. When they reach that age, they are adults and should be ready to choose one life or the other, but there's nothing tying them to it. Some decide to wait longer in the human world before they make the transition. Others think they want to be human and live decades that way, and then change their minds. And then there are some," her eyes seemed to flicker toward Stephana, "who aren't given the choice."

"She's talking about me," Stephana said. "It's alright, Aurora. You don't have to be so careful. I know what I am." She looked at me. "I didn't know I was a hybrid until I was a teenager," she said. "I was raised by my mother in the human world. She and my father didn't have a relationship. They never did. I was the result of a drunken night they describe very differently. She didn't even think he knew I existed. She didn't tell him she was pregnant or tell him when I was born."

"How did you find out?"

"The same way most teenagers find out the things that are kept from them by their parents. I started asking questions when things didn't make sense to me. When you're a kid, you just go along with what people tell you because it's all you know, and you don't have any reason not to believe them. You don't have any context, so when something doesn't make sense, you don't realize it. Then when you get older, you understand the world around you more, so you notice the little details that don't add up. I started to notice those little details, so I asked my mother about them."

"And she told you?"

"Not immediately," Stephana said. "Did you expect her to just be like 'yep, Stephana, you are the bastard child of a one-night stand of dubious consent with a vampire who I barely escaped from with my life'?"

"I have a feeling taking the straight forward approach might have saved you a lot of awkward conversations," I said.

"It probably would have," Stephana admitted. "But my mother didn't want me to know. She never wanted me to find out who, or what, I really was."

"How did you finally get it out of her?" I asked.

"I didn't," she said. "I don't think she ever would have told me. But my prodding got someone's attention. I still don't know who. I probably never will. Someone, though, figured out who I was and took the information back to my father. By that time, I was an adult. Barely, but an adult. Beyond the age of maturity for a vampire. I'd been asking questions for years, trying to find out who my father was and why my mother had been lying to me for so long. When my father found out, he came for me. My mother tried to keep me from him. She even warned me he could be dangerous, but I didn't listen."

"Of course, you didn't."

"By that time, I was so curious about myself and about him, I couldn't resist. I thought he would just tell me about himself and his world, and that would be enough. But it wasn't for him. As soon as he found out he had a child, I became his focus. He thought I had been stolen from him. It wasn't even about loving me or wanting a relationship with me. He saw me as rightfully his and was furious he hadn't had the opportunity to mold me as a child. He was especially angry I had gone beyond maturity and hadn't been transformed. To him, that was an offense to all vampires because he came from a once powerful family. It was disrespectful that the last member of his lineage was living as a human. He wanted to change me."

"What happened?"

"I didn't want to be changed," she said. "At least, I hadn't made that decision yet. I didn't know enough about it. All I had ever known was the human world. The idea of leaving all of that, completely changing what I thought my life would be like was too much. I needed more time to think. But my father wasn't having any of it. He told me it shouldn't be my choice, that he was my father and what he wanted for me was all that mattered. To him, no human was the equal of a vampire.

The thought that a human -- a woman at that -- would defy him or try to have any control over anything involving him was outrageous. It infuriated him. He convinced me to come back to the Underworld with him to show me around. I should have known it wouldn't be so easy. While we were here, I saw things I never wanted to see. The way the species treated each other. The way they treated others of their own kind. It was horrifying. I didn't want anything to do with it."

"Then how did you end up here?"

"I told my father I'd made my decision, and I didn't want to change. I wanted to stay human. Of course, he didn't accept that. It became a literal fight for my life. I ran. I did everything I could to avoid him, and I did, for many years. I spent the next two decades of my life hiding and moving constantly just to try to stay out of his grasp. Finally, he found me, and he forced me through the transformation. Out of retaliation, he made me suffer the entire four days. Right up until the last second. I had to go through all of it. He kept me locked in a cell, tied up, and came to taunt me every few hours. He'd count down the minutes, reminding me I only had four days. I prayed for death. I would have happily gone through every moment that it would take for me to die if I knew I would have that end. Not having to live as a vampire and give my father what he had wanted all along would have been worth the brutality of the end of my life. But I didn't get that relief. In the last twenty minutes of the four days, he came to my cell and sat beside me. He talked to me as the minutes passed, telling me why this was what was right for me. Then he forced a syringe full of his blood into my mouth. I fought against it, hoping I could resist long enough for the time to pass. But I couldn't. I was so weak after lying there for four days, and he was so much bigger and stronger than I was. There was nothing I could do. The second a single drop of his blood went down my throat, it was over. I was over."

"How long ago was that?" I asked.

"Long enough," she said.

"If you didn't want to exist like this, why didn't you…" I hesitated.

"Kill myself? Let a hunter kill me?" She shook her head. "There was a short time when I considered it," she admitted. "But then I thought about what I had gone through. I knew there were others who were struggling. Not just vampires. Other species. Other people who came to the Underworld, either not by their own bidding, or thinking it would be something else. I wanted to be there for them in a way that no one was for me. So, I committed myself to making the most of the existence I was given."

"What happened to your father?" I asked.

"He made the wrong person angry," she said simply.

23

Stephana's words hung heavily in the air, but I had to push past them. There was still more I needed to know and to understand.

"What about Darian?" I asked. "If the entire Prime family was killed that night, how did Darian become Prime?"

"The vampires have a very strong concept of hierarchy," Aurora said. "There isn't just one Prime. The Underworld has several vampire factions spread out across the cities and surrounding areas. Each of these factions has its own Prime. Some of them have been in control for centuries. But even with Immortal creatures, there is the possibility of destruction. If a Prime is destroyed and they have a blood mate, that mate will take over. If there is no mate or the mate cannot reign for one reason or another, and they have a suitable child, that child will take over reign of their faction. In a situation like this when the entire family was killed at the same time, there has to be a different way of choosing the next leader. The advisors and most trusted confidants of the former Prime select the next leader. When this family was killed, the advisors chose Darian."

I was considering the implications of Aurora's words when the door to the cabin opened again and Diane stepped inside. The rest of the Dragon were no longer with her, and I immediately had a sense of worry that whoever she had gotten in touch with to be my trainer had refused.

"He's ready for you, Hayden," she said.

"Who is it?" I asked.

"His name is Artemis," she said.

"Where is he?" I asked.

"Follow the path behind the cabin to the next clearing. He's waiting for you there. Aurora, Ashe, and Stephana can wait here."

"We can't go with him?" Ashe asked.

"No," Diane said. "This training is for Hayden. He needs to learn to control himself and use his powers without anyone else's influence. The three of you give him strength and help him to get in touch with more of his abilities, but there's no guarantee you will always be there when he needs that support. Hayden, you have used your abilities before?"

"Some," I said. "I think."

"But only when you were angry or afraid?"

I nodded.

"Yes," I said. "It seems like I can only really tap into them when I have strong emotions."

"Right," Diane said. "And it's good that you can do that. You'll need your magic and your vampire abilities the most when you are in danger or need to accomplish something beyond human capabilities. But you can't always rely on those intense emotions, or on the women being there with you when you need the boost of your link. You have to learn to use your abilities on your own, whenever you need them."

I kissed each woman on the cheek and headed out of the cabin. The path leading through the woods at the back was much more defined than the path we had taken to get there, and I quickly found myself in another clearing. I only saw dirt and a squirrel. There was no one there. I really hoped the squirrel wasn't my trainer. I hadn't been able to suspend my disbelief that much yet. The squirrel noticed me standing there and skittered away, leaving the clearing empty.

Maybe I had to show initiative by entering the clearing first. I took a few steps into the clearing. Nothing changed.

I stood there for several more minutes, looking around at the still woods and empty clearing. Was this another riddle? Maybe they were trying to tell me all I needed was inside, and I should just reach out to the trainer within. That would seriously piss me off. I was about to go back to the cabin when I noticed a man walking toward me from the trees.

He walked into the clearing with his hands clasped in front of him. A grin spread across his face as he slowly made his way toward me. He stopped a few feet away from me. He didn't say anything, but kept staring at me. I was starting to get really impatient. Finally, I couldn't take it anymore.

"Dude, what the hell?"

"Artemis," he said.

"Yeah, I'm aware. I've been standing around waiting for you."

"Patience is a virtue of the strong," Artemis said in a gravelly voice.

"Are you being serious right now?" I said.

This was getting ridiculous. He still hadn't moved an inch and I was getting the distinct impression that he was fucking around with me.

"I am always serious."

"Okay, cool," I said, throwing my hands up as I started toward the path. "I'm going to go back to the cabin now. When you're done with the whole Kung Fu routine, you come let me know."

"Catch me."

"What?"

And like that, he vanished. I looked around wildly, but there was no trace of him. It was like he had literally disappeared into thin air, but I knew from what the women had told me about the abilities of the warlocks, this was extremely unlikely. Suddenly, from about fifty yards away, at the edge of the clearing, I saw him step out from behind a tree. He waved at me.

"Catch me, Hayden."

This had to be one of the dumbest things I had ever done, but I figured I should at least play along. I began to run toward the tree, using some of the incredible speed I had developed since I had made my full turn. I was almost all the way to the edge of the clearing when I saw him vanish again. His laughter filled the air around me and I stumbled to a stop. I spun to find the source of the laughter and saw him, now on the other side of the clearing. He was sitting with his legs crossed on the ground.

"What the hell?" I yelled and ran toward him.

I barely got a few steps before he vanished again and reappeared just a few feet from me. Frolicking through the woods wasn't exactly my vision of training my magic. I felt like I was in a perfume commercial.

"Your speed is no match, Hayden," he said after vanishing across the clearing again.

"How... how did you do that?"

"Magic. Magic you can do, Hayden. You just don't realize it yet."

"No," I said. "Stephana told me even warlocks can't just travel like that. At least, most can't."

"And you don't believe I'm powerful enough to do that?" he asked.

"No," I answered without hesitation.

Artemis gave a mirthless laugh.

"You'd be right in thinking I haven't learned the skill of instant travel," he said. "It's something I hope to master one day. But that doesn't mean I can't mimic it, exactly like you just witnessed."

"How?"

"Speed," he said. "Like you have, only greater. And invisibility."

"Invisibility?"

"Yes," the trainer said. "I am one of very few warlocks these days who teach that skill. As you can imagine, it's not one that the powers that we necessarily want many to know and use."

"Why not?"

"A species that has been embroiled in war for so many years? You'd like to think that everyone is on the same side, but that's not reality. A being capable of going unseen by anyone around him has an incomparable advantage. Using such a skill hasn't been outlawed, exactly, but it's strongly discouraged. Anyone thought to be training another warlock in using that type of skill is very closely scrutinized and sometimes doesn't emerge from the situation unscathed. I'll just leave it at that."

"Then why do you want to teach me?" I asked. "If it's so dangerous, why would you train me in it?"

"Diane tells me you are needed," he said. "You need to have as much skill and control as you possibly can. Besides, I'm not one who has ever responded well to the limitations of wartime reign.

Like most of Lunaris, I have a much different vision for how the Underworld should be controlled."

"What's your vision?"

"That doesn't matter," Artemis said. "My vision can never come to be if there is still war. The first step is finding peace, or at least bringing an end to the current conflict. Then we can move forward. I told Diane I would train you as much as I could, and that's what I'll do. She seems to think you have a lot of potential. She thinks there's something in you. It's up to me to help you find it.

"Concentrate. Concentrate on time itself. So far, you have only focused on your body. What it can do, and the gifts it brings. You must also focus on your mind. Your mind is where the magic resides. Instead of trying to catch me, concentrate on what you would need to catch me."

"I don't know what you mean."

"Time. You need time. Time to get to me before I can leave. Concentrate on slowing everything down. Your breath, your heart, your blood, everything. Slow everything down."

"I thought you were going to teach me to become invisible," I said.

"You're not there yet," Artemis responded. "We

have to start somewhere. For now, I want to see if Diane was right about you. Let's see if you are as amazing as she thinks you are."

It felt like a challenge and I was more than happy to step up to it.

"What do you want me to do?"

"Slow everything," he said.

"I don't know what you mean," I said again, becoming more frustrated.

"Figure it out. Slow down everything inside you and then turn it outward and slow the world around you."

As he spoke, I could feel it happening around me. Everything was slowing down. My breath grew deeper in my diaphragm, my heart beat slowed, and my mind began to focus on the man in front of me.

"That's right," he said. "Focus on slowing down. The air, feel it getting thinner, resistance is lessening. The world is allowing you to manipulate it. Now, walk."

I walked forward a few steps. My speed seemed normal, but I looked around in wonder, noticing that nothing else seemed to move. Blades of grass were stuck motionless. I crunched over them like fallen leaves. I walked to him and I saw him, slowly, blink. Suddenly, time sped up. The air grew thick, and the ground softened below me. It wound up and I could hear the sounds of the world return, even though I had barely noticed their absence.

"You learn quickly," the man said.

There was a note in his voice that said he was impressed, but that it royally pissed him off too. It was obvious he'd come here not expecting anything from me. Diane told him I needed help training my warlock side, but he had no way of knowing how much of my abilities I had already discovered, or the extent of my potential. To be honest, neither did I, but I wasn't lining up to join warlock preschool. He wanted to take the approach of breaking me down and humiliating me so I would respect him and learn at his feet. Instead, I surprised him and showed him training me was going to be more of a challenge than he might have thought.

"Like that?" I asked.

"Yes. It takes years for many to learn this skill. You did it on your first try," he paused for a moment and looked at me through narrowed eyes. "Who are you, Hayden?"

"What else can you teach me?" I asked, ignoring the question.

The man paused for a moment, his eyes still locked on me, searching mine. He reached into his pocket and pulled out a small gold-colored ball.

"Do you know what this is?"

I cocked my head at him.

"A golden snitch?"

There was zero recognition on his face, so I decided to move on.

"I don't know, a marble?"

"A test."

"A test? How is this a te-"

Before I could finish, he threw it into the air.

Oh, shit. It really was a snitch, whether Artie here knew it or not.

As the ball began to come back down again, it stopped. I looked around to see if time had paused again, but everything was still normal. A bird flew overhead, darting around the floating golden ball.

"Catching something that falls is one of the first things a mage learns. Many days are spent learning how to keep glass balls from falling fast enough to shatter. Then you learn how to gently lower it. Then you must learn how to stop it. Then," the ball began to rise gently even further into the air, "you must learn how to make it rise again. You have moved things before with your mind, haven't you, Hayden?"

"Yes."

"How?"

"I don't know. I didn't know what I was doing. I just did it."

"You must focus not on the ball, but on the air around it. It is similar to time, and how you must manipulate it around you, only you must now focus that on an object. Focus on the ball, and the space around it. Remove the pressure from above that is forcing it down and place it below, to keep it up. Try it."

I tried to do what he asked, and the ball darted toward the ground. I panicked and felt my mind squeeze painfully as I focused on the ball. It stopped in midair, just inches from the ground.

"Yes, that's it. Now, hold it there. Hold it, Hayden."

I could feel my mind squeezing like my brain was in a vice. My eyes burned, but the ball held.

"That's enough for now. One day, Hayden, you will do more. One day soon," he began, but was cut off.

The ball was rising.

I didn't answer, but continued to focus on the

ball. I tried to remove the air from around it and place it below. I pushed with my mind until I saw it rise even higher. It was now ten feet above us, and flying higher, faster. Suddenly it exploded upward, shooting as if it was attached to a rocket. It flew high into the distance until it disappeared into the white sky. I let go of it and looked at the man in front of me.

"Was that good?"

He reached out his right hand, and while his eyes were still locked on mine, the ball fell into his waiting palm.

"Yes. Very good."

"Then I think we can move on."

24

Artemis had tried to be the one to decide when the training session was going to end, thinking I was too tired to continue, but I kept pushing him. Finally, it was me who said we could call it a day. Night had fallen, and Artemis looked exhausted. The expression on his face told me his body was drained and his mind had been pushed beyond what he had been prepared to give. The final bright blue glow of a spark of magic I sent into the sky illuminated, his head shaking back and forth as he watched me.

"We'll do more tomorrow," I said.

It wasn't a request.

"Tomorrow," Artemis said.

I was tired but still buzzing with adrenaline

when I got back to the cabin. The women were waiting for me and looked up with anticipation in their eyes. I grinned and kissed each of them.

"Does that mean it went well?" Aurora asked.

"You can say that," Artemis said. "Goodnight."

He walked out of the cabin and I laughed.

"What did you do to him?" Stephana asked.

"Taught him not to underestimate people," I said. "Should we go back to Stephana's house?"

"Not tonight," Ashe said. "It's too far, especially since you're supposed to be back here tomorrow for more training."

"There's a house nearby we can use," Stephana said. "It will be much more comfortable than staying here."

We left the cabin and made our way back through the woods and to the car. We drove along the edge of the woods for several minutes before turning on to a wider path. Aurora directed Stephana, and we went deeper into the woods. Finally, a shape appeared on the horizon ahead of us. It was dark against the deep blue of the night sky, but it was enough to see that the house was far bigger than the cabin. Stephana parked the car and we climbed out. I craned my neck to see the sharp turrets of a gothic style house.

"This is my kind of camping," I said.

"Not very outdoorsy?" Ashe teased.

"Oh, I can do outdoors," I said. "But if I have the choice between hunkering down in an empty cabin or a rickety tent, and staying somewhere that looks like this, I'm going to choose this any time. Even if it does look like something out of Scooby Doo."

"I promise there aren't any monsters in there waiting for you," Ashe said.

"I think he's with the monsters," Stephana said as we climbed the steps onto the wide front porch.

"By that logic, *he's* the monster, "Aurora said. "He's a vampire *and* a warlock."

"Well, shit," I said. "Maybe we're going to find Shaggy and the gang in there after all."

Stephana grinned at me as she drew a key from the small bag she carried with her.

"Where did you get that?" Ashe asked.

"Diane," Stephana answered. "She said we'd be safe here, and it would be easier to stay here during your training."

"It looks good to me," I said. "Do you know where the bathroom is? I could use a shower."

"How about a bath?" Stephana asked.

She had a mischievous look in her eyes and I

fell into step behind her as she led me to the dramatic staircase to the side of the foyer. The other women followed and soon we found ourselves in a large bathroom. The outside of the house looked archaic, but it was obvious the inside was well taken care of. The clawfoot bathtub in the middle of the room was massive and deep. Stephana reached in and turned on the faucets, then turned to me. Reaching for the bottom of my shirt, she started tugging it off over my head. From behind me, I felt Aurora's body mold against mine as she slipped her hands around my hips and released the button on my pants. Ashe lowered herself to her knees and untied the laces of my boots. She guided my feet out of them as Aurora pushed my pants down and freed my cock into her hands. It was already hard, eager for her touch, and she indulged it with several long strokes. I leaned back against her and rested my head on her shoulder while Ashe pulled my pants away from my feet. Stephana took my hands and guided me toward the bathtub. I stepped in and sank down, groaning as the hot water immediately relaxed my muscles.

Stephana picked up a curved metal bowl from the floor beside the tub and filled it with water. She poured it over my head, and I tilted my head back to let it stream through my hair. Aurora took a sponge from where it dangled from the showerhead and poured fragrant gel soap into it. Lather formed in her hand as she squeezed it. Ashe walked around to the other side of the tub so she could kneel beside it and let her hand trace my body beneath the water. Her fingertips ran along my muscles as Aurora used the sponge to swirl lather across my skin and Stephana washed my hair. I closed my eyes and gave myself over to the luxury of the women bathing me.

I was tired from the hours of training, but the experience of discovering my abilities and learning to control them was exhilarating. The touch of the three women only awakened me further and I felt energy and desire rushing through me. The feeling of the sponge vanished, and I opened my eyes to see Aurora stripping out of her clothes. She stepped back up to the side of the tub and I slid over to the edge to nuzzle my face into the apex of her thighs. Her body smelled warm and sweet, already eager for my touch. My tongued delved into her folds and I was rewarded with a deep moan. Ashe's hand continued to stroke my cock and I mimicked the rhythm on Aurora's pussy.

Stephana moved away from the tub and I heard her taking off her clothes as well. She replaced Ashe's hand with her own so Ashe could undress, and a moment later I felt Ashe climb into the tub with me. Taking my mouth away from Aurora, I sat up and gathered Ashe into my arms. She slid into my lap and I ducked my head down to suck one of her breasts as I massaged the other. Ashe tucked her legs to either side of me and lifted her hips to stroke her clit over the head of my cock as Stephana continued to stroke the base.

When Stephana released me, I sank deeply into Ashe. I kissed her for a few seconds and then turned my head toward Stephana to let my mouth play over her pearl. She lifted her leg and set her foot on the edge of the tub, opening herself to me. My tongue dipped inside her and Stephana dug her fingers into my hair. I reached to the other side of the tub and let my hand find Aurora's thigh. My fingers ran up the inside along her tender skin and found the wet warmth of her opening. I stroked her in tight circles, creating a complete circuit with the three women. We lost ourselves in each other, indulging in each other's pleasure as much as our own. I was enraptured by the feeling of the three women surrounding me, and the intensity of the rush they caused. Every second made me feel more fulfilled.

I took my mouth away from Stephana and replaced it with my hand, turning to Aurora to offer her the attention of my tongue. In my lap, Ashe rolled her hips, grinding against me so my cock stroked deep inside her. She tucked her hand between her thighs and I looked down to watch her fingers play over her clit as she tossed her head back. Moans of pleasure poured from between her lips and I felt myself quickly losing control. I held myself back, not wanting it to end yet, and pounded harder into her as Ashe toppled into her climax. Her body tightened and spasmed around my cock until she finally relaxed. I kissed her and eased her off of my lap and down into the water. As she settled back to relax, I stood and took Aurora by the hips. Turning her around, I entered her. She arched her back to push me deeper and I wrapped my arm around her hips to swirl my fingertips over her peak as I thrust inside her. Stephana walked around the tub to stand beside Aurora and I reached over with my free hand to plunge my fingers as far into her as I could. I moved my hand at the same speed and rhythm as my hips and soon both women were whimpering, getting closer to their own climaxes.

I stopped holding back and let myself give in to everything I was experiencing. My body shook, and a primal roar tore from my lungs as my cock throbbed and spilled out into Aurora. I felt her walls tighten around me at the same moment, and Stephana clench down on my fingers. We rode through the peak of our orgasms and then I sank back down into the water. Ashe parted her thighs so I could lie back against her, and she kissed softly along the side of my neck as she poured warm water from her palm onto my chest. After a few lazy moments, I reached behind Ashe and unplugged the drain. We stood and turned on the shower so the four of us could get clean before bed. When we finished, we dried off and walked naked through the house to where we'd left our bags when we came inside.

"Sleep with me tonight?" Aurora asked as we walked up the stairs toward the bedrooms.

I nodded.

"Absolutely," I said.

I kissed the other two women goodnight and we parted ways, so they could head in the opposite direction down the hallway, while Aurora and I went into the large master suite. My body was humming with satisfaction, but seeing Aurora's silky, unapologetically curved body walking across the room reminded me of the undercurrent of hunger I always felt. She lifted her arms over her head and bent back to stretch her back, causing her tattoo to spread over her ribcage. I walked up to her and bent my head down to run my tongue along the ink embedded in her skin.

"This," I whispered as I kissed each letter, "is so sexy."

"Mmm," she murmured, running her hand along my back as I traced the word with the tip of my tongue.

Serendipity.

I rose up to my feet and gathered her against me. Our mouths met as she entwined her arms around my neck and let me guide her back so we toppled into bed together.

25

"Tell me more about your father," I said later as I held Aurora in my arms.

She was curled into the crook of my arm and she made a questioning, murmuring sound as she adjusted her position to sit up and look into my face. Her chin rested on my chest and then she lifted her head to prop it with her hand.

"What do you want to know?" she asked.

"About his past," I said. "Was he born to vampire parents? Who is his family?"

"I don't know," she said.

"You don't know?" I asked.

She shook her head.

"I don't really know much about his past, Hayden. That's kind of a risk of being a vampire.

When you live for centuries and never lose your ability to have children, it can get a little difficult to keep track of your entire lineage, especially when many of them are killed off like mine were."

"What happened?" I asked.

"What do you mean?"

"Like you said, you have this extensive lineage, but all I've met is your father."

"That's all who's left," she said.

"Exactly. So, what happened? Where did everybody else go?"

Aurora sighed and kissed the middle of my chest before sitting up further so she could look at me more comfortably.

"Vampire hunters might sound ridiculous, or like they are something of bad horror films, butthey are very real. There aren't as many of them now as there used to be, but years ago they were an incredible threat. That's part of the reason our kind made a massive migration into the Underworld, and for the most part live our lives here."

"The Underworld hasn't always existed?"

"It has, in one form or another," she said. "But vampires weren't as quick as many of the other species to isolate ourselves away from the humans.

We found we could blend in with them without a tremendous amount of effort."

"Because most of what humans think about vampires is a whole bunch of bullshit?" I asked.

Aurora laughed.

"Essentially," she said.

"See? I'm learning."

She smiled and playfully nipped at my lips.

"Vampires preferred to integrate into society because it was easier to get access to blood. Of course, years ago, it wasn't as easy to get fulfillment of our need for lust among the humans. But, when you could find one of them willing to go for a tumble, it tended to be pretty dynamic. When you are as hopelessly repressed as humans a century or two ago, finally giving in when it is still forbidden tends to be explosive. But that's not why we started leaving. Even though most of what humans think of vampires is completely wrong, the fear exists and is intense. Fear that strong is one of the most dangerous things in the world, and for us, it led to the uprising of hunters who devoted themselves to weeding out those they thought might be vampires and destroying them. Unfortunately, just because those hunters thought they were vampires doesn't mean they actually were. A lot of humans lost their lives because they were misunderstood."

"I didn't think vampires as a whole were so magnanimous," I said.

"What do you mean?" Aurora asked.

"The hunters killed off a lot of humans because they thought they were vampires, right? Isn't that why the vampires decided to live in the Underworld?"

Aurora laughed.

"You are adorable for thinking that," she said.

In one swift movement, I flipped her over onto her back.

"I don't think I like you calling me adorable," I said.

"I can call you anything I want," she giggled.

I made a teasing growl in the back of my throat and kissed her hard, then rolled back over.

"If that's not why, then what changed everybody's mind?" I asked.

"There were always vampires who lived in the Underworld," she said. "After a while, the hunters got better at differentiating between humans and vampires, and more vampires were starting to die. Vampires started seeking refuge in the Underworld, but were still spending most of their time among the humans. Eventually, one of the hunters followed a vampire into the Underworld, and there was a massive upheaval. There was a huge loss of life and the hunter brought back more information that allowed even more deaths among those who lived with the humans. Vampires decided it was too risky to continue living that way, and retreated back among their own kind. But the damage was done. So many had been destroyed, and because a lot of them were in the powerful families, their loss was particularly felt."

"A lot of them were your family," I said.

She gave a single nod.

"That's my understanding," she said. "So, I know very little about the family that came before my father, and honestly very little about my father, too. I was born to him a very long time ago, and barely had a relationship with him when I was growing up. When we were at the palace and I was telling you about the maze, I told you I didn't see very much of him when I was a child. I was raised by my mother and the other women of the palace, and didn't have much contact with my father at all. I didn't even really start getting closer to him until after my transition, and even then, it was still really tenuous for a long time."

"Why?" I asked.

"I wasn't exactly the model daughter he wanted," she said. "As a trusted and powerful advisor to the Prime and his family, he had strong ideas about what was appropriate and proper, and how I should behave."

"It's strange to think of him not being Prime," I said.

"Because that's all you've known of him."

"No," I said. "That's not it. It's the way he acts, the way he interacts with other people. It's just obvious he thinks of himself as being entitled to the power and influence he has. It just seems like he's had that level of power for a lot longer than he has."

"Well, Darian has been in power for a long time. Just because he wasn't actually Prime doesn't mean he didn't have influence. I told you I grew up in the palace. To be honest, life hasn't really changed all that much since my father started his reign. He just has even more people who see him as influential as he's always seen himself."

"So, you didn't want to stay around and behave yourself, is what you're telling me?"

"Basically," she agreed. "I had adventures to go on. I wanted to see and experience so much more than I could just by sitting around here. I was wild, and I liked it that way. I didn't want anybody to tell me how I was supposed to act or what I was and was not allowed to do. It just wasn't me. So, I pushed against him and refused to submit to what he wanted from me. There really wasn't anything he could do about it, to be honest. I'm sure he could have ousted me as his heir and sent me out on my own, but what difference would that have made? I was already spending so little time at the palace. If I was in the Underworld at all, I was with the other factions where nobody knew who I was and didn't care who my father was. I developed my taste for the other side many years ago, and while I could never spend my entire life outside of the Underworld, I could also never be like my father and not go at all."

"But he does go," I said. "Nakatomi Tower."

"That is barely the other side," she said. "It's the only place outside of the Underworld he goes, and when he does, he is heavily guarded and escorted from one point to the other. He doesn't want anything to do with the human world."

I grinned at her.

"Is that why you came after me?" I asked. "Mean Daddy doesn't like the human world, but you are fascinated by it and want to be a part of it? Is this a *Little Mermaid* situation, only rather than me having to figure it out with no voice, it was under threat of death and dick loss?" I thought that over for a second. "Damn. That would not be a popular reboot."

I noticed Aurora staring at me blankly in that way she did so frequently.

"I'm not sure how to respond to that," she said.

"You don't know Ariel?" I asked. "Alright, we are putting everything on hold for a while so we can get you more educated about human culture. I just put my very masculinity on the line to give an intricately crafted and custom princess reference, and you didn't even get it. Of course, in retrospect I might have gone with the princess who shares your name, but a comparable situation just hasn't shown itself yet."

"You truly fascinate me, Hayden."

"Well I *am* fascinating," I teased. "When did you come back? When did you decide to reconcile with your father and do the prodigal daughter thing?"

"The prophecies Malakan made about me really stuck with me," she said. "Throughout my entire existence, I thought about what he had said and what it meant. I didn't know if I completely believed it, honestly. It's hard to when it's something so strange and not even a part of your species, you know?"

"No, I have no idea what you are talking about, " I said.

She laughed.

"I guess you don't. But for me, warlocks had always been almost a taboo. In my world, they were a really touchy topic you didn't talk much about with people unless you knew them very well. Our kinds would go back and forth between being completely against one another and being tentatively linked, and there was never a consensus. There were always those who hated the other species, and there were always sympathizers. No matter what the climate at the time, you had to be careful talking about it because you never knew what a new person would think or who they might know. Malakan had been a part of my life for as long as I can remember, and I trusted him, but I still didn't really understand his ways or his magic, and I wasn't sure I believed in his ability to make predictions like that. Prophecies aren't something that happen all the time. It's not like the mages are just wandering around throwing prophecies at everybody like fortune cookies."

"You don't know fairy tales, but fortune cookies, you know," I said.

She shrugged.

"The point is, what he said had always followed me around. No matter what I did to try to get out from under it, or not think about it, it was always hanging over me. So, when the first war started, I was...unnerved. I don't know why exactly, but that's when I started sticking closer to my father. When things settled down, I went back to traveling and to spending more time on the other side, but I had moved back into the palace, and that's where I stayed."

"Why does your father look so much older?" I asked. "What happened to him?"

Aurora shook her head again.

"Dark magic," she said. "That's all I know. Black Magic touched him at some point and aged him. He's never talked to me about it."

"What happened to your mother?"

As soon as I asked it, I wished I hadn't. The way she had talked about her mother, I knew they had been close when Aurora was younger, but she hadn't mentioned having her around even after her changing ritual. Something horrible must have happened to her, and I shouldn't have brought up something so painful. Aurora just stared at me.

"The same thing that happened to my father," she said darkly. She shook her head as if to ward off memories that had started to creep into her mind. "Why does it matter? Why does any of this matter, Hayden?"

"I was just curious," I said. "I'm still trying to figure it all out. Besides, it doesn't look like I'm getting any help with the manual, so I'm going to have to be the one to write it, so anyone who comes after me won't be as confused as I have been."

Aurora laughed and settled back into my arms so we could go to sleep. Thinking about the next day and everything that was to come, I finally let myself close my eyes and rest.

26

I dropped down onto the ground and leaned my head back against a tree. Squeezing my eyes closed, I willed the world to stop spinning around me and for my stomach to stop doing flips. I was completely exhausted, but it was not my body that was drained. My muscles were tired and definitely felt the exertion I had been putting out since before the sun came up, but I could have kept going. I felt enough energy and strength running through me to keep me going for hours more. It was my mind that felt like a wet towel that had been rung out. It was enough to keep me on the ground, ignoring Artemis shouting at me.

"Get up," he demanded. "Get off the ground. You need to keep going."

"I need a break," I told him.

"Do you think you're going to get a break when you're in the middle of a battle?" he asked.

I opened my eyes, just so I could roll them at the trainer. He was a touch too dramatic for me. He should have had a pointy hat with stars and a flowing cape. Oh. Fuck. That's right. Not a wizard. I'd made one joke about him using his enchanted brooms to gussy up the clearing for us and was subjected to an insufferable speech on the differences between mages, wizards, sorcerers, and spellcasters. There was a tremendous amount of flailing and gesturing, and I checked out part way through, so I didn't catch all of it. At some point, I was sure another comment would slip, and I'd get to listen to it all again.

"Spare me the scare tactic shit," I groaned. "We're not in battle right now."

"The purpose of training is to prepare you for situations you could find yourself in at any moment," Artemis said. "You're not always going to have the luxury of knowing when a battle is going to happen, or when you might be facing off against somebody who wants nothing more than to kill you. Do you honestly think if you got into a fight this instant, your enemy would give you a few minutes to prepare yourself and rest your mind? No, he wouldn't. The second he sensed any sort of weakness in you, he would destroy you. You have to be able to defend yourself. Now, get up."

I groaned again as I pushed myself up from the ground, using my back against the tree like a lever to get me back to my feet.

"This is nowhere near as much fun as I wanted it to be," I commented.

Artemis had been walking away from me, but he turned back to glare at me.

"What do you think this is, a fucking summer camp? Are we going to take a break after this and go make a birdhouse out of popsicle sticks?"

I laughed, putting my hands on my hips.

"So, you can talk like a person," I said. "All it took was me pissing you off enough, and you stop with all the mystical, whimsical crap."

I felt a blast of energy hit me in the stomach and I shot backwards, slamming into the tree. I slid down and landed in a heap where I had been sitting.

"I guess you didn't have a chance to get ready, did you?" Artemis asked.

"That was dirty," I said, getting back to my feet.

"Then remember it," Artemis said. "Use it."

"And here we go again, back to the mystical, whimsical crap. What are you talking about?"

"The whole purpose of you being here it to get you in touch with your Magi powers," Artemis said. "They are in you. They were born already in you. You just have to find them and be able to use them. One of the strongest tools you have is your memory. Being able to reach back into your own past and find the moments that fuel you the most gives you strength. When you are able to look back, you can gather all of the power and all of the strength from any moment in your life and use it when you need it. That's what you need to be able to do."

"I don't understand," I said.

"Have you ever been able to do something you didn't think was possible just because you were angry? Or because you were thinking about something that upset you?"

"Of course," I said. "That's why I'm here. That's how I knew there was something different about me."

Artemis nodded and took a step closer to me.

"It pains me to say this, so I want you to understand I will say it one time, and one time only. You may very well be the most powerful warlock of our time. Your capabilities and skills could far outshine even the greatest names we know, more than Saint Michael, even more than your own father. But if you don't learn to discipline yourself and use what you have, you will be a waste. There are many who believe that the strongest of the warlocks are able to manipulate their own memories and use them against others. It's not something I can do or that I've even ever seen done, but I believe it's possible, and I believe you can do it. If you are able to isolate these very specific moments in your life, you can then use them to strengthen you and make you capable of anything. But it is extremely difficult, and it is very dangerous. It is discouraged by virtually every warlock in existence. It is generally understood that reaching into your own past and manipulating what you have already lived can be disastrous. If you don't take this seriously, Hayden, you could destroy yourself and everything around you."

I drew in a breath. That was definitely worse than being chewed out by a teacher for goofing off in class. None of them had ever threatened me with mass destruction before. I didn't know what I was supposed to say to Artemis. This seemed like one of those moments where I was supposed to prostrate myself on the ground in front of him and beg for his guidance as my mentor. I wasn't about to do that. Instead, I nodded.

"All right," I said. "Tell me what I have to do."

"Think back," Artemis said. "Go as far back as you possibly can. Think about your earliest memories; what you still carry with you from when you were a child."

"I don't have many memories from when I was a child," I told him. "That's a problem I've had most of my life. I don't remember being little. I have a few flashes of what I think are memories from when I was a little bit older, but nothing really concrete until well into elementary school."

"Those memories are there," Hayden. "They don't go away. That's what people use to excuse themselves from not being able to hold on to what has happened in their life. Every moment you have ever lived, every word you have ever said, every breath you have ever taken, every decision you have ever made. All of them are still there inside you. You just have to find them to be able to hold them in your hand and use them. Look back. Look back now and find those moments."

For the next hour, I followed Artemis's guidance to search for memories I wasn't even sure I had. I was able to grasp at flashes, finding new wisps and hints of moments I had long forgotten. By the end of it, though, I still didn't feel like I had found anything useful, and my brain had gone back to feeling like mush. I stood in the middle of the clearing, my hands on my knees as I leaned over, trying to steady myself again.

"I don't know what I'm looking for," I said. "How am I supposed to find all these memories if I don't even know what they are?"

"What matters to you, Hayden?" Artemis asked. "What is it that you want to know?"

"What do you mean?" I asked.

"You have questions in your eyes," he said. "I can see them. What is it that's weighing on you so much? Find those questions and then look for the answers."

I straightened and let out a long breath.

"Who am I?" I asked. "People told me things about who I am and where I came from, but I don't understand any of it. What happened to me? How did I come to live with my foster family?"

I stopped myself there. Artemis shook his head, coming toward me.

"Don't you think I know who you are?" he

asked. "Don't you think I've known since the second I saw you?"

I hesitated. I knew it could be a trick, and I didn't want to walk into it.

"I don't know what you're talking about," I said.

Artemis smiled, but I wouldn't say it was a pleasant expression.

"Yes, you do," he said. "I know exactly who you are, Hayden. That's how I know how powerful you are. That's why I mentioned your father. Stephana didn't have to tell the Dragon who you are in order for us to know. Some of them aren't sure, but there isn't a single doubt in my mind that I'm standing before the son of the Archwarlock. You are so much more than anyone will tell you. I am a hybrid, born with only half warlock blood, but you were crafted into a hybrid. You were born with the full strength of a warlock and then given the power of a vampire. You were raised among the humans and took upon yourself the qualities of them as well. Not many in the Underworld respect the humans the way I do. I understand that, although they do not have the abilities and the features of our kinds, they are powerful in their own way. You have all of it,

Hayden. All of it is in you. You need to find it and use it."

I was shocked by the revelation, but something about him knowing who I was took the pressure off my shoulders and made me relax.

"I want to know what happened to me," I said. "I want to know how I ended up where I was, with who I ended up with. How is it possible for a warlock baby to be kidnapped by a vampire in the Underworld, and show up as the child of a very normal human family? Not even an eccentric or weird or unusual in any way, human family. Like, the lives in suburbia kind. I had chores and an allowance , just like every other kid in my neighborhood. There's a disconnect there I just can't figure out."

"That's completely understandable," Artemis said. "It's a lot for you. But as I said, those memories are in there. You can find them if you look hard enough."

I closed my eyes and tried to tap into my ability to search for my memories. I needed to understand what happened at the very beginning of my life, so I could understand the rest of it. I saw the inside of that church. I knew there were no vampire nuns running around, scooping up babies and distributing them out to human families. I know Ty had something to do with it. I needed to find something, anything, that would help me understand those critical moments that completely changed the trajectory of my entire existence. I don't know how long I stood there, digging through the deepest corners of my mind until I got the briefest glimpse of something that could be a memory. It went past me like a breath of wind. I was barely aware that it was there until it was gone, but then it sank in. I fought harder to find it again.

I thought back to what Artemis said about holding the memories in my hand, and I tried to do just that. I reached for the memory, grabbing onto it and dragging it toward me. Suddenly, it was there. It was sitting in the palm of my hand and I fell into it so thoroughly it was like I was experiencing those moments again. I was being carried and I couldn't see anything around me. I was incredibly warm, almost to the point of feeling like I was suffocating. Whoever was carrying me must have been huge, because I felt tiny in his arms. Then I realized it wasn't that he was so big, it was that I was so small. I must have been a baby, and I was wrapped in a blanket as I was being carried. The memory faded, and I fought to regain it.

When it came back, I felt even hotter. It was hard to breathe and everything around me was completely dark. I knew for sure this was when I was a baby, and I was experiencing my own kidnapping again.

The pressure around my face was so strong I couldn't even cry. But around me I could hear muffled voices. One of them sounded angry.

"How could you be so stupid and careless?" one voice asked. "How could you let something like this happen?"

"I'm sorry," another voice said.

It took only a second for me to recognize that voice as Ty's.

"You're sorry?" the first voice yelled. "That's all you have to say for yourself? You're sorry? Do you have any idea what you've done?"

The screaming continued, the words becoming indiscernible as the memory faded.

27

"What do you think it meant?" I asked.

I was back in the cabin with the women sitting around me. The sun had set a few hours ago, and Artemis had left. I swallowed the bite in my mouth and reached for another of the chocolate chip cookies Stephana and Ashe had baked for me during my training.

"What do you mean?" Aurora asked. "I think it was clear what that meant. It was a pretty straightforward memory. You remembered being kidnapped just a few days after you were born."

"But I don't understand," I said. "Why was I there? According to Artemis, if I was able to pull it forward with that much detail, then it has to be a real memory. It's like what Malakan said about the visions that I had during the ritual. Even if I don't understand them, they are what they are. So that memory is real. That's how it happened. but I don't understand it."

"Why not?" Ashe asked.

"Because I was in the room when Ty was being yelled at. The voice sounded different, I'm guessing because it was so angry, but I can only assume it was Darian yelling at him."

"Of course, he was yelling at him," Aurora said. "He had just told him he had lost the baby my father had told him to bring back."

"Exactly," I said. "Ty was standing there in front of him telling him that he had lost me. So why was I there? Wouldn't he be able to see me if Ty was standing there carrying me?"

"Maybe he wasn't carrying you," Stephana said. "You said it was hot and you couldn't breathe. Maybe you weren't actually in his arms. He could have put you in his bag or wrapped you in something. It was cold when he was supposed to go out and get you, but it would have been warm inside the palace, so he would have taken his coat off when he went to talk to my father. You could have been wrapped up in it."

"Cold?" I asked. "What do you mean it was cold?"

"It was winter," Aurora said. "One of the coldest in years."

"My birthday is in August," I said.

Aurora exchanged glances with the other women.

"No," she said. "It's not. You were born in the winter. Your birthday is just a few weeks from now. That's why all of this is getting so tense. The anniversary of your birth and kidnapping is almost here, and a lot of people are calling for war in memory of it. I thought you knew that."

I felt like somebody had kicked me in the face.

"No," I said. "I didn't know that. I've celebrated my birthday in August my entire life."

The reality that I had yet another thing I didn't know about myself settled over me. I didn't even know my own birthday. I didn't know where I was born or when I was born. I didn't know anything about who I was or who I was supposed to be, not even the most basic details. It only made me hungrier to find out what actually happened.

"Are you all right?" Stephana asked.

"I think I've had enough training for now," I

said. "I want to get back to what needs to be done right now. We need to find Ty."

"I agree," Aurora said.

"Where do we look?" I asked.

"We go where people talk," Ashe said. "If we can't find him directly, we go somewhere people might have heard from him and try to sniff him out from there."

"Solomon's Fang?" Aurora asked.

Ashe nodded.

"We'll go to the Underworld side," she said. "Somebody there might have seen him or heard where he was going. That will at least give us a starting point."

It was strange walking into the bar a couple of hours later. After all of the events of the last couple of days, walking into a place where everyone was sitting around casually, talking and laughing, felt surreal. It felt like I was portraying some sort of character, like I was swaggering into the bar and reciting lines. In a way, I guess I was. A few people looked up when we walked in, but for the most part, they seemed completely unaffected by our arrival. We walked up to the bar and took the row of empty stools in the corner. Stephana and Aurora sat for a few seconds, then got back up and started wandering around the bar, talking to people at the various tables. Ashe leaned across the bar toward the bartender, who was standing a few feet away rubbing a glass with a cloth. It was almost comical, like she was doing it just because that was something bartenders were supposed to do.

"Hey, Chloe," Ashe said.

The girl looked up at her and smiled.

"Hey, Ashe," she said. "It's been a while since I've seen you around here."

"I know," Ashe said. "Things have been busy. You haven't happened to have seen Ty recently, have you?"

The blonde bartender shook her head.

"No," she said. "Not that I know of. Are you looking for him?"

Ashe nodded.

"Yeah," she said. "It's kind of important we find him."

"Give me a second," Chloe said.

Her eyes slid over to me and I could feel her checking me out the way Ashe had when I first saw her.

"Chloe?" Ashe said.

The woman jumped slightly, tearing her eyes away from me.

"Oh, right. I'll right back."

"Could you try not to distract people so much?" Ashe said, narrowing her eyes at me playfully.

"I'm sorry," I said. "I can't help it that I'm totally irresistible."

She scoffed.

"That's the problem," she said. "You really can't."

Chloe went to the other side of the bar and I saw her lean toward two men who were sitting on the stools opposite us. She whispered for a few seconds and then they shook their heads. She nodded and moved on to a woman sitting at the corner. She was closer now and I could hear her talking.

"Have you heard from Ty?" she asked. "Anytime in the last few days?"

"No," the woman said. "Not recently. Is something wrong?"

"Ashe is just looking for him," Chloe said.

"Well, if she tracks him down, tell him he's pissing off a lot of people. We tried going through the portal yesterday, and he wasn't there to let anybody through. There's people on the other side who want to get back, too, and nobody's able to use it. He sealed the portal when he went through it, so everybody is stuck until he decides to come back."

Ashe looked at me.

"So, we know for sure he's still in the Underworld," she said.

"Not necessarily," I said.

"What do you mean?"

"If he could seal it going one way, he could seal it going the other," I said. "It's entirely possible he went back through when nobody was around, and sealed it again."

"Why would he do that?"

"I don't know," I said.

Chloe returned, shaking her head.

"Sorry," she said. "It doesn't seem like anybody has seen him recently."

"Thanks for asking," Ashe said.

"Do you want to leave?" she asked me when Chloe walked away to help a guy who was shouting at her from the other end of the bar.

Out of the corner of my eye I saw her grab a spigot and spray him with water. He stumbled back and stopped shouting long enough to wipe the drops out of his eyes.

"Wow," I said. "Chloe doesn't take shit."

"No," Ashe said. "She most certainly does not.

And that's part of the fun of the Underworld. Not quite as many rules. You get belligerent at a bar, the bartender will spray your ass like an angry cat until you calm down, and there's nothing you can do about it."

I laughed.

"It's seems weird to have a bar here," I said.

"Not as weird as you'd think," she said. "A lot of vampires, especially ones who were changed when they were older, are more likely to keep drinking alcohol than they are to keep eating. Tastes better when you're a vampire. Goes down smoother. You know it won't kill you even if you way over do it."

"That's a definite bonus."

She smiled.

"That, and I think any kind of people are always going to be drawn to spending time with other people, and there are few places where that's as easy as at a bar. You come here, you sit down with a beer or a cocktail, you laugh with your buddies. Or you sit and cry out your troubles. Someone is always going to be there to talk to you and help you through. And more than just vampires come in here. Not anywhere near as many, of course, but you'll see the occasional fey, shifter, or demon in here. Sometimes a ghost or a lycan."

"Are all of those actual things, or are you just seeing how many you can throw at me and I'll believe you?"

She grinned at me but didn't answer.

I watch Chloe pick up the glass she had wiped and bring it to a tap. She pulled the handle and red liquid poured out into the glass. My stomach lurched, and I looked away. Ashe looked at Chloe and I heard her laugh.

"Tomato juice, Hayden," she said.

"Bullshit," I said. "Nobody has tomato juice on tap."

She shrugged.

"I was just trying to make you feel better," she said.

"They don't have a person down in the basement hooked up like a floppy keg, do they?" I asked.

Ashe laughed.

"No," she said. "There is no person with a perpetual IV sitting down there in a cage or anything. The blood comes from donors."

"Raiding the Red Cross seems pretty fucked up," I said.

"We don't raid the Red Cross," she said incredulously. "That blood has stabilizers, anyway. Not delicious. Donors who come to *us* to donate. There are humans who get a kick out of playing vampire. They willingly offer up their blood and we collect it."

"Delightful."

I looked around the bar, trying to get my mind off what she had just told me. It was fascinating to see the exact mirror of Solomon's Fang on the other side. It looked just like the bar I wandered into the night of my reunion without any idea of what would happen because of that one decision. Memories of what did happen within minutes of me going in, and then the next day, flashed through my mind and my cock jumped.

"So," I said, leaning closer to Ashe. "If this is the exact replica of Solomon's Fang on the other side, does that mean your apartment is here, too?"

"It's Chloe's apartment when it's here," she said.

I mocked a pout and she leaned closer.

"But the VIP suites are here."

28

As soon as the door to the VIP suite was closed, I grabbed Ashe and pushed her up against the wall, lifting her up so her legs were wrapped around my waist. She grabbed my head and pulled it toward her to catch my mouth in a deep, seeking kiss. Her tongue swirled hungrily with mine and I knew she had been thinking the same thing I was the entire time we were sitting at the bar. We kissed that way for a few seconds before I let her drop back down to her feet and started working at the button and zipper of my pants. My eyes followed Ashe's hands as she pulled off her shirt and tossed it away, then pushed her pants down over her hips. I didn't let her take them all the way off. Instead, I grabbed her when they were at her knees and whirled her around to face the bed against the wall.

Pushing her forward, I yanked her hips back toward me and slid her panties down. She looked back at me over her shoulder and I watched her eyes close and her mouth open in a gasp of pleasure as I slammed my hard cock into her. Already hot and wet for me, her pussy closed around me, and I groaned. Ashe arched her back, causing her hips to lift and the angle of her body to change so I could plunge even deeper. The skin of her thighs and round ass bounced against my thighs with each hard pound, but there was enough of her still covered by her clothes to make it even more erotic. I bit down into my bottom lip as I grabbed tightly to her hip with one hand and her shoulder with the other, using the position for leverage to pound even harder and faster. The hand on her shoulder moved into Ashe's hair and I wrapped the silky red strands around my hand to tug her head back.

She moaned loudly, and I saw her take one hand from the mattress so she could tuck it between her thighs. Her fingers played with her clit, and her body started shaking as she rocked her hips back to meet mine. Suddenly, she shoved herself back against me to let me plunge as deep into her as I could physically get and reared back from the bed to lean against me. Her head dropped back onto my shoulder and I felt her pussy clenching around my cock as she shook and gasped with the orgasm running through her. I pulled the cups of her bra down so I could grab her breasts. They felt heavy and swollen in my hands and her tight nipples pressed into my palms. I ran my mouth along the side of her neck as I continued rolling my hips into her, wanting to ride every one of her spasms. Finally, she fell forward again like she couldn't hold herself up anymore. Her hips rolled in slow circles to find every bit of sensation I could offer her. I was just pulling out of her, ready to finish, when the door opened.

"Am I interrupting something?" Aurora asked.

The tone in her voice told me it didn't really matter to her if she was interrupting it or not. In fact, she might be happy she was interrupting. Ashe stood up and smiled.

"I just finished," she said. "You can have him all to yourself."

She gave me a lingering kiss before pulling her panties and pants back into place and walking over to her shirt. Aurora grinned and came toward me. I knew neither of the women minded sharing me.

We had fun playing together. But sometimes it was nice to be one-on-one and really get to concentrate on each other. The time being out of Ashe was long enough that I felt completely back in control and ready for Aurora. I turned around and sat on the bed to watch her undress. She didn't have the same rush and urgency that Ashe had when we came into the room. Instead, she took off each article of clothing slowly, lingering over the fabric gliding off her skin and dropping them to the floor in a pool at her feet. I savored the exposure of every inch of her skin and enjoyed watching the sway and curve of her body as she walked across the room toward me.

Ashe stayed long enough to watch Aurora reach for my shirt and pull it off over my head, then climb into my lap. I heard her give an appreciative moan from the door as she walked out, just as my cock sank into Aurora. Her head fell back, and I ducked mine forward to fill my mouth with one of her luscious breasts. She rocked her hips slowly, grinding into me so I barely moved inside her, but it was just enough to send waves of powerful sensations along my shaft. Even with the adrenaline and arousal coursing through me, I felt myself relaxing as I tightened my hips and met each thrust of her riding me. It was a different experience being inside Aurora than it was either of the other women. The sex was incredible with all of them, but being with Aurora was an elevated experience. Our blood bond made it more than just our bodies as the connection let us feed off of each other.

I knew this was especially true for Aurora. Because of my warlock blood, she was fully reliant on me. I was her only source of everything she needed to keep going, from the passionate lust of our bodies to the blood she needed to survive. As if she could hear me thinking about the blood, Aurora lifted her head and licked her lips. She didn't say anything, but her eyes locked on my neck. Her fingertips traced the vein that ran alongside it.

"May I taste you, Lord?" she asked.

Her voice was rumbling and rich, and it sent a shiver through me. But I hesitated. I remembered the pain of the first bite and the days of my thigh feeling like it was on fire. She could sense my hesitation and she lifted my hand, cupping it to her cheek. Nuzzling her face against my hand, she made a soothing sound.

"Don't worry," she said. "It's not like the first

time. Your transformation is complete now, Hayden. My bite is no longer toxic to you. The first bite can be very painful, but after that, many find it extremely pleasurable."

I pressed my hands to the back of her hips and rocked her harder against me, then tilted my head to the side to reveal my neck. She grinned and leaned forward. I felt her tongue gliding across my skin and she drew in a deep breath. A warm sensation filled my body and the pleasure of being buried deep inside her intensified. As Aurora sucked at my neck, she began to ride me harder. I growled in my throat, guiding her hips harder and faster as our passion spiraled higher. I was glad I couldn't see my blood draining out of me, but the feeling of her suckling, gaining from me what she needed, was one of the sexiest experiences I had ever had. It made me come harder than I ever had before, drawing everything from me as I roared and pulsed inside her, reveling in her body milking mine in both intense ways.

Aurora and I were still tangled up together on the bed when the door opened again, and the other two women came in. She and I sat up, reaching for our clothes as Ashe and Stephana perched on the end of the bed.

"Did you find out anything?" I asked. "Has anybody seen or heard from Ty?"

"No," Ashe said. "A few new people came in to the bar, and we talked to as many of them as we could, but it doesn't seem like anybody has any idea where he is or where he might have been. But we did hear something else."

She and Stephana looked at each other.

"What?" I asked. "What did you hear?"

"A particularly rowdy group of vampires came in just a few minutes ago," Stephana said. "It seems like this was not their first stop of the night. They were already a pretty loud and seemed to be really enjoying themselves. One of them ordered a round and they did a toast."

"To what?" I asked.

"To whoever killed Malakan," Ashe said.

This perked up my ears and I got dressed as fast as I could so I wouldn't miss any of the conversation.

"What?" Aurora asked, sounding horrified.

"Yep," Stephana said. "Apparently, there are all kinds of rumors floating around about what might have happened to him and his house. It's no secret it burst into flames."

"I thought nobody knew about that house," I

said. "I thought it was complete secret that he even had it."

"That's the thing," Ashe said. "None of them seemed to really know where the house was actually located. They knew it had exploded and burned down, but not where it was. Now, the people in Final View know he had a place inside the cliff. I don't know if that means they only knew about the stone chambers, or if they actually knew about the house itself, but none of them really strike me as people who are particularly social with anybody outside of their community. They tolerated us the times we went through, but I'm not really expecting an invitation to the next block party."

"So, how did they know about the house?" I asked.

"That's the big question, isn't it?" Ashe asked.

"All those vampires are obviously extremely anti-warlock," Stephana said. "When they were talking about the explosion, they were thrilled by it. They thought it was absolutely great that somebody destroyed not just the house, but conceivably, Malakan himself. They went on to applaud whoever it was who called for the hit, and then whoever it was who lit the fire."

"So, they know it wasn't an accident," I said.

"It seems that way," Stephana said. "None of them seemed to think that he might have done it accidentally. They were all completely convinced it was an attack. But that's what we said, anyway. If Malakan did this himself, he would want to make it look like somebody did it to him. So, in that way, it's working out exactly as he wanted."

"If that's what happened," I said. "And we still don't know."

I was feeling frustrated and angry. The thought of people sitting right downstairs cheering the loss of Malakan infuriated me and I wanted to go down and confront them.

"Did anyone else say anything?" I asked.

"Yes," Ashe said. "As a matter of fact, they did." Her lips curled into a smile that seemed to say she found particular significance in the exchange. "There was another table sitting nearby listening to everything, and they took objection to the celebration."

"What did they say?"

"They told the loud guys to shut up and stop being so disrespectful. Yes, Malakan was a warlock, but he was aligned with the vampires. He left his own kind in order to help ours, and that means he deserved respect and honor, not to be murdered and then have his memory assaulted. They said they didn't want to believe anyone would do something like that, and hoped it was some kind of accident. If it wasn't, they wanted whoever was responsible to be held accountable."

"So, some thought it could be an accident?" I asked.

"Yes," Stephana said. "And then another table piped in and said they thought it was something else all-together."

"What did that mean?" I asked. "If it wasn't an attack and it wasn't an accident, what did they think it could be?"

Ashe shrugged.

"They didn't elaborate. They just said there could always be another explanation."

"Everybody's talking about it," I said. "But nobody seems to know what actually happened."

"Right," Ashe said. "But I think the point is people are talking."

"What do you mean?"

"Nothing gets people angrier faster than a story that can be told several different ways. When something happens, and it can be explained by different people from different angles, no one is satisfied by it and everyone gets up in arms, ready to defend their perspective and tear down those who oppose them. This conflict has been simmering for a long time."

"Maybe this is just the thing to get it hot again," I said.

29

I WANTED TO GET BACK DOWN INTO THE BAR TO talk to the vampires who had been involved in the argument about Malakan. We finished getting dressed and headed out of the suite, but I noticed as soon as we got into the hallway that I couldn't hear the voices from downstairs anymore. When we had first come up , it was almost as loud in the hallway as it was down in the bar itself, but at that moment it was quiet. Voices were almost imperceptible, subdued. It was obvious the raucous group Ashe and Stephana told us about weren't down in the bar anymore, and I wondered what made them leave. I briefly envisioned Chloe chasing all of them out with her water spigot, but when I got to the bottom of the steps and looked toward the bar,

I knew that wasn't what happened. I stopped, the women running into my back behind me.

"What is it?" Ashe asked.

I nodded toward the bar.

"Look who's here," I said.

"What is my father doing here?" Aurora asks. "The Prime isn't usually seen in a place like this. Especially my father. I didn't even think he knew what Solomon's Fang was."

"Apparently, he does," I said, almost more to myself than to her.

Feeling every muscle in my body tense, I started toward The Prime where he sat at the bar. He turned as we approached, and I saw his eyes widen. He jumped up from his stool and reached for me, grabbing me by my shoulders. I had the compulsion to push him away, but I held it back. I needed to keep myself under control. As of right now, I still didn't know much about him, or how he was involved in all of this, and he didn't know who I was. No matter what I was feeling for him at that moment, I had to stay as calm as I could and not give anything away.

"Hayden!" he exclaimed. "Aurora, Ashe, Stephana. I'm so glad to see all of you. I've been so worried. When I realized most of you weren't in the palace anymore, I was so afraid something had happened to you. I looked everywhere and couldn't figure out where you might have gone. I've been looking for you for two days."

He was acting completely frantic, like he had been terrified when he couldn't find Ashe, Aurora, or me, but I got the feeling that was exactly what it was... acting. Nothing about his voice or widened eyes seemed genuine, just like when he first heard about Malakan's death, and it only put me more on edge.

"There were things we needed to attend to, Father," Aurora said.

"But you didn't even tell me you were leaving," Darian said. "You were there, and then the next morning you were just gone. I had just learned my dearest friend and confidant had been killed, then my child went missing. How did you expect me to feel?"

"I am an adult," Aurora said. "I'm not a little girl and you don't need to know where I am at every moment. I don't need to ask your permission to go anywhere. Hayden is my Lord. Wherever he goes, I will follow, always. There's nothing you can do about that."

There was a heaviness in her voice, almost like

a warning, and I reached for her hand, squeezing it reassuringly. She needed to stay calm, too. This wasn't the time for her to overreact and inadvertently let her father know what was going on. I watched the Prime's reaction to Aurora's words carefully. Just as I expected, a flicker of darkness rolled through his eyes, like a brief storm. Then he pushed it away and resumed the look of fear and worry.

"You might be an adult, Aurora, but you are still my child. You are still my responsibility to keep safe, and I was worried about you. Nobody knows what horrible accident befell Malakan, or what else might have happened to him, and to not know where you were was terrifying."

He sounded like he was trying to muster up some tears, and I felt disgust bubble in my stomach. There was definitely something else going on. This was not a father who was genuinely worried about his daughter. To Aurora's admittance, they were closer than they had been when she was growing up, and even in her early adult years, but they still didn't have a particularly strong link. Certainly not strong enough to warrant such a degree of frantic concern and executing a one-man search party into the dregs of Solan City to find her. This definitely wasn't the first time Aurora had just walked away from the palace without telling her father where she was going, and from the stories about the war I had already heard, I knew it wasn't the first time she had left in the midst of conflict or tragedy. There was another reason Darian had come after us, and I wanted to know what it was. I couldn't help the feelings of anger toward him, as much as I tried not to show them. When I looked at him, I could only see the man who had arranged for my kidnapping in the days following my birth. I could only see a person so ruthless they were willing to put a newborn baby's life at risk just to hurt their rival, and to make themselves look good when they hopefully brought the two species back together years later. It was someone I couldn't stand to share space with. This was the man who had taken the life I was supposed to have, and I wanted vengeance for it. But first, I needed to know what actually happened and why.

"I'm sorry," I finally managed to force through my throat. "There were things that I needed to take care of, and I brought them with me. Like you said, nobody knows what happened to Malakan, so I didn't necessarily see any reason to be afraid."

I had chosen my words specifically, and wanted

to know how he would react to them. I was rewarded by his dark eyes sliding over to me. He looked like a snake in the seconds before he tried to wipe away the expression.

"That's the thing with you young people," he said, his voice slower now. "You don't understand that there is always a reason to be afraid."

"Father," Aurora said. "Why would you say something like that?"

The Prime looked over at his daughter.

"Because it's true," he said. "We live in very uncertain times, Aurora. Our world is in conflict, and whenever there is turmoil like this, there are threats everywhere. You might feel safe because you know your surroundings, or secure because you know who you are, but you never know where danger might lurk."

The thought sliced through me that when he looked into my eyes, Darien might see the baby he had condemned.

"Like I said, there were things we needed to do. As you can see, we're safe. I'm sorry if you worried about us," I said. "But I will always keep Aurora, and Ashe and Stephana, safe.

Darian looked at each of us. We were all tense, none of us having sat or relaxed since we walked up to him. Though we hadn't specifically discussed it, it seemed each of us instinctively knew not to tell Darian who I was or what we knew. Finally, he took a step back from us.

"I'm glad to have found you safe," he said. "I can go back to the palace now. Come home soon, Aurora."

It seemed very deliberate that he mentioned only her name. He walked out of the bar, and we all exchanged glances. Making our way to one of the tables in the far back corner of the bar, we sat down.

"I've been thinking a lot about what we should do next," I said. "I think we need to go see my foster family."

"Why?" Ashe asked.

"They are a part of this," I said. "They're going to know how I came to live with them when I was a baby. They can give us information nobody else can."

"What if they don't know anything? What if they thought it was just a regular foster situation?" Aurora asked. "Do you really want to walk into your house and say, 'hey Mom and Dad, I really appreciate you adopting me at all, but I just found out that I was born a warlock and now I'm a vampire too. I really need to know what happened when I was a baby so I can figure all this out and fight a massive war'?"

"I would probably select different words than those," I said. "I don't really think I need to get into the details quite that much. Besides, they never adopted me."

Stephana looked at me strangely.

"They didn't?" she asked.

"No," I said, shaking my head. "We were really close, and they were always good to me. I called them Mom and Dad, and they would say I was their son and tell me they loved me and all. But they never brought up the idea of adopting me. Never."

"Did you ever ask them about it?" Ashe asked.

"No," I said. "To be honest, I didn't even know it was an option until I was already almost a teenager. That sounds ridiculous, but like I said, I don't have memories of being a small child really. I mean a few flashes here and there, a couple of isolated moments, but nothing like a real record of when I was younger or memories of day-to-day life. I don't remember ever having an awareness being a foster child as being so much different as any other child. It was just how my family worked.

It wasn't until I was older that somebody mentioned to me that they knew somebody who was a foster child who had been adopted by their family. At that point, it didn't seem to make any sense that I would want to change my life that drastically. Nothing was wrong or unfulfilling, or any of those other things you might find in a brochure. So, we just never talked about it. We're still close, though. I mean, as close as a lot of adults are to their parents. We keep up, talk every so often. I go home for the holidays every couple of years."

"Didn't you live in the same city as them?" Aurora asked.

I slid my eyes over to her.

"Are you really going to lecture me on my responsibilities toward my parents?" I asked.

"If anybody's going to do that, it's me," Stephana said.

I laughed.

"Okay, so I didn't go see them as much as I probably could have, but we have a good relationship. Maybe they'll be able to tell me more about how they got me." A thought went through my mind and I slammed my fist on the table. "Shit," I said.

"What?" Aurora asked.

"I can't," I said. "Without Ty, I can't go through the portal."

"Well," Ashe said, glancing over at Aurora.

"What is that?" I asked. "What is that look?"

"You might have an option," she said. "It's not the best one, and you have to understand it's a one-time thing."

"What is?"

"Because a blood price was paid for you to go through the portal the first time, you have one chance to go through it without the portal keeper being there to help you. Just once."

"Everybody doesn't have to pay the blood price?" I asked.

"No," Ashe said. "That's up to the keeper. Virtually everybody is required to at least one time, but if they are traveling with someone who has already paid the price or has been let through by the keeper before, they usually don't."

I dropped back against the seat with an incredulous sigh.

"That son of a bitch," I said. "He did that just to fuck with me."

"It happens," Ashe said. "But it's fine. I paid as your proxy, so it's done. You have one chance to move through the portal without Ty."

"What about you three?" I asked.

"We should be able to go with you," she said. "It's a little bit like train-hopping, but if we are all touching, we should be able to all go through at the same time. But you have to understand, we won't be able to get back. Without Ty, there is no getting back to the Underworld."

"Then we stay until we figure out where he is and make him bring us back."

30

"I REALLY DON'T UNDERSTAND HOW THIS WHOLE portal thing works," I said. "Obviously, there are going to be times when the portal keeper isn't there to watch over the portal, and it's not always going to be a situation where as the people who want to go through it have already paid the blood price and saved their one free ticket until they might need it. And they can't just stop people from going from world to world when they want to."

"Of course, they can," Aurora said.

She was so matter-of-fact about it, it struck me silent.

"Oh," I said a few seconds later. "Well, damn. That doesn't seem like a very efficient public transportation system. There has to be some sort of plan in place in case something happens, some sort of interim portal keeper or something. A co-keeper, a replacement keeper, a vice keeper. Something."

"Portal keepers are appointed by the Prime," Ashe said. "Just like Ty was appointed by Darian after the incident, all portal keepers get their assignment from The Prime. They are the only ones who are able to operate that. The portal is linked specifically to them, and only they can allow others to utilize it unless that other person has a specified passage, such as the free ticket from the blood price, as you said. If something happens and the current portal keeper dies, another one has to be appointed by the Prime. That's the only way one can be put into power."

"So, this isn't a 'Santa's suit' situation," I said.

The women looked at me blankly and I realized they didn't understand the reference.

"A what?" Stephana asked.

"A Santa's suit situation," I repeated. "You know, if something happens to Santa Claus, whoever finds his suit and puts it on then becomes the new Santa?"

My eyes flitted back and forth from Aurora to Ashe to Stephana.

"No," Aurora said. "That's not how it works. Nobody has to put on Ty in order to become a portal keeper. "

The image of Ty's skin hanging in a closet like hooded footie pajamas was almost too much for me.

"I actually just meant nobody could step in and take over his responsibilities,"

"We're going to find Ty," Ashe said. "He isn't dead. If he was, we would know by now. He's somewhere, and we will find him."

I nodded.

"I know," I said. "I'm just thinking about the portal. I've gotten used to being able to jump back and forth, you know."

I hoped I sounded as casual as I was trying to. The truth was, the thought of going back to the other side and not being able to come into the Underworld was unnerving. I didn't like the thought of being separated from the world I had adopted as my own.

As soon as the thought went through my head, I realized I hadn't adopted the Underworld as mine. It was mine already. It had been my entire life, even though I didn't know it. That was the world into which I was born, and the one I was meant for. Finding it wasn't a discovery of something new. It was coming home. I didn't want to think about not being able to go back through the portal because I didn't want to be separated from it again. I didn't want anything or anyone being able to tell me where I could go, or that I was being held back from this place and these people.

"We don't have to go," Aurora said. "We can stay here and keep looking for him, if you want to."

"No," I said. "I need to go back there. We need to figure this out. If we don't know where Ty is, then we have to go about finding the information we need in another way. The only place we're going to find it is on the other side. I understand the risk, but I accept it. It'll be fine. I know I'll make my way back here."

I noticed the women looking at each other again and I let out a sigh.

"What?" Ashe asked.

"You're doing it again," I said.

"What are we doing?" Aurora asked.

"You're giving each other that look."

"What look?" Stephana asked.

"That look that says that all of you know something that I don't know because I haven't gotten to that chapter in the stupid fucking manual yet. What is it that I don't know?"

"Ty is only the keeper to that portal," Ashe said.

I rolled my eyes so far up into my head I figured I'd probably be able to see some of my memories just by examining my gray matter.

"What do you mean Ty is only the keeper to *that* portal?" I asked. "I thought there was only one portal from the other side into each city. That's what you told me."

"I told you there was only one *official* portal," Ashe said. "There is only one recognized and regulated portal from city to city. It's the only one that anybody is supposed to know about or use."

"I don't understand," I said.

"If something happened and you absolutely had to travel back to the Underworld, going through the portal Ty guards may not be the only option. We might be able to find one of the black-market portals, like the one over the water at Final View. To be fair, the actual existence of the portals is widely debated. There doesn't seem to be any general consensus over whether they're there or not, or if the ones that do exist are still active and usable. But there are rumors and all of us have heard stories about people using them."

"Perfect," I said. "Why didn't you tell me about that before? That changes everything."

"It's not that easy, Hayden," Aurora said. "These aren't just other portals where you are going to be able to step through into a nice alley. These things are unregulated, unmonitored, illegal portals created by people you probably don't want to associate with."

"At this point in my existence," I said, "I can't really make any judgments about who I do and I do not want to associate with. In the last few days, I've come into contact with a whole lot of people I probably never would have had anything to do with in any other circumstances. No offense to any of the three of you, because you are fantastic and I'm really enjoying my time with you, but I never particularly saw myself as someone who was going to be spending a tremendous portion of my time hanging out with a bunch of vampires. We're not going to get into the lycan and the demons and the shifters and the werepeople and the Kraken and the fairies and the wind monsters."

"Some of those aren't real things," Ashe said.

"Not the point," I shook my head at her. "If there's a way to travel between worlds, I'm going to take it."

"Those who say they exist, or who report to have used them, say they are extraordinary dangerous," Stephana said. "There's no guarantee you're actually going to end up at the destination you wanted. Or that you'll survive the passage. And the price to use them isn't like the blood price Ty required. A price is charged of every person who goes through the portal, and sometimes it is much more than you would be willing to pay. But, because they don't charge you until after you've already traveled through, you're essentially screwed."

"Well," I said, "I'm sold. Sign me up for a timeshare."

"Hayden, you need to take this seriously," Ashe said.

"Look, I do take it seriously. I take all of this seriously, but frankly, telling me it's dangerous isn't going to stop me. Making my way through the rum-runner tunnels of some vampire gangsters sounds delightful. Even if it didn't, though, do I really have a choice? If I go through the portal at Solomon's Fang, and then I need to get back to the Underworld, I'm not going to have the opportunity to say I'm not going to do it because it's not safe. I have to do what I have to do. Find out where the black-market tunnels are so at least I can be ready. We need to go as soon as possible."

"I think I should stay behind," Stephana said.

"What?" I asked.

"You're going to need a contact in the Underworld," she said. "You're going to need somebody who's able to keep track of what's going on here, and who can look for some of the black-market portals. "

"You're right," I said. "You stay here and keep in touch with me. Ashe, you should stay too. Keep me up-to-date on what's going on at the Fang."

"I will," Ashe said. "If I hear anything about Ty or Malakan, I will get in touch with you immediately."

"Good," I said. I turned to Aurora. "Aurora," I started.

She shook her head adamantly.

"Don't even try it," she said. "There's no way I'm staying behind while you go to the other side.

You're just going to have to deal with me coming right along with you."

I grinned.

"You know what? I wouldn't have it any other way."

31

I PACKED MY BAG WITH FRESH CLOTHES AND OTHER things I might need on the other side. I had no idea how long we might be gone, or what might be waiting for me in the remnants of the life I'd left behind. Carrying it, and Aurora's bag, the group walked to the portal. We waited until there was no one else in the alley and there was a lull in the people passing by on the sidewalk. I hugged Ashe and then Stephana, giving both a kiss.

"We'll let you know if anything happens," Ashe said.

"So, will we," I said. "If we find out anything, we'll call you."

"Be safe," Stephana said. "Remember, there are plenty of people on the other side who know about our world, and you never know who might be looking for you. Don't feel comfortable there just because it is familiar."

"I won't," I said.

We hugged one more time and Aurora and I stepped up to the portal. I wrapped one arm tightly around her waist, remembering what she said about her being able to travel with me like a train hopper if we were touching. I wanted to be touching her as much as possible. The last thing I needed right then was to get through to the other side and end up in the basement of Solomon's Fang with only part of her body with me. That was a complication I could really do without.

"Are you ready?" Aurora asked.

"Absolutely," I said.

Without looking back, we braced ourselves and activated the portal. I was relieved when I felt the brick wall giving away beneath my hand and was able to step through. My knees buckled under me when I got into the basement and I landed face down on the floor, the bags draped over my shoulders smashing into my stomach and knocking the breath out of me.

"That was graceful," Aurora said as she stepped over me.

"I'm still not exactly used to traveling through the portals," I said. "And I'm not exactly traveling light here. I had two checked bags and a carry on."

She flashed a grin at me as I climbed to my feet.

"What do you think's going on up there?" she asked, her eyes lifting to the ceiling like she was looking up into the bar above us.

"Probably the same thing as always," I said. "I don't know how quickly word passes from the Underworld to here, especially when the portal isn't active."

She nodded, but I couldn't decide if she was relieved to hear that or didn't believe me. We walked through the basement and up the stairs, and even before I opened the door, I knew something was strange. I didn't hear any voices coming from the bar, and when we stepped in I didn't see anybody there. It wasn't like the first day when I walked down the steps from the VIP Suite and it was still too early in the morning for anyone to be there. It was definitely a time of day when plenty of people would usually have trickled in and taken up their seats at the bar. But not today. The room was empty, and the lights were dim.

"What's going on?" Aurora asked.

I shook my head.

"I don't know," I said.

We crossed through the bar cautiously, but nothing happened. I had halfway expected a member of the Shade to pop up from behind the bar or for Artemis to drop down from the ceiling and tell me it was part of my training. Instead, the entire room stayed completely still and silent. I reached out for the handle on the door and realized it was locked.

"It doesn't look like they ever opened today," I said.

"They don't close," Aurora said. "I mean, to other people, it looks like it's closed, but anybody from the Underworld knows Solomon's Fang is always open."

"Not today," I said.

I turned the heavy deadbolt and we walked out onto the sidewalk. The cold air nearly sucked the breath out of my lungs. The temperature had dropped quickly in the time I had been in the Underworld, and all around us the changing of the seasons was obvious. It wasn't as eerily abandoned out here as it was inside the bar, but it still didn't feel as busy and hectic as I was used to it feeling. I wondered if that was just because I had gotten accustomed to the tenser, higher energy of Solan City or if something really had changed.

"What should we do first?" Aurora asked.

"I'm going to call my foster parents," I said. "I'll make sure they're at home."

I pulled my phone out of my pocket and called my mother first. It rang twice and then clicked off. I looked at the phone, puzzled, and then called my father. It was entirely possible Mom was out doing something. She was nothing if not involved. One of the things I did remember about her from when I was younger was that she was constantly a part of one cause or another and doing whatever she could to help people. Looking back on it, it should have struck me as strange that I was the only foster child they ever had. My dad's phone didn't even ring. It went straight to voicemail, but I didn't leave a message. I didn't know what to say.

"What's wrong?" Aurora asked.

"Neither of them is picking up," I said. "That's not like them. At least one of them is reachable all the time. Where the fuck is everybody?"

Out of the corner of my eye I noticed Aurora was looking at her phone. The expression on her face changed.

"Hayden, look at this," she said. "This might

explain why they didn't answer the phone."

"Why?" I asked, moving closer to her.

"Because they might think you're dead."

"What?" I asked, snatching the phone from her hand and looking at the screen. "Son of a bitch."

Aurora had searched my name and all the results said I was missing and presumed dead. I scanned through a few of them before handing the phone back to her.

"What did it say?" she asked.

"Since I've been gone for well over a week and nobody has heard from me, they figured I wandered off somewhere and either died of an overdose or was murdered," I said. "Nothing like disappearing to find out how people really see you."

"Why would they say that?" she asked.

"The night I met you, I was supposed to be going to my high school reunion," I told her. "It has been a few years since anybody saw me, and I wasn't exactly at the peak of my life, so to speak. I went from being popular and successful, on my way to the career of my dreams, to fat, aging, and scraping together tips from delivering pizzas just so I could pay the rent."

"Why did you even try to go?" she asked.

"Honestly, I have no idea. I didn't want to see anybody there and I definitely didn't want to start reminiscing about my glory days, considering they were far behind me. I don't know. Maybe I thought if I went back, I would somehow magically be that person again. Something about being near my old classmates and surrounded by the place where I found all my success would sink into me and I would be on top of the world again. But, when I got there, I knew that wasn't going to happen. I just couldn't bring myself to go in, so I took a walk and found Solomon's Fang."

"And the rest is history," Aurora said with a smile.

"That's right," I said. "As it turns out, though, people were actually expecting to see me that night. When I didn't show up, they started trying to track me down, went to my apartment, called my job. Nobody knew where I was. I guess they figured the reunion was just too much for me."

"How does it make you feel?" she asked.

I laughed and looked over at her.

"Did you really just ask me how that makes me feel?"

Aurora shrugged.

"It seemed appropriate for the situation,"

she said.

I let out a sigh.

"Well, I can now say I have lived two lives and in both was presumed dead when I wasn't, so that's a thing."

"I think you've lived three lives," Aurora said. "But third time's a charm."

"You're just full of old clichés, aren't you?" She smiled, and I couldn't help but lean over and kiss her. "You know what's interesting, though?"

"What's that?" she asked.

"All of these people who think I'm dead pegged me for a loser. They have no idea that I'm actually one of the most powerful beings in the world. And that I'm sleeping with three super hot chicks."

Aurora laughed and shook her head.

"So, I take it you're not too torn up about people in this world thinking you slunk off and died?"

"I mean, when you put it like that, it's not the most pleasant thing in the world. I'd rather them have a better story for how I died, but surprisingly, it doesn't bother me. It's actually kind of a relief. This world screwed me. And I don't really have anything in it that matters enough that I want to hang on to it, except maybe my foster family. But even they are just a tenuous grasp because I don't see them a ton anyway. The reality is, my life in this world crashed and burned a long time ago, and I really have no interest in trying to salvage it. Now that I have the chance to, I'd rather lean into the idea of being dead, and be able to just walk away. I am very committed to my new existence, and I'm ready to embrace it full on."

Aurora turned and wrapped her arms around my waist, pulling me close and tilting her head back to look into my face.

"I'm proud of you," she said.

"Good. Now, what do you say we go do some haunting?"

"Where do you want to go?" Aurora asked. "Your parents aren't answering the phone. Do you want to just go to their house?"

"No," I said. "I was actually thinking about it. They aren't the only ones who have information. I still want to talk to them, but we might be able to get a more direct line by going to the office of the foster agency. If we can find my records, we can figure out exactly who handed me over to my foster parents, and even how I ended up in the system to begin with."

"Do you really think your record is going to say

kidnapped from a warlock?" she asked.

"I sincerely doubt it," I said. "But whatever it says could be a clue. There might be something in there that tells us when I was brought to the agency or who brought me there. Then we could use that to trace it back further."

We started walking down the sidewalk, and out of the corner of my eye I saw Aurora watching me.

"What's bothering you?" she asked.

I shook my head.

"Nothing," I said. "I'm fine."

"You're thinking about something," she said. "What is it? What's wrong?"

"I'm just wondering what the records would say about how old I was when I got to the agency. All my life, I thought my birthday was in August. I've always been the summer baby and joked that's why I love going to the beach and skinny-dipping. Now, it turns out I was still four months away from being born in August. I should love skiing and drinking hot cocoa or whatever shit winter babies do. It just kind of messes with your head."

"I know," Aurora said. "I'm sorry."

I reached over and took her hand.

"It's fine," I said. "It really is. Sometime soon, I'll know everything."

32

"Do you know where the foster agency is?" Aurora asked.

"No, but it shouldn't be too hard to find out," I told her. "We lived in the same place my whole life, as far as I know. I can't imagine there are too many overlapping agencies handling foster care children. I think there's just one office that oversees a fairly large area. All we need to do is find that office, go in, and ask if I can see my records. I don't think they are sealed the way some adoptions are. Hopefully, now that I'm an adult, they'll let me look at them."

"You mean, now that you're dead."

The comment hit me, and I realized I didn't think it all the way through.

"You're right," I said. "If people think I'm dead, there's no way I'm going to be able to just walk into an office and talk to people. They're either going to see me walk through the door and think they're seeing a ghost, or it's going to blow my cover and I won't be able to get out of it."

"So, we can't go in and ask to see your record. Doesn't mean we can't do it without asking."

There was mischief in her voice, and I smiled.

"Why, Aurora. Am I to believe you are suggesting some criminal behavior?"

"Why don't we just think of it as a brief unauthorized tour of the foster child care system," she said. "Worst case scenario, we get caught and I tell them I'm an undercover reporter who's doing an exposé on how the foster care system works, and I wanted an inside look at the office."

"I wouldn't have thought you would even know what an exposé piece is," I said.

"There's journalism in the Underworld," she said. "The late news is always gripping."

"I can imagine it is," I said.

"Besides, I told you, I spent a lot of time on the other side. I know people do weird stuff like this, and sometimes get away with it. I'm sure I would be one of those people."

I look at her quizzically.

"And why do you think that?" I asked.

"Remember when Ashe told you I'm a princess and you should treat me like royalty?" she asked.

I didn't realize Ashe had told her about that admonishment, but I nodded.

"Yes," I said.

"Everybody should," she said, smiling. "I always get what I want."

The way she said it left no doubt she was absolutely right.

I pulled up the information about the foster care agency and checked the hours of the office.

"They're closed," I said. "It's a little bit of a hike from here, so by the time we get there, everybody should have left for the night. We might come across a custodian or a night security guard, but they probably don't have anything on the Shades."

"I think we'll be alright," Aurora said.

We made our way through the city as fast as we could, and the entire way we were traveling, all I could think about was that I felt like a ghost. It was a strange way to be thinking about it, but there I was, in a world that had already written me off. In just a matter of days, they had decided I had with met some sort of miserable and pathetic end, yet, here I was, moving among them. A few times, I caught people glancing at me a second time after they passed or staring at me hard from across the street like they thought they might recognize me. But nobody said anything or made any indication they thought they knew who I was. There were a couple of times I was tempted to wave my arms around over my head and make a creepy *'oooooooooooo'* sound just to see how people reacted. But I refrained. I was trying *not* to draw attention to us.

Finally, we made it to the stark structure containing the foster care system offices. A chill that had nothing to do with the weather settled through me as I looked at the building. The bags crossed over my chest had become cumbersome, and I wished we had found somewhere to drop them before coming here. But we had already come this far, so there was no point in turning back now. I glanced at the small parking area behind the building. I only saw one car in the very far back corner, but it very well could have been there for months. It didn't have a very used look about it.

"It looks like everybody's gone," I said.

"Are you sure?" Aurora asked.

"Getting second thoughts about Aurora, ace

reporter?"

"If I don't have to do it, I'd really rather not," she said.

"Fair enough," I said. "I don't see any cars in the parking lot. There's a parking structure just a little bit away, and it's conceivable some people parked in there and walked down here, but for the most part, it looks like the building's empty."

"Perfect," she said. "How should we get inside?"

I stepped back so I could look at the building. There were no balconies or outcroppings that would have let us climb up to one of the top windows. The bottom windows had bars crossed over them that would prevent accessing the glass panes.

"Let's go around the back and see if there's another way," I said.

Glancing around to make sure nobody was watching us, we got closer to the building and walked carefully around the perimeter, examining it to find any door or window we might be able to sneak through. We had just gotten around to the back of the building and found a gray metal door at the top of two short concrete steps when we heard voices. I grabbed onto Aurora's arm and pulled her down, so we were crouched in the shadows beside the small porch. A few seconds later, a man and a woman showed up at the door. He held the door open as she walked through. She was staring down at an open folder on top of a stack of others in her hands, and they were talking about the difficulty of a particular case. Neither one of them had any awareness that we were just feet away from them.

"Are you sure you got everything you need?" the man asked.

He was standing at the door, holding it open with his back, and it immediately occurred to me that was the way we were going to get in. I looked around the porch, and my eyes landed on a brown rubber doorstop. It looked like it had been brushed aside and forgotten, but it was exactly what I needed.

"I'm pretty sure," the woman said.

"Great," he said.

I concentrated on the door stop, staring at it with all of the energy and intensity I could muster. Artemis's voice was in the back of my mind, and I used it to focus my concentration and call forward the same ability he had used to toss me back against the tree. The man stepped away from the door and it started to swing closed in that slow, lazy way of heavy metal industrial doors. Even with the slow pace, , I didn't have much time. It's not like I could just stand up and run through the door in front of them. Focusing harder, finally, the doorstop wiggled and then scooted across the concrete. I had to keep my excitement in check, so I could keep focusing on it. A few seconds later, it rose up and I forced it forward with my mind, wedging it into the corner of the door so it blocked it from closing completely. The man was already down the steps and approaching the woman and didn't notice the door didn't close all the way.

My head was pounding when I finished, but Aurora was beaming at me.

"That was amazing," she whispered. "Your training is really paying off."

"Yeah, remind me not to do that much until I get more used to it. That was exhausting."

The man and woman leaned close like they were talking softly to each other. They suddenly stepped away from each other and hurried around the side of the building. I could only assume they were headed toward the parking deck at the end of the block.

"Come on," I said to Aurora.

We ran around the side of the porch and up the steps. I grabbed the handle of the door and yanked it open so she could go inside first. Making sure the doorstop wasn't still in place, I let the door close.

"He didn't even look back to make sure the door shut all the way," Aurora said.

"It's amazing what a hard dick and a short skirt can keep you from noticing," I said.

The door opened onto a darkened hallway. The only illumination came from emergency lights, up toward the top of the walls. We made our way slowly down the hallway, listening for any indication of others who might be inside.

"Where do we go?" she asked.

"I doubt they keep twenty-eight-year-old records in the main offices," I said. "Most of that kind of stuff is done by computer now, but that long ago, they probably did a lot of it by hand. There's got to be a records room around. Look for a door to a basement."

We checked the plaques next to the doors on either side of the hall. All were just names of various workers, and we turned at the end of the hall onto another. A flight of stairs brought us a partial floor down onto a landing with a single bulb still burning above a door. I pointed to the small sign beside it.

Records.

"Got to love the government," I said. "Labels for everything."

"What are you going to do about that?" Aurora asked, pointing to the keypad under the doorknob.

"Shit. I hadn't noticed that. It requires a code to unlock the door."

"Did Artemis teach you anything about hacking computer systems?" she asked.

"No," I said. "That didn't exactly come up."

"Oh," she said. She looked at the keypad again and let out a sigh. "So, what are we supposed to do now?"

I thought for a few seconds, then started up the steps again.

"We need to find the break room," I said.

"Break room?" Aurora asked.

"Yep. I need a soda machine."

"Is now really the time for you to be feeling nostalgic?" she asked.

Fortunately, the break room was in the next hall over, and the lack of a door made it easy for me to walk right in toward the illuminated soda machines in the far corner.

"Not nostalgic," I said. "Destructive."

I examined the front of the machine and saw it didn't have a coin slot. Aurora stepped up beside me and pulled a credit card from the side pocket of her bag, which was still hanging on my shoulder. She swiped it through and I selected four drinks. Scooping them into my arms, I headed back to the records room. I popped open two of the cans and handed them to Aurora then popped open the two others.

"What are we doing?" she asked.

"I might not be able to hack the door open, but I could probably break-the-hell-out-of-the-keypad the door open."

"Using soda?" she asked skeptically.

"Okay, are you ready? On the count of three, pour it all over the keypad."

"Is that going to work?" she asked.

"To tell you the truth, I don't really know. But it's what I've got right now, so all we can do is try."

I started the countdown and on one, we both poured our cans of soda onto the keypad. Part of me was hoping for dramatic sparks and sizzling sounds, but instead, I got a pathetic sounding wine and the backlight of the buttons went out.

"I think it worked," she said.

"Only one way to find out," I said.

I pulled on the handle of the door, and it swung open.

"Vandalism for the win," Aurora said.

We went into the records room and I turned on the light. Row after row of filing cabinets sectioned off the royal blue industrial rug. I walked up to one of them and saw they were arranged by year. At least that would narrow it down. That was a relief.

"My file will be in one of these cabinets," I said, indicating the three with the correct year range on them. I pulled open the first one, and a thought made me sink down to my knees.

"What do I look for?" I asked.

Aurora came up beside me and knelt down.

"What do you mean?" she asked.

"If I was just a baby when my parents got me, did they name me? Or did I have a name when I went into the system?"

"I don't know," Aurora said.

"What was my name when I was born?" I asked. "You were around then. You remember when I was taken. What was my name?"

Tears formed in her eyes.

"I don't know," she said. "Your parents hadn't announced it. There's a warlock presentation ceremony for when babies are born, but you hadn't had one yet."

I give a resigned nod.

"Just another piece of the puzzle," I said. I looked back at the filing cabinet in front of me. "I don't think they would have had my parents name me," I said. "That's not part of being a foster parent. That means I had a name when I came into the system, or at least I was given my name once I got here. So, let's look for that."

I took one of the filing cabinets and she took another. We flipped through all of the files, then moved on to the third cabinet. By the time we were done, I felt exasperated and confused.

"Nothing," I said. "There's no mention of me at all."

"Maybe that wasn't your name," she said. "Or maybe you didn't have a name. A few of these don't list the names of the child. One of them could be you."

She was trying to sound as optimistic as possible, but I could tell she was doubting every word she said. I nodded, and we started going through the files again. We compared every file that didn't have a name with the birthdate my parents always told me, and the one Aurora said was really mine.

We looked at the months around those days, and even ones in other years. None of them seemed connected to me. My foster parent's names weren't in any of the files, and the information tracing the movement of each of the children through the system eliminated them as options one by one.

"I don't have a file," I said. "I wasn't ever placed in the foster system."

"It doesn't make any sense," Aurora said. "Why would your parents tell you that you were a foster child if you were never in the system?"

I shook my head slowly.

"I don't know," I said. "But it explains why they never adopted me. They didn't have any records for me. They had a birth certificate, but that's easy to forge."

Aurora was about to respond when I heard a sound above us. I held up a finger to quiet her.

"What was that?" she asked.

"It sounded like a door," I said. "I think somebody's in the building."

Adrenaline started pumping through me again like it had when we had been in the palace. I had the same feeling I did when I realized someone was listening to us. Someone was following us again. I crossed the room quickly and flipped the light switch. Darkness descended on us and Aurora stepped up to my side.

"What are we going to do?" she asked.

"We need to get out as quickly as we can," I said. "I don't think there's going to be a whole lot of finessing this. When I open the door, run."

I picked up the bags I had put down and strapped them across my chest again. Tightening the buckles on the straps, so they were closer to my body and easier to carry, I reached for the door. I threw it open, and Aurora burst out of the room. I followed her, nearly slipping in the soda on the floor. We scrambled up the steps and ran through the building toward the door to the outside. I could hear footsteps above us, and I knew whoever had followed us could hear our escape. It didn't matter, we just needed to get away from the building as fast as possible. We ran until we were several blocks away, then I yanked Aurora into an alley and pressed us against the brick wall of the small clothing shop beside us. Our breath was ragged and deep, but it began to slow as we waited. No one came after us.

"I think we got away," I said.

33

Aurora and I stood in the hallway, staring at my apartment door. It was covered with black dust, and it was obvious the police had been here looking for fingerprints. At least that was reassuring, in a way. They didn't just decide I had slid down into the sewer to become one with my kind and gave up on me. At least they put forth the modest effort and time investment to see if anything bad happened to me.

"Are we still going to be able to get inside?" Aurora asked.

"We should be able to," I said. "My rent is paid up through the end of the month, so until they either find by body or turn everything over to the next of kin, the landlord can't just take back over.

Of course, my landlord is kind of an ass, so anything's possible."

I dug through one of the pockets in my bag and pulled out my keys. The one to my apartment fit easily into the lock.

"Well," Aurora said. "At least we know they didn't change the locks."

"Step one accomplished," I said.

The lock engaged, and I opened the door. In front of us, my apartment was in chaos. Not that it was ever in the best condition, but the mess in front of us definitely wasn't all me. Drawers were opened, and the contents spread out, the cushions on my furniture were tipped over, and there was fingerprinting dust on virtually every surface. My mail had been opened and spread across the kitchen table. Even my trash looked like it had been dug through.

"Were you robbed or did the police search your apartment?" Aurora asked.

"You know what? I'm not sure. Maybe a little bit of both?"

I led her further into the apartment and we surveyed the damage. My TV and video games were still there, so I came to the conclusion I hadn't actually been robbed. Unless the robbers were extremely discerning, which was always a possibility.

"So, you went missing, and the police came here to what? See if you were dead? Find out if you had been kidnapped?" I shot her a glare and Aurora winced.

"Sorry," she said. "My point is, why did they do this? What did they think they were going to find?"

"I don't know," I said. "Like I said, I didn't exactly live the most squeaky-clean of lives before I walked into Solomon's Fang. It's entirely possible they thought I'd gotten onto the bad side of some of the people I used to run with. In that situation, fingerprint dust would absolutely be a necessity."

"You look like you barely know where you are," Aurora said.

"I kind of feel that way," I admitted. "It doesn't feel like my place anymore. I mean, I know it is. I'm looking around and I'm seeing my stuff, my dirty socks, my overdue bills. All that, totally mine. But it just doesn't feel familiar anymore."

"Are you ready to go?" she asked.

"Yeah," I said. "Just let me grab a couple of things and we'll leave."

I went through the apartment and took a few

things, shoving them into my bag, then walked out without looking back.

"Where to now?" Aurora asked.

"Well, now that I'm homeless, I'm not sure."

"You are not homeless," she said. "You have a palace in the Underworld, and we can get a home of our own if you want. Maybe Ashe will finally leave that apartment above Solomon's Fang."

"That sounds good," I said.

"And for now," she said. "We get a hotel room. We figure it out from there."

We made our way to a nearby hotel and I lurked in the corner of the lobby under the brim of a hat, hoping nobody looked at me too hard while Aurora walked up to the desk to check in. The man behind it looked concerned, and she leaned closer to murmur something in his ear. His expression turned to surprise and then interest, and he nodded. Aurora took the credit card she had pulled from the bag again and slid it across the desk toward him. He took it, swiped it, and handed it back to her with a key card. I saw her wink and wiggle her way across the lobby toward the elevator. I waited until the elevator was open and stepped inside to hurriedly follow her.

"What was that all about?" I asked when the doors slid shut.

"Sometimes it takes a little bit of creative convincing when the people working don't like that I don't have identification to check in with," she said.

"Creative convincing?" I asked.

"I might have suggested to him that I'm extraordinarily good at sucking."

A loud laugh burst out of my chest.

"He has no idea," I said.

"Nope," she said with a mischievous grin.

"So, what's with the no identification?"

"I can't get an ID," Aurora said. "At least not here. They are available in the Underworld, but most people don't have them. Getting one here is a hassle I just don't feel like going through. I don't have a birth certificate because I was born in the Underworld before birth certificates were a thing. I know you said they're easy to forge, but it's not quite as easy when you don't have any form of identification or any reference point. I could probably get one if I wanted to, but I don't really feel like going through all the red tape. Keep in mind, it's not like I would only have to do it once. When you don't age at all, things start to look suspicious within just a few years."

"It looks like you get along just fine," I said.

She grinned at me.

"Thank you," she said.

"How about the money?" I asked. "If you don't have an identification and as far as I can tell, you don't have a job, how do you have a credit card?"

"There's no need to worry about money," Aurora said. "We have access to all the money we will ever need."

The elevator opened, and we went into our room. It felt good to drop all of the bags I was carrying. The bed looked soft and warm, and for the first time all day I realized how tired I really was. I wanted to flop down onto it and sleep until I felt like I could think straight and my muscles stopped aching.

After a long shower, I put on pajamas and climbed onto the bed. Aurora was sitting on the edge of the mattress brushing out her hair, and the expression on her face made it seem like she was a thousand miles away.

"What are you thinking about?" I asked.

She glanced back over her shoulder at me.

"Something's missing," she said.

I looked over at the pile of bags on the floor.

"I can't think of anything else we might need," I said.

"No, not that," she said. "I mean in all of this. There's a piece missing, and I think I figured it out."

"What is it?" I asked.

"Malakan," she said.

"What about him?" I asked.

"You started questioning what happened the minute you saw the house go up in flames, didn't you?" she asked.

"Yes," I said. "It seemed off. There was something about it that didn't make sense."

"I don't think he's dead."

It came out of her all at once, like she had been trying to hold it back, and wanted to say it as quickly as she could before she could question herself.

"You don't?" I asked.

She shook her head as she turned to face me fully.

"No," she said. "And I know you don't either."

"I don't," I admitted. "I haven't almost from the beginning."

"I think he started the fire himself. It would

explain how fast and intense it was, and why there was no body."

She was saying all the things I already had, but I knew it wasn't for my benefit. She was coming to terms with it herself.

"He escaped through that hidden entrance," I said. "He caused the explosion, knowing it would burn fast and intense, but it would only go a certain distance from the house. He must have had it timed perfectly so as soon as I left, he triggered whatever it was that started the explosion and got enough of a distance away from the house that he would be safe when it went off. He didn't have to go through that entrance right at that minute because he knew I wasn't going to be able to see anything other than the flames. Then, when I was gone, he slipped out."

"But why? Why would he do that?" she asked.

"All I can think is that he wanted to make sure people, maybe somebody in particular, thought he was dead, so they didn't track him down and make sure he really was."

I yawned, and Aurora reached out to stroke the side of my face.

"We should get some sleep," she said. "You can't keep running yourself into the ground."

I tucked myself between the cool sheets and flipped the blankets back to give her space to crawl in with me. She curled up against me and rested her head on my chest. I kissed the top of it and closed my eyes.

"Where do you think he went?" I asked a few minutes later when I couldn't fall asleep.

"I don't know," Aurora said. "But if Malakan is still alive, he did what he did for a very specific reason. Remember what you said about everyone hearing about it. He wanted to make what happened was known. He didn't want it to be a secret. This wasn't a subtle move. If he's still alive out there somewhere, he's waiting for something, and it relies on everybody in the Underworld thinking he died in that fire."

"What about me?" I asked.

"What do you mean?" she asked, lifting her head and propping her chin on her hand so she could look at me.

"He obviously did it when I was there so I would know it happened. But does he want me to think he's dead, too? Or does he believe part of me will know he's still alive and come find him?"

Aurora leaned forward and gave me a soft kiss.

"I don't know," she said. "I do know he trusted

you. If he didn't, he wouldn't have let you go to that house. He could have performed that ritual anywhere. In the stone chambers, at the palace, even at Stephana's house. He preferred his house for the most important of his rituals, but they didn't usually involve other people. He could have brought the orbs with him anywhere, just like the warlocks did when the Prime family underwent the ritual. But he specifically decided to have you come to his house, so he could perform it there. That wasn't by accident. He wanted you to see it then, and maybe he wanted you to come back."

"So, I could witness the fire," I said.

"Maybe."

She kissed me again and rested her head on my chest. A light sigh told me she was asleep almost instantly. I thought back to the ritual and the horrifying vision I had of my future. Holding Aurora closer, I kissed her again, silently swearing to her I wouldn't let that vision come true.

34

By the time Aurora woke up the next morning, I was already dressed and waiting for her.

"What's going on?" she asked.

"We need to get back to the Underworld," I said.

"We came here to talk to your parents," she said. "We haven't even gotten in touch with them."

"I know," I said. "And we will, but for right now, we need to get back there and talk to Ashe and Stephana."

"Why don't we just call them?" Aurora asked.

"Somebody was following us when we were in the office last night," I said. "They were following us when we went to the city, they were listening to us when we were in the palace. Somebody is trying to find out what we know and what we are doing. If they're going to go to the extent of all that, don't you think they will have thought to listen in on our phone conversations, too? What we realized about Malakan isn't something we can talk about in front of anybody but us. We can't risk someone hearing us and bringing that information back to whoever is at the root of this. You are right. Malakan is alive. He has to be. And that means that fire at his house is just a part of something much bigger. Like you said, it wasn't subtle. He didn't just slink away or disappear. He made a big ass show of faking his death, which means there's somebody out there who wanted him dead for real. We can't talk about anything we've found out about me, about him, or about anything else through any channel that might be overheard. We need to get back to the Underworld so we can talk to them face-to-face."

"But we can't," she said, swinging her legs out of the side of the bed and standing up. "We already went through the portal. We explained to you that you can only use it one time without Ty there, you said you understood."

"I did understand," I said. "And I thought it

wasn't going to be a problem, but now it is. We have to get back there, and that means we're going to have to find one of the black-market portals. That's the only way."

Aurora looked like she wanted to argue with me, but she knew it wasn't going to do any good. I'd made my decision, and there wasn't anything that was going to change my mind. The thought briefly flickered through me that she could refuse to go along with me, and I would have to face the danger of the black-market portal on my own, but then it disappeared. I knew I wasn't going to go without her, and I knew just as much she wouldn't let me.

"I know where to find one," she said.

I stared at her.

"What?" I asked. "You said you didn't even know if they existed, and you had only heard stories about them."

"I know," she said. "I didn't want to encourage you to think of them as a viable option. We weren't exaggerating when we told you these things can be unbelievably dangerous. The thing is, they only get more dangerous and more unstable with time. The approved portals are regulated. They're monitored, and the power contained in them is closely balanced and carefully controlled. That's one of the main purposes of having a keeper who is specifically assigned to keep watch over any given portal. It's not just about protecting the portal or monitoring who is passing through. It's about protecting people from the portal as well. The power of the portals can become unstable and horrible things can happen. People have been known to go into the portals and never be found again. Some have been torn to pieces and only parts of them show up at their destination. Some end up in far-flung places and have no idea how to get back. These are portals that were created by people who wanted power and control. They wanted to be able to move through the Underworld undetected, and to hold dominance over others."

"I'm not going to let that happen," I said. "If you know where one of these portals is, it means you've used it before, and you got through just fine. If you can do it, I can too."

"It's been a long time, Hayden."

"It doesn't matter," I said. "Aurora, this is what we need to do. Bring me to the portal."

"I don't think I find your sense of humor

funny," I said, looking down at the manhole cover at my feet.

"If only it was a joke," Aurora said.

"Seriously?" I asked. "This is actually one of the portals? One of the big scary mysterious black-market portals is a manhole?"

"The manhole isn't the portal," she said. "It's just how we get to the portal."

"I don't know if that's better or worse," I said.

"We can turn back," she said.

"Absolutely not," I said. "We've gotten this far. If the Ninja Turtles have taught me anything, it's that sewers are the perfect place to go when you are an outcast, and they are frequently full of pizza and people who will help you."

"I don't think that's quite what we're going to find," she said.

"Only one way to find out," I said.

I leaned down and moved the cover out of the way. I hoped no one was watching us at that moment. Fortunately, we were in an alley behind an abandoned warehouse and hadn't seen anyone, but if they were, I could only imagine how strange it looked for us to walk down the alley with our bags, then disappear down the manhole.

I climbed down a narrow, creaking metal

ladder into exactly what I would have envisioned as the bottom of a long-forgotten sewer. Cringing, I looked around to see if I could identify where the portal might be located.

"This is lovely," I told her.

"I wasn't exactly going through the most delicate and elegant phase of my life," she said.

"Someday I want to hear stories about you when you were younger," I told her.

"You're going to need to set aside a lot of time for that," she said.

"Well, you're in luck, because it seems I have plenty of time on my hands."

She smiled, then pointed down the wet, slimy sewer toward a large hole.

"That way," she said.

"Is that the portal?" I asked.

"You really are hopeful, aren't you?" she asked. "No, that's not the portal. Just another step in the process."

The long, winding passages continued for what seemed like miles with nothing happening. Aurora and I fell into silence and I waited for her to tell me when we were close to the portal. Finally, we came around a bend and I heard voices. They fell silent when we turned the corner.

I scanned the narrow sewer passage quickly, seeing the portal just beyond three men. All three stared but said nothing.

"Let us pass," said Aurora from beside me, and I marveled at her.

Even standing ankle deep in a sewer, she still commanded respect.

"Not without payment," one of the men said.

He didn't wait for a response but leapt toward me. I grabbed him in mid-air and tossed him backward into the wall of the sewer, sending him crashing into the wetness below. The other one, who had been inching forward, hesitated for a moment, giving me an opportunity to face him. He clenched his fist and came forward, but I was already there to meet him. I sent a blow crashing into his stomach and lifted my knee to catch his jaw. Strength was flowing through my body as adrenaline kicked in, and the knee lift had broken several of the man's teeth. As he landed on the ground, he spit some of the pieces out and looked at his partner, who was now standing again.

"Get the girl," one shouted, and they both charged at her.

A blur of movement followed. The anger and power were still surging through me as I turned toward him. My body shot through the air, slamming into his chest and crushing him against the wall. I heard bones crack and he collapsed to the ground. Whirling around to face the last man, I met his eyes. His fists clenched and released by his sides and his jaw twitched, but he didn't come at me.

"Go," he growled.

Aurora and I started for the portal and out of the corner of my eye I saw the man reach for a knife in the waistband of his pants. I let my anger reach out for the knife and snatch it from his hand. His eyes widened as he watched the blade slice through the air in front of him and embed in his thigh without me touching it. He let out an animal-like cry and I pushed Aurora ahead. We ran for the portal, diving through just before the man caught up with us.

When I opened my eyes again, I had no idea where we were, but we were in one piece. That was a start. Peeling myself from the ground, I noticed we were at the edge of a broken, crumbling road and I could see the city in the distance. Without a word, we started to walk.

We had been walking through the city from

where the portal had dropped us for almost an hour before I could bring myself to talk through the anger.

"When all this is over," I said, "I'm going to magic all those fucking things sealed." I looked over at Aurora and found her staring at me. "That's right. You heard me. I said magic."

She laughed.

"You know what I just thought about?" she asked.

"What?" I asked.

"My tattoo," she said.

"Is your tattoo particularly funny?" I asked.

"Not the tattoo itself," she said. "But how it applies to us. It says serendipity. Do you realize if my father's plan had actually worked out, and you hadn't been whisked away to the humans, we would have been raised together? I mean, I guess by that point I had already been raised, but I would have known you as a tiny baby and watched you grow up. We would have spent our lives together. You would have likely spent a lot more time with my father than I did because he would have been trying to groom you into his perfect little reconciliation gift for the warlocks, but I would have seen you every time I was at the palace. I can only imagine that when you were sent back to your warlock family, we would have stayed in touch because we would have gotten close over the years."

"I don't think I'm following you," I said.

"We still ended up together," she said. "In a completely different way than we would have been if it had worked out that way, but we're still spending our lives together. It's serendipity."

I stared at her for a few seconds. I didn't think that was actually what that word meant, but I decided it wasn't really my place to argue. She was the one who had it inked into her skin. It could mean whatever she wanted it to. Besides, I liked her explanation. It made me feel even more connected to her and to the life I was intended to live. Like, somehow, she was a link I would have found no matter what. My destiny.

"Do you think we would have found each other if your father had never planned what he did?" I asked.

"I think so," Aurora said. "Again, not in the same way." She looked at me sideways, her eyes tracing me up and down. "Well, I don't know.

Maybe it would have been in the same way. After all, I wasn't spending a whole lot of time at the palace at that point in my life. Maybe we wouldn't have interacted very much and then I would have come back when you were grown."

I stopped in my tracks. I knew Aurora was being flirty and playful, but what she said made realization hit me like I've been punched in the gut.

"He knew," I said.

Aurora stopped and looked at me.

"Who knew what?" she asked. "Malakan?"

"No," I said, shaking my head and quickly closing the space she'd made between us so I was close enough to lower my voice to a whisper. "Not Malakan," I said. "Your father."

"What about my father?"

"He has known all along. He knows who I am."

"Hayden, I don't…"

"Think about it," I said adamantly. "Why else would he be so insistent that I die rather than have you finish the change for me?"

"He wanted to protect me," Aurora said. "I've never considered making a blood bond with anybody before, and he wanted to make sure I was making the right decision. He didn't know you or anything about you and wasn't sure I was thinking it through."

"No," I said, shaking my head. "That can't be the reason. He was absolutely adamant I not go through the change. He wanted me dead. It's because he didn't want me to survive and have the opportunity to find out who I really was. Think about how he fought me, and then how he reacted when I beat him and took your blood. If he was really a father who was so protective of you, and so determined I wasn't the right person, why would he be happy?"

"What do you mean? He was happy because I was."

"Aurora, think about it. People don't change their minds that fast. Your thoughts about somebody and your emotions about the situation aren't on a swivel like that. He wasn't going to go from being completely against us being together to being thrilled you had chosen me just because I beat him in a fight. Keep in mind it wasn't like you were standing there offering me your blood. I took it from you. For all he knew, I was just going to walk out of that room and never see you again. I mean, not caring about any type of connection between the two of us. He had no idea what was going to happen, and yet he acted like it was the greatest thing he'd ever witnessed. His mood changed completely because it had to. He couldn't risk getting on my bad side before he could figure out how to stop the backlash from my return."

35

"He never said anything to you, Aurora?" Ashe asked.

We had finally made it to Solomon's Fang and were huddled in a corner of the bar, more aware than ever of the eyes on us and anyone who might be in close enough proximity to hear what we were saying. Aurora shook her head.

"No," she said. "Nothing. I can't believe he knew." She sounded completely stunned. "How could he possibly have known something like that, and not said anything to me? As soon as he realized that I had bitten Hayden, how could he not come to me and tell me he knew who he was?"

"Because he couldn't," I said. "Remember, he wouldn't have wanted to make me suspicious, or for there to be any chance of me finding out about my past. The two of you aren't exactly the Underworld's answer to the Brady Bunch. He probably felt like he couldn't trust you. He had no idea how you would react if he told you who I was. He might have hoped you would have just let me die, but he would know in the back of his mind there was also a good chance you would save me because of who I was. He didn't want to risk that."

"Do you think..." Aurora started.

"Yes," I said, already knowing what she was going to ask.

"What?" Ashe asked. "Do you think what?"

Aurora and I looked at each other.

"It's the reason we came back here," I said. "We needed to talk to you. but we can't do it here. Can we go to your apartment?"

"Sure," she said. "Just let me get the bar covered."

Aurora and I went up to the apartment and waited in silence until Ashe walked in. She looked like she was still trying to process what we'd told her. I understood what she was feeling. I was still trying to process it, too. She sat down on the couch between us and leaned back so Aurora and I could still see each other.

"It's about Malakan," I said.

Aurora and I explained our theory to Ashe.

"He must have known you would question it," she said when we were finished. "He wouldn't plan it like that if he didn't want you to."

"Why do you say that?" I asked, wanting to hear her reasoning to find out if it was anything like mine.

"By now, everybody in Solan City and the surrounding areas knows about the fire. There would be no reason for him to make it happen when you were there just so you would know about it. He knew news about it would spread quickly, and everybody would know within days. The only explanation for why he would do something that dramatic when you were right there is so that you would recognize it for what it was. He didn't want you to know about the fire. He wanted you to know about what wasn't happening. He trusted you would figure it out."

"But what if I didn't?"

"Then you wouldn't be what he needed you to be," Aurora said. She sounded like she understood. "If you didn't realize it, or you didn't put the pieces together and figure it out, then it just meant you weren't going to be able to do what he expected of you."

"So, this is some sort of really messed up test?" I asked.

"I don't think it's like that," Aurora said. "The point of this isn't to test you. There has to be more to it than that."

"Then we don't have any choice, do we?" I asked. "We have to find out what it is. Ashe, have you heard from Ty?"

"No," she said. "I still haven't. I've tried to call him a few more times, but his phone is going straight to voicemail, which is still full. Everybody who's coming here, though, I've been asking about him. Other than people complaining about him not being at the portal, nobody seems to have any information."

"Then I guess we're heading back to the sewer," I said.

"What are you talking about?" Ashe asked.

"We have to go back to New York," I said. "Aurora and I tried to find my file at the foster agency, hoping it would give us some information about how I ended up with my parents. But we found out I don't have a file there. I was never actually placed in foster care. We have to go back and talk to my parents. They're the only ones are going to be able to tell us how they found out I needed a home and who brought me to them."

"Do your parents live in a sewer?" Ashe asked.

"No, they don't live in a sewer. That's just how Aurora and I got back here."

"One of the portals?" Ashe asked, sounding unsure.

"We took one of the black-market portals to get here, we'll have to take it to go back."

"But if it doesn't leave us off anywhere near where it started?"

"We cross that bridge when we get to it," I said.

**"How did you know?" Aurora asked.

"I didn't know it was going to be an actual fucking bridge," I grumbled as we walked across the unstable rope bridge we appeared on after going back through the sewer portal.

It ended up being a much easier process to go through the second time. Apparently, the fight had gained us some sort of street cred that earned us our way back through. At least for that time. I couldn't help but feel the permission was given begrudgingly and with the hope that we would come back and try again so they could demand the payment they were denied.

"I'm just glad more of the planks on this thing weren't missing," Ashe said. "Falling through and landing on my ass after going through that portal would not have been a good continuation of the day."

"Do you realize just how disturbing it is that the end of that portal was on a rope bridge behind an elementary school?"

Aurora looked up toward the weathered school building with its broken windows and boarded up doors. Spray paint was slashed across the walls and a bundle of sleeping bags in one of the doorways told me at least one transient called this place home.

"It doesn't look like this place has been used as a school for a long time," she said.

"Maybe that's because kids kept disappearing off the playground because they fell through the fucking portal," I said.

"I'd prefer to think the portal was put in place after the school already closed," Ashe said.

I reached the end of the bridge and got off the rickety wood. All of us getting onto solid ground without it collapsing seemed like a miracle.

"How far are we from your parents' house?" Aurora asked.

"I'm not sure," I said. We started off for the schoolyard as I tried to orient myself. We walked a few blocks and things began to look familiar. "We should call for a ride," I told them. "We could walk from here, but it would take a really long time, and I think it would be best if we got there as quickly as we can."

The car arrived within a few minutes, and I was silent throughout the ride. I was trying to figure out what I was going to say to my parents. They probably thought, like everyone else, that I was dead, and I was about to just show up at their house. They still weren't answering their phones, so I had no choice but to surprise them. I didn't want to scare them, or upset them, but I needed answers. I'd run out of other options for trying to find the answers I needed other places, so it was down to confronting them. I reassured myself I was doing what was right, and that once they got over the initial shock, they would be happy see me, and to know I was doing well. It would be interesting to try to explain to them what I was doing, exactly, but that would come.

By the time the car pulled up in front of my parent's house, I felt like I'd given myself enough of a pep talk. I braced myself as we walked up the sidewalk, readying myself for their reaction, but the door opened before I even got a chance to knock. My father was standing there, looking out at me like I had just shown up as expected to Sunday night family dinner.

"Good to see you, Hayden," he said.

I stood there with my fist still in the air, the unfulfilled knock waiting to happen.

"Owen," Aurora gasped beside me.

I turned to look at her, my hand falling to my side when I saw the shocked expression on her face.

"Hello, Aurora," my father said. "You look as beautiful as ever."

"What's going on?" I asked, looking back and forth between my father and my mate.

"Come on inside," Dad said. "Your mother's waiting."

"Waiting?" I asked.

We followed him through the front door and down the short hallway into the living room. My mother was sitting on the couch, sipping tea out of the same rose-patterned teacup I remembered drinking out of from some of my earliest memories. It was because of that cup that the smell of herbal tea always made me think of roses.

"Molly," Aurora said before I could even greet my mother.

Mom smiled at her.

"Aurora," she said. "I was hoping Hayden would bring you with him. It's wonderful to see you."

"Seriously, what the hell is going on?" I asked. "I came here because I needed to ask you about when I came to live with you. I don't know how you know Aurora, but she…"

"We know," Mom said.

The rest of the words disappeared in my mouth.

"You know?" I asked.

"Yes Hayden," Aurora said. "I know them from Solan City."

"No," I said, shaking my head. "That can't be true."

"It is," Dad said. "We've known Aurora for more than fifty years. But it's been a long time since we've seen her."

Aurora met my eyes again. "Owen and Molly were each born to vampire families. They come from the Underworld and used to live near the palace. They decided not to go through with the change when they reached the age of maturity.

Instead, they came here to live out their lives as humans."

I stared, open-mouthed, between them.

"But why?" I asked.

Footsteps came from the hall leading to the bedrooms and Ty stepped into the room.

"Because they couldn't stand to live under Darian any longer."

36

I lunged at Ty, the fury bubbling up in me so I couldn't control it anymore.

"You stole me!" I screamed at him. "You fucking stole me from my family, and then you lost me."

Aurora and Ashe both grabbed onto me, trying to yank me back as I clawed at Ty. I stepped away from him, and my father moved between us.

"Hayden, you need to stop."

"Why should I? He destroyed my life. He took away everything I should have been and should have had."

"So, that's what you feel about your mother and me?"

His voice was so quiet, calm, and controlled, it

sucked the adrenaline out of me and I realized what I had said. The women released their grip on me when they realized I wasn't trying to get to Ty anymore.

"I'm sorry, Dad," I said. "I didn't mean it that way. It's just that Ty…"

"I know what he did, son," Dad said.

"You do?" I asked.

"Of course, I do," he said. "So, does your mother. That's why we're here. Let him talk to you. Let him tell you what happened."

My father stepped out of the way to clear the space between Ty and me, and it took everything in me to keep myself from lunging at him again. My fists clenched by my sides, I stared at him.

"Go ahead," I said.

"Yes, Hayden," Ty said. "I did kidnap you. I am the one who took you from your parents when you were a baby. I already told you that. I've been honest with you about that."

"Only after I found out elsewhere," I said through gritted teeth.

"I know," Ty said. "But I would have told you the truth. And what you need to hear is that I lost you on purpose. There was no accident about it. I took you from the palace, away from Darian. I brought you here to Owen and Molly, so they could be your foster parents. But I did it with the understanding that they would never tell you who you are or what you were meant to be."

"Why?" I asked. "What gave you the right to decide what my life was going to be like?"

"Nothing gave me the right," Ty said. "But Darian gave me the opportunity. What he told everyone isn't true. He didn't want to use you as a unifying force with the warlocks. That was never his intention. You were meant as a weapon. You were going to be raised in the palace, coming to learn to trust and rely on the vampires, and to hate and be suspicious of your own kind. Then he was going to use you to infiltrate and manipulate the warlocks, so he could continue to build his plan of genocide. It's all he's wanted all along. Power. That is why he orchestrated the deaths of the Prime family seventeen years before you were born."

Aurora gasped, and when I glanced back at her I saw her hands pressed over her mouth.

"No," she said.

"I'm sorry, Aurora," Ty said. "But it's true. He wanted to start the war. He wanted to take the power completely for himself. He's never believed in unification or reliance on each other. Darian has never believed in cooperation or even civility between the vampires and the warlocks. He hated the warlocks because of the black magic that aged him when he was young and virile, and he wanted to reclaim more of it by taking the power of the Prime."

"How did you find this out?" I asked.

"I overheard it," Ty said. "I wasn't supposed to know, but as soon as I heard it, I knew I couldn't let it happen. I made the decision that that I was going to take you away, so he couldn't use you like that. I knew the trouble it would cause, but I was committed to it. I agreed to take the fall myself so no one else could be blamed. It didn't matter to me. There was nothing Darian could do that would make it not worth knowing I had saved your life, and the lives of everyone who would have been wiped out by Darian's plan. There was only so much he could do to punish me without the scrutiny of his advisers and the public. He did the worst he could, but there hasn't been a single day I haven't known I did what I was supposed to do. I did what needed to be done."

"So, what?" I asked. "You brought me here and just expected me to live a normal life?"

"Yes," Ty said. "I knew Owen and Molly

would take care of you. They have always wanted a child but didn't want to bring one into the world who would be obligated to the species. I have always trusted them, and I knew they understood the turmoil and horror of what had been happening in the Underworld. They would be able to protect you, and they would keep you away from all of it. You could just live. And eventually, after a very long life, you would die. Warlocks have extremely long life spans, but they are more likely to die earlier when they are among humans because of the illnesses that exist here in the other side that aren't in the Underworld."

I stared at him, unsure of how to react.

"So," I said, "your big plan I was hoping I would catch a cold and die before someone noticed I was a hundred and fifty years old?"

"Essentially," Ty said. "I didn't say it was the perfect plan, but it was what I could figure out in the very short amount of time I had to make a decision. By the time I found out what Darian was actually planning, everything had already been put into place. He had already chosen me to be the one to take you from your parents. Your warlock parents. I only had a few days to come up with what I was going to do to make sure his plan didn't work."

"I'm sorry we didn't tell you," my mother said from the couch.

"I'm not," my father said.

"You're not sorry you lied to me my entire life?" I asked.

"No," he said. "I'm not. When I agreed to take you in, I gave Ty my word. He was planning to do something utterly selfless and courageous, and all he asked in return was my confidence. The only request he had of us was that we would never tell you about the Underworld, where we came from, or your past. The less you knew, the safer you were. Ty knew as well as I did that if you found out, you would be in incredible danger. I had to make that promise to him, and I had to keep it. Up until now, we haven't seen or spoken to Ty in twenty-eight years. When he made the final agreement with us and walked away, knowing a few days later you would be brought here, we both knew we wouldn't be able to interact anymore. We couldn't communicate because that could be linked. Somebody could trace us to each other and eventually figure out what happened. For the last twenty-eight years, I had no idea what was happening in the Underworld or what had come of Ty. No matter what he says, Darian could have done so much more to him than he did. I am well aware of the capacity the Prime has for cruelty and evil. The fact that he didn't submit Ty to so much more, whether he did it in public or in a way that no one would ever have known, is a testament only to how great a man Ty is."

"We never meant to hurt you, honey," Mom said. "The intention was for you to live a normal life, free from the dangers of Darian's plan. That's all."

"Ty," Ashe said, "in all this time, you never thought to tell anybody what happened? You've watched our world go through years of war. You knew there's more to come. At no point did you think it might be a good idea to let somebody know Hayden was still alive? You could have ended the fighting and the suffering if you just told everyone what happened and brought him back."

"Doing that would have caused far more fighting and suffering," Ty said. "I had made my decision, and there was no turning back on it. It wasn't just about saving Hayden's life, or preventing him from having to live knowing he was the cause of the implosion of the warlock race. I did it for that, but I also did it because I wanted to stop Darian as much as I could. I wanted to stop him from being able to destroy the warlocks from the inside. I never believed in total power of the vampires, or the separation of the warlocks."

I shook my head. "But that doesn't answer everything," I said. "Who brought me here? How did Philip get wrapped up in it, so he lost his job, too? How did Darian orchestrate the deaths of the Prime family? Did anybody know what he was doing, or what he did after? I still don't understand why or how this happened."

"I'll do my best to answer your questions," Ty said. "I never thought it would come to this. I had no way of knowing you would eventually wander into the bar. It's like you were drawn there."

"I was," I said.

This changed everything. I was so much closer, and yet at the same time felt even further away. There was still so much left to know.

EPILOGUE

"You knew who I was as soon as you saw me, didn't you?" I asked.

"I wasn't positive," Ty said. "It seemed so out of the realm of reality that it could possibly be you, but I knew you. When I saw you in the basement with Ashe, it hit me. I recognized you instantly, almost like I had seen you as an adult, even when you were a baby. I don't know if that makes any sense. As soon as I saw you, though, I knew I was seeing you again, and the only explanation I had was it was you. I knew your eyes. I could predict the shape of your face. I knew your warlock parents well, and I could see both of them in you so clearly. What was funny is I could see Molly and Owen, too. The way you spoke, the way you laughed. Even some of the movements you made, reminded me of both of them."

"That's why you came to Ashe's apartment and asked me all those questions," I said.

"Yes," he said. "It didn't make any sense to me. I couldn't figure out why you were there, or why you weren't talking to me like you knew who I was. The only explanation I could come up with when I first saw you was that Owen and Molly had gone against what they had promised me and told you how to get to the Underworld. I figured now that you were an adult, they thought you could handle it, or that you should know and be able to make your own decision."

"Shouldn't I?" I asked.

"It doesn't matter, does it?" Ty asked. "Regardless of how it happened, you ended up back there. I just thought if they told you, they would have told you about me. They didn't know about my demotion, or that I would be the portal keeper at Solomon's Fang. But they did know going to that bar would be the only way he would find your way into the Underworld, and that there was a very good chance you would run into me there. You just never reacted. I never got even a glimpse from you that you knew anything."

"Because I didn't," I said. "I was just completely stoked a gorgeous woman had picked me up in a bar, and then another one was waiting for me in the morning." I looked over at my parents. "Sorry," I said.

"No reason to be," Dad said. "They're irresistible, especially after a bite. And with Aurora giving you the blood-bond bite, there was nothing you were going to be able to do to resist either of them."

On the list of conversations I thought I would have with my parents during my lifetime, this was not one of them.

"Even after you asked all those questions, you still didn't say anything," I said.

"I still wasn't completely convinced," Ty said. "It just was too much."

"You didn't even ask me what my parent's names were," I said. It was the first time that had occurred to me. "You asked me who my parents were, and when I said I didn't know my birth parents because I was raised by a foster family, you didn't ask anything else. If you had asked what their names were, you would have known."

"I know," Ty said. "Something stopped me. Maybe I just wasn't ready to really come to terms with it. But when we went to see Malakan, there wasn't any doubt left. He looked right into me, and he knew what was happening."

"Your failures," I said. "He commended you for taking responsibility for your failures. He didn't actually mean it. He was talking about me, but he didn't mean you failed. He was telling you he knew who I was."

Ty nodded.

"Yes," he said.

"Then where did you go? "I demanded. "You just disappeared."

"I know," Ty said. "I left the tavern because I could feel everything snowballing. I knew eventually all hell was going to break loose, and I wanted to try to figure out as much of it on my own as I possibly could. I left so I could come here and warn your parents about everything that was happening. They needed to know what was going on. They were relieved to find out you weren't dead, but also horrified you ended up in the Underworld."

"But then he told us about what you have been doing," Dad said. "He told us about how brave you were when you rescued Ashe, and how you fought the Shade. I'm so proud of you, son. I've known your whole life you had that in you, and I am so proud to have raised you."

"Thank you," I said.

"Why didn't you answer your phone?" Ashe asked. "We've been trying to get in touch with you for days. You got here and told his parents, so why didn't you come back?"

"Because I needed to go find Malakan," he said.

"You believe he's still alive, too," I said.

"Of course I do," Ty said. "It just didn't piece together. He probably knew Darian was going to eventually find out who you were, if he didn't already know, and there was no way the Prime would want you wandering around the Underworld knowing you are a hybrid, much less the son of the ArchWarlock and the bonded Lord of his daughter. Darian would think of you in the same way he thought of himself. That means he believed you would go immediately to the warlocks, and that would be the end of the vampires. That gave him only one the option. He needed to eliminate the only other person who he thought would know who you were. He knew Malakan knew because Aurora sent you to him. She knew as soon as she met you something was different about you, too, though she never would have been able to figure it out. But Malakan knew. He knew who you are even before he looked at you. Darian would need Malakan gone, and the old warlock knew that."

"So, he went ahead and took care of it for him," I said.

"Yes," Ty said. "That's the only explanation I can believe. We need to find him, Hayden. If we're right and he orchestrated that fire for himself, it's because he's somewhere waiting for you. It wasn't an accident that he told you he would train you in your warlock ways just before the fire. You are meant to be extraordinarily powerful, and you could change the course of the future. Some backyard training by a Lunaris hybrid isn't going to cut it. Your world needs you now. Both of your worlds."

SIGN UP FOR UPDATES

For updates about new releases, sign up for the mailing list below. You'll know as soon as I release new books, including my upcoming new series, as well as sequels to *Vampire Mage*.

https://www.subscribepage.com/joshua_king

ABOUT THE AUTHOR

Joshua King is a Sci-Fi, Fantasy, Urban Fantasy writer that loves a killer story mixed with a few ongoing fantasies. Strong gorgeous women, super evil villains, precarious situations, and a normal dude that gets transformed into making it happen are all part of the fun.

When not writing, he's watching movies, traveling the US with his wife and son, or paying homage to the God of War. He's hoping to entertain you and give you a few minutes of heart-racing fun or mind-bending mystery in the various worlds he's created or the ones he plans to create.

Made in the USA
San Bernardino, CA
28 February 2019